The Christmas Cookie Club

ROSEMARY WHITTAKER

The Christmas Cookie Club

Rosemary Whittaker

Also by Rosemary Whittaker

A Sugarloaf Valentine
A Sugarloaf Mix-Up
A Sugarloaf Surprise
A Sugarloaf Christmas
A Sugarloaf Easter
A Sugarloaf Secret
A Sugarloaf Summer
A Tale of Two Christmases
A Boxful of Christmas
The Cinnamon Snail
Sunshine State
The Wattle Birds
The Feijoa Tree
The Villa Mimosa

Stopwatch Publications

First printing, 2024

ISBN-13: 978-1-922651-53-2

This book is a work of fiction. Names, characters, places, and incidents are the product of the author's imagination or are used fictitiously. Any resemblance to actual events, locales, or persons, living or dead, is coincidental.

Published by Rosemary Whittaker
www.rosemarywhittaker.com

The cover design includes artwork licensed from Lio Putra, Eveleen007, Dmitry Naumov, Liudmyla Povorozniuk, Terry123, vikusah_art, DMVector and KrikHill.

For my readers, with huge gratitude for all your encouragement and support.

Chapter One

My laptop pings, and my heart sinks as I see yet another message from my manager, Caroline.

Hi, Lucy, could you run your eyes over this again and make the translation sound a little more … charming?

I open the attachment. There's nothing like starting a Monday morning with a deep dive into a brochure on skin blemishes. I roll my eyes as I scroll through the endless jargon, wishing the coffee machine hadn't chosen today of all days to break down.

Does Caroline seriously expect me to give this a sprinkle of fairy dust and throw in a happily ever after? Because if there's one thing the German language is known for, it's charm.

I start typing, smoothing out the edges of phrases like *enlarged pores* and *unsightly blemishes.* I hate wasting my time turning a facial cream update into the equivalent of a romance novel. And all for a boss who will no doubt change her mind by this afternoon and demand I rewrite the entire thing in a more professional tone.

I'm barely onto the second page when my screen pings again. *Urgent: Quick Turnaround Required.*

I know what's coming. Yet another badly written piece of copy for me to transform into the sort of German that won't make the recipient fall asleep before the end of the first paragraph. This job was supposed to launch me into the cutting-edge, dynamic forefront of modern language translation. Instead, I'm trapped in a cycle of endless revisions and last-minute requests for product descriptions I don't care about.

'Lucy, have you finished that brochure for Berlin?' asks Mark, appearing next to my desk.

'Almost. I'm busy making it gripping yet easy to read.'

He raises an eyebrow. 'Do I detect a note of cynicism? Everything you write needs to be "easy to read". That's pretty much our whole brand. We make contemporary and accessible beauty products for the modern European. All our ad copy has to be clear and accessible. That's why we hired you.'

'I know. I'll finish this face cream copy as quickly as possible. Then I have to make a start on Caroline's thing about non-paraben deodorants. She says the marketing team is expecting a final version by the end of the day.'

He nods and disappears. With a sigh, I click on the document again.

'Easy to read!' I mutter to myself. If only I could translate my way out of here. I used to love language – the way it can bridge gaps and create connections. Now it feels like a tedious puzzle I'm being paid to solve, with absolutely no reward at the end.

It's almost noon, and I've barely made a dent in my work. I won't have time for lunch today. Panic creeps in, tightening its grip around my chest. I push myself harder, typing furiously, and then the screen freezes.

'No, no, no!' I mutter, jabbing at the escape key. But it's no use. My computer, in a masterstroke of timing, has decided it's done for the day. If only I could join it.

I pick up my desk phone and call IT, praying someone is available. A voice answers after a few rings.

'This is Dave,' says the world's least enthusiastic tech support agent.

'It's Lucy,' I say. 'My computer's frozen. I can't access anything.'

'Have you tried restarting it?'

'I didn't want to lose what I was doing.'

Dave sighs deeply, as if my request has wounded him personally. 'Someone will be along shortly,' he says and hangs up.

I pull out my mobile phone so I can answer emails while I wait. I open my inbox and see a follow-up message from Caroline.

Lucy, are you anywhere close to finishing that deodorant copy? The Berlin team is asking.

I resist the urge to hurl my phone across the room and instead politely reply that I'm waiting for the IT department – whose spirit animal is the sloth – to fix my computer. With any luck, she'll call Dave and tell him to get a move on. He may listen to her.

I skim through the rest of my emails and decide they aren't important. The Germans will just have to wait for my computer to be fixed before they get their brochure. Although I can't imagine they're really looking forward to receiving such a dull document.

I haven't eaten anything since early this morning, and I have a long afternoon ahead of me. It annoys me to think my colleagues in Germany are probably eating their lunch right now. I was accidentally copied on a document explaining that our European offices have strict rules about working hours and proper time off. I've never dared tell Caroline I saw it. She believes longer hours equal greater productivity, and lunch breaks are only for the weak.

I fish a granola bar out of my bag and eat it as quickly as I can in case she walks past and sees what I'm doing. I could tell her I'm eating lunch at my desk, but she'd be sure to see my screen is off and make some sarcastic remark I could really do without today.

Not for the first time, I wonder why I took this job. It looked great on paper, but it was never the sort of translation work I'd been dreaming of. Mum and Dad told me it would look good on my CV, and I suppose they were right. But they don't have to work here. Yet again, I calculate the minimum time I can spend at this company without looking like I'm a quitter.

My phone rings. I swallow my last bite rather too quickly and start coughing.

'Hello?' I manage, wondering whether it's someone from the Berlin office, in which case I ought to have said, '*Guten Tag!*'

'Lucy?' says Caroline's irritated voice. 'Have you finished that document yet?'

'Almost. But my computer –'

'I can't think what's taking you so long. I sent it this morning.'

I don't tell her it was two pages of the most badly written ad copy I've ever had the misfortune to read, and that I had to rewrite the entire thing before I could even think about translating it into German. Knowing my luck, it will turn out she wrote it herself. She's annoyed enough already without me insulting what she probably considers to be shimmering prose.

'It's my computer,' I explain. 'I was in the middle of writing a sentence when –'

'Don't bother,' she interrupts me. 'I've heard it all before. Sort it out, and get that document to me within the next hour, ok?'

She rings off, leaving me staring at my phone and wondering where she's sitting today. I don't have the best aim in the world, but if she's in one of the nearby cubicles, I should be able to lob my phone and hit her with a carefully planned throw. I'd have to pretend it wasn't my phone, but it's password-protected, so she'd probably never know.

I look at my phone again and change my mind. Anonymity isn't possible when you've been stupid enough to choose a bright pink case decorated with giraffes. It seemed a good idea at the time – something to cheer myself up on a dull winter's morning. If only I'd had the forethought to buy a plain blue one like everyone else. But there's nothing I can do about that now. My phone will have to remain unlobbed for the present.

It rings again, and I give a squeak of frustration. What does she want to tell me now – she has a twenty-thousand-word novella for me to translate about the importance of choosing the correct foundation?

I pick it up and jam it to my ear. 'What now?'

There's a pause before anyone speaks. Have I just signed my own letter of dismissal? I scrabble around for something to soften my answer, but my brain has given up for the day. Caroline will just have to deal with it.

'Lucy?' says a voice. It's pleasant and low-toned – nothing like Caroline's high-pitched, cut-glass shriek.

'That's right,' I say.

'It's Mum.'

My shoulders sag in relief before tightening again. There can only be one reason for her to call me in the middle of a busy workday.

'What's wrong?' I ask. 'Has something happened with Dad?'

'Dad's fine,' she says in a reassuring tone. 'I'm sorry. I didn't mean to worry you.'

'Are you sure he's ok?'

'Perfectly sure. I've just spoken to him, and he sends his love.'

'Just spoken to him? Where is he?'

'He's at home,' she says. 'But I'm not.'

A fresh wave of panic surges over me. 'Is there something wrong with you?'

'I'm fine too,' she says. 'If I could just –'

'You can't be fine!' I say. 'You're calling me during the day, and you aren't with Dad. Tell me what's going on!'

'I'm doing my best,' she says. 'But you keep interrupting me. I promise that Dad and I are both well. It's Gran.'

My heart sinks. 'What about her?'

'She's had a fall, and they've taken her to the hospital. They say she's broken her hip, and they're operating this afternoon.'

I let out a breath. 'That doesn't sound too bad. Will she be alright?'

'As far as I know. They don't seem too worried.'

'That's good.' I hesitate. 'I'm glad you told me, but couldn't it have waited until I got home this evening?'

'Not really. You see, it's Humphrey.'

I consider this for a moment. 'That is a problem.'

'I know,' she says. 'I'm looking after him at the moment. I drove down to Honeywell as soon as I heard. I can stay with him tonight, but I have to get back home to Dad by tomorrow evening. One of the neighbours is kindly sleeping over at our house, but she can't stay a second night.'

'How about Gran's neighbours?' I ask. 'Couldn't one of them look after Humphrey?'

'I'm trying to find someone, but I haven't had any success so far. Most people in the street are a similar age to her, and I don't know anyone else who lives in the village these days.'

There's a long silence. She doesn't break it, but I know what she wants to ask. I want to help. I really do. But there's no way I can. I'm up to my eyes in work, and it's only going to get worse in the run-up to Christmas.

'I'm sorry, Mum –' I stop, staring around the office. Am I about to tell her that what's going on here is more important than making sure Gran isn't desperately worried about her beloved dog? Am I about to tell myself the same thing? Not a hope.

'Don't worry,' she says. 'I knew it wasn't likely. I'll sort something out.'

'I was about to say I'm sorry I can't get there this evening,' I say. 'But I can catch a train tomorrow morning. I could be with you around lunchtime.'

Her voice is thin with relief. 'Oh, Lucy, that would be wonderful! Are you sure?'

'Perfectly sure. It's about time I took a few days off.'

'But what will your manager say? You told us she can be rather difficult at times.'

'I don't remember saying that. I guess I must have been having a bad week. Caroline will understand.'

'That's wonderful!' she exclaims again. 'I'm so grateful, Lucy. Please thank her for me and tell her it shouldn't be for too long.'

I look at my blank computer screen, then at the double doors at the far end of the office. There's no sign of Dave or any of his IT minions. If previous experience is anything to go by, no one will turn up for hours. In the meantime, Caroline will stop by my desk every five minutes or bombard my phone with messages asking why I haven't anticipated all her unreasonable requests and produced these documents by sometime last week. If I'm not here, and my phone mysteriously runs out of battery, she can't do any of that.

I push back my chair, pick up my bag, and sling my jacket over my shoulder.

'I'd better get going,' I tell Mum. 'I have a lot to do before tomorrow morning.'

I ring off and, without looking at anyone, I walk towards the door.

Chapter Two

There's no direct train the following morning, and I have to change twice. I settle into my seat on the final train and stare out at the frosty countryside. When did I last take this trip? I remember passing fields with golden haystacks and helping Gran pick apples from her Bramley tree. It must have been sometime in September. Three months ago.

I should visit her more often. I know how lonely she's been since Grandpa Ed died. But there's always so much going on at work that I lose track of time. I resolve to do better in the future. I hate to think of Gran having to move out of her cottage due to lack of proper support. She's lived there since she was married, and it would break her heart if she had to leave. But I mustn't get ahead of myself. The important thing is for her to recover from her operation. We can worry about everything else later.

Mum is waiting for me when the train pulls into the station. She's the only person on the tiny platform.

Her face lights up when she sees me. 'Lucy! I'm so grateful to you for coming at such short notice!'

She enfolds me in an enormous hug. It's familiar and comforting, but I feel the usual wash of guilt when I realise I haven't seen her recently either.

'How's Gran?' I ask.

'She came through the surgery well. I stopped in at the hospital before coming to meet you. She's been in a fair amount of pain, and she's woozy from whatever they've been giving her for it. I told her you were coming to look after Humphrey. She seemed pleased about that. You can pop in and see her this afternoon.'

'How will I get there? Do taxis venture out as far as Honeywell, or is there a bus?'

'There's no need for that,' she says. 'You can drive her car. It's insured for the whole family.'

Gran sold Grandpa's station wagon after he died, saying it was far too big for her and that she hated driving it. She recently bought herself a brand-new hatchback. Apparently, she's very pleased with it, although I understand Humphrey was less impressed. He's never liked cars, but I hope he's got used to this one by now. If so, he and I can take some walks in the New Forest. Otherwise, we'll have to stick to the lanes around Honeywell.

I ask about Dad as we drive to Gran's cottage.

'He's doing well, all things considered,' Mum says in the cheerful tone she always uses when she talks about him. 'The insurance company has finally settled, so we can get the house properly adapted for him, which will make all the difference. And don't forget it's still early days. His physiotherapist is doing wonders. Dad won't be in a wheelchair forever.'

She tells me this every time she sees me. I'm never sure which of us she's trying to persuade.

'What about the other driver?' I ask.

'As far as I know, he's fine now, which is something to be thankful for. There's no point in two lives being ruined.'

I'm not sure I'd be so forgiving in her place. The driver whose car hit Dad's a year ago was uninsured, and he'd lost his licence several months previously after being caught drunk driving. Personally, I'd like to see him in prison for the rest of his life rather than only two years. But Mum is a far nicer person than me. She and Dad get on with things without discernible bitterness. It's the best way, but I don't think I could ever be like them.

I put all this out of my mind as we turn into Bramble Close. It's a small cul-de-sac with just nine houses.

Mum pulls up outside the cottage at the furthest end and switches off the engine. 'Here we are, love. Let me help you with your bags.'

'I'm fine, thanks. I didn't bring much with me. I didn't think I'd need it. Mostly jeans and thick boots so I can take Humphrey for lots of muddy walks.'

Mum unlocks the front door, and we're greeted by loud barking.

'That's enough, Humphrey!' she says as he comes pelting down the hallway to greet us. He skids to a halt and looks up at me with suspicion.

I bend down to scratch his ears. 'Don't be so ridiculous! You know perfectly well who I am. We played tug-of-war with Gran's cardigan last time I was here, remember?'

'With Gran's cardigan?' asks Mum, puzzled. 'Why would you do a thing like that?'

I set down my bags at the foot of the stairs. 'It wasn't my idea. Humphrey was trying to bury it under the apple tree. He wasn't happy when I tried to take it off him, and it turned into quite a tussle. By the time I got it away from him, it had no buttons, and one sleeve was torn right off.'

I smile at the memory. 'Gran came out and found us. She said a magpie must have pulled the cardigan off the washing line and pecked holes in it and that Humphrey had wandered outside and found it. He looked up at her with those big, innocent eyes as though he'd never been near a washing line in his life and was shocked to think his fellow creatures could be capable of such a terrible thing. I didn't argue. You know how Gran refuses to hear a word against him. She could find him standing in the kitchen eating tonight's steak, and she would claim the butcher had dropped by with some samples and asked Humphrey to do a taste test.'

'I hope he won't be too much of a handful for you,' says Mum.

'We'll be fine. Won't we, Humphrey? Just leave my clothes alone, and we won't have a problem.'

I look around the hallway. 'This cottage is always so neat. I have no idea how Gran does it, especially with him around.'

'Your grandmother has always been very house-proud,' says Mum. 'She taught me from an early age that there's a place for everything, and everything should be in its place.'

'I hope I can maintain her exacting standards. Tidiness isn't my strong suit. But it should only be for a few days. And I can lock Humphrey out in the garden while I'm cleaning.'

I catch his eye and laugh. 'I'm only joking. I'll need you to scrub the bathroom for me each morning.'

Mum follows me upstairs. 'I thought you could sleep in the spare room while you're here. I've made up the bed for you. I slept in Gran's bed last night, but I've stripped it and washed everything this morning. Perhaps you could make it up again once the bedding is dry?'

'No problem,' I say. 'Or Humphrey can if I'm too tired.'

We go back down to the kitchen, and Mum shows me where she's put the coffee.

'Gran only drinks tea,' she says. 'But I know you're a coffee fiend.'

'Guilty as charged. Especially today. I've already drunk about five cups. My job is giving me a serious caffeine addiction.'

'How are you enjoying your work?' she asks. 'I hope it wasn't too inconvenient for you to take time off.'

'Not at all,' I assure her. 'It's about time I took a proper break. The last time I had a week off was when I came to stay with you and Dad in July.'

She frowns. 'You need to take better care of yourself than that. No job is worth putting your physical and mental health on the line.'

'It isn't that bad. And Caroline has said she wants us to use up our annual leave rather than rolling it over to next year. I'll use that as a bargaining chip if I have to stay here for longer.'

Mum still looks worried. 'Don't jeopardise your chances of a promotion.'

'Make up your mind,' I say. 'Either I should take my holiday allowance or I shouldn't.'

'I'm sorry,' she says. 'I worry too much.'

'Yes, you do. But that's understandable. First, there was Dad's accident, and now there's Gran. You have a lot on your plate. Please don't add me to your worries. I can look after myself. I'm looking forward to spending some time in the countryside with plenty of fresh air and exercise. Humphrey will see to that.'

She looks at her watch. 'It's almost one o'clock. Why don't I make us something to eat before I leave?'

'Even better,' I say. 'Why don't I make us something to eat while you take a break? Knowing Gran, the larder will be full of delicious things. And if I can't find what I need, I'm sure Humphrey will be only too delighted to show me.'

Chapter Three

Mum leaves after lunch. I'm going straight to the hospital once I've seen her off, so we have to leave a disconsolate Humphrey behind in the house. The overstretched NHS might take a dim view of him accompanying me. I could pretend he was my emotional support dog, but I doubt anyone would believe me. I can't think of any physical or mental condition that would be improved by the addition of a giant, over-active canine of indeterminate heritage.

'He'll be fine by himself for a little while,' Mum assures me. 'He's been as good as gold each time I've had to pop out for a few minutes.'

She hesitates. 'He chewed one of the sheets in the laundry basket, but I'm sure he didn't mean to.'

'You sound like Gran,' I tell her. 'There's nothing Humphrey could ever do that she wouldn't excuse.'

'He'll be fine,' she says. 'He'll quickly get used to having you around.'

'I hope so. But I can't stay here forever. We need to make some plans.'

Her face is anxious. 'I know. I felt terrible asking you to drop everything and come down here at a moment's notice, but I couldn't think what else to do.'

'You did the right thing,' I say. 'I wasn't complaining. But if Gran ends up staying in the hospital for longer than we expect, either I'll have to stay here or we'll have to find someone else to look after Humphrey. I can't imagine my landlord would let him stay with me in London, and the poor love would hate it. He needs to be in his own home and see all his usual people.'

I hand Mum her overnight bag. 'Is this all you brought with you?'

'It's all I had time to pack. Give Gran my love when you see her, and let her know we have everything under control. There's no reason for her to worry. She needs to concentrate all her energies on getting better.'

'I'll tell her,' I promise. 'And please give Dad my love too and tell him I'll come and see you both as soon as I can. I'll be there for Christmas if not before. With or without Humphrey.'

Her face creases with worry. 'I don't think …'

'I was joking,' I reassure her. 'Gran says Humphrey gets carsick after just a couple of miles. And I'll be facing a lifetime rail ban if I try to smuggle him on the train and he chews all the seats. Anyway, I'm sure Gran will be home long before Christmas.'

I feel a slight sense of panic as I watch her pull away. While Mum was here, I had someone to turn to – someone who would answer my questions with her usual calm good sense. Now I'm all on my own, and I'm not sure how I'll cope.

I tell myself to stop being so defeatist. If Mum can cope with everything life has thrown at her, I should be able to manage a small thing like this. I have no idea how our family would have survived if she hadn't been there to hold everything together last year. Christmas was a nightmare, with Dad in hospital after the crash, and no one knowing whether he would wake up at all, let alone recover enough to walk again and lead a normal life.

We still don't know how things will end up, but he's doing far better than any of us imagined possible. He's back home now, which was his first goal. He's still in a wheelchair, which he finds hard to accept. But, considering how bleak things looked last year, we have a lot to be grateful for. It's a shame everything has fallen on Mum. I feel the familiar pang of guilt that I haven't been there for her as much as I'd have liked to be. I originally suggested giving up my job and going home until Dad recovered, but she wouldn't hear of it.

'That's the last thing we need,' she told me rather more firmly than usual. 'Your father and I are so proud of everything you've done. We couldn't bear to see you throw it all away. What would make us both the happiest would be for you to stay where you are and keep following your dreams.'

But I'm not sure I am following my dreams. After I graduated, I was too busy looking for work in an overcrowded field to think much about the future. When I got my current job, I was so determined to hang onto it at all costs that I didn't stop to consider what those costs might be. I don't have time to think about all of that now, but it's something I need to consider when this crisis is over.

I arrive at the hospital twenty-five minutes later, thankful not to have been caught in the rush-hour traffic. I ask the way to Gran's ward and take the lift to the third floor.

A nurse coming out of the ward sees me and stops. 'Were you looking for someone in particular?'

'Lavender Hollis.' I say. 'She's my grandmother. She was admitted yesterday after a fall, and she had surgery on her hip. Is it possible for me to visit her?'

She holds open the door for me. 'Of course. She's in that bay over by the window. I'm sure she'll be delighted to see you.'

Gran is lying in bed, looking paler than usual. Her eyes are closed, so I sit in the chair next to her until she wakes up. I wait in silence for ten minutes, wondering how long I should leave her to sleep.

A nurse appears with a tray of medicines. 'Lavender Hollis?' she says, and Gran opens her eyes.

The nurse hands her a plastic cup containing three tablets and a glass of water. 'Time for your pain killers.'

She gestures towards me. 'And it looks as though you have a visitor.'

Gran's face lights up. 'Lucy! How long have you been here?'

'Only a few minutes,' I say, leaning over and kissing her cheek. 'I didn't want to wake you.'

I take her hand. 'What have you been getting up to?'

'I don't remember,' she says. 'Your mother tells me I fell down the stairs, but I have no memory of it. All I know is that I woke up in the hospital. They told me they'd put a pin in my hip, and I'd be here for a few days.'

Her face is pinched with anxiety. 'I'm so worried about Humphrey.'

'There's no need to worry,' I reassure her. 'Mum looked after him last night, and I'm here now. I got to Honeywell at lunchtime, and he and I are getting along fine. I won't go back home until we've sorted something out for him.'

She still looks worried. 'He's an enormous responsibility.'

I laugh. 'In every sense of the word.'

'You won't put him in the kennels?' she asks. 'You know his history.'

None of us likes talking about it, but we all know about Humphrey's early life. He was poorly treated as a puppy and ended up in a shelter. Gran adopted him soon after Grandpa Ed died, and the pair of them have never looked back. It's a match made in heaven, but Gran has to be extremely calm and gentle with him at all times, no matter what he gets up to. She's always said she has no difficulty with that, and I can see why. Humphrey is one of the most charming and lovable dogs I've ever met, despite his many quirks.

'I promise we won't put him in the kennels,' I say. 'Mum told me he didn't settle there the one time you tried. He needs to stay at home in familiar surroundings, and we'll make sure he does. Humphrey and I will be quite comfortable together in your lovely cottage. He's promised to show me all the local walks.'

Her face relaxes. 'You're a good girl, Lucy. I'm so sorry about all this.'

'Don't be silly. Which of us has not, at one time or another, fallen down the stairs and ended up in hospital? Perhaps not in hospital exactly, but I fell down the stairs at home on my eighteenth birthday. I may or may not have drunk more than was wise at my party. The jury's still out on that.'

'I remember that,' she says. 'Your mother was terribly upset, but your father thought it was funny.'

'I'll bet he did. Mum takes things so seriously. I can't think how she and Dad ended up together, but I'm glad they did. They balance each other out.'

'They do,' Gran agrees. 'And your mother hasn't had much to laugh about this past year.'

'I know. She's been amazing. She's held everything together and never once complained.'

'And now I've added to her worries,' she says. 'That's the last thing I ever wanted to do.'

'No, you haven't. I've told her to leave everything to me and not to worry about a thing.'

'But you'll have to go back to work soon,' she says. 'Who will look after Humphrey then?'

I give her a reassuring smile. 'Mum always says the way to solve even the biggest problem is one step at a time. And Humphrey's living situation is my first step. Do you have any friends or neighbours who could stay with him for a week or two?'

'I don't think so. He likes to sleep in his own bed. He doesn't adapt well to unfamiliar places.'

'Then we can look for someone to care for him in your cottage,' I say. 'That shouldn't be too difficult. There must be dog sitters in the area who could help out.'

'I've tried that once or twice,' she says. 'But it hasn't worked out. Humphrey is rather territorial about people he doesn't know sleeping in his house. I had a friend visit me last year. He prowled up and down the landing all night, barking outside her room every few minutes. We had to book her into a bed-and-breakfast the next day so we could all get some sleep.'

'That makes it more difficult,' I admit. 'But Mum says he was fine with her last night, and I'm not expecting any problems while I'm here. Humphrey and I have always got along very well together. Try not to worry about him. I'm sure I can find a solution that works for all of us.'

Gran doesn't look convinced, but she doesn't say anything more. Her eyelids have started to droop. I expect the painkillers are kicking in, which is a good thing. Time for me to leave and let her rest.

'I should get back to Humphrey,' I say. 'I've been gone for a while, and he'll be ready for a walk. Hopefully, we'll meet some other dog owners, and I can ask them if they have any suggestions.'

She nods sleepily, and I lean over to kiss her goodbye.

'Is there anything else I should know about before I go?' I ask. 'Quirks with the hot water or the central heating?'

She shakes her head. 'It's all quite straightforward. Call your mother if you have any questions. She knows the cottage like the back of her hand.'

'Then I'll leave you to have a lovely sleep. I'll come in to visit again tomorrow afternoon.'

Her grip on my hand tightens. 'Don't forget about the cookie club.'

Have the painkillers done their work too well and caused her to hallucinate?

'The cookie club?' I ask cautiously. 'Is that something Humphrey likes to eat? Where do you keep them?'

'The club,' she repeats. 'Don't forget about it.'

I'm about to agree that I won't and tiptoe away before she can become more agitated, but something stops me.

'I'm not sure what you're talking about, Gran. Did you say I shouldn't forget about a cookie club?'

Her eyes are almost closed now, but she speaks clearly enough for me to hear. 'That's right, dear. The Honeywell Christmas Cookie Club. You'll be in charge of running it this year.'

Chapter Four

Humphrey is delighted to see me when I arrive back from the hospital. I'm not sure what he got up to in my absence, and I don't have the energy to enquire too closely. The important thing is that he hasn't broken into the larder, so I should be able to feed us both this evening.

I find his harness and lead and take him out for a walk. We head in the direction of the water meadows but turn off well before we reach the boggiest parts. I don't want to have to rescue him from a marsh in the middle of winter.

It was bad enough when I brought him here last summer. He came home plastered in mud, and I had to help Gran give him a bath. It took the two of us almost an hour, and the bathroom was a swamp by the time we'd finished.

It isn't as though Humphrey dislikes baths. His eyes light up at the sound of running water. It's more that he hasn't grasped their purpose. As far as he's concerned, a bath is just an opportunity to displace enormous volumes of water. Getting himself clean is an alien concept to him, one I doubt he'll ever understand.

I may have to face that challenge before Gran comes home, but it's a treat I'm happy to put off for as long as possible. I know she gives him regular baths, but I'm not sure how. Perhaps she calls in reinforcements. I must remember to ask her when I visit tomorrow. And I need some clarification on that cookie club thing too.

Humphrey has a lovely time running around the field and chasing the local crows, although actually catching anything seems to be another idea he doesn't quite grasp. I really don't want him to catch birds, but it would be nice to think he had the ability if he ever needed to survive in the wild.

Humphrey's idea of being a hunting dog is to let out a volley of barks loud enough to alert even the deafest wildlife before running around in excited circles for several seconds. Only then does he take off in the general direction of the birds, which are of course long gone. He returns to me each time with a puzzled expression that seems to say he senses there's something wrong with his technique, but he can't quite figure out what it is. After which, he sees another bird, and the entire process starts again. Still, it keeps him happy. I hope he runs off enough excess energy to sleep well tonight, even without Gran in the house.

We don't meet any other dogs, so I can't ask their owners for dog-sitting suggestions. Maybe it's too cold for dog-walking. The temperature has dropped sharply since this morning. I wonder whether we might have snow tonight, and if so, what Humphrey will think of that. He and I could build a snowman together tomorrow. He may prefer us to make a snowbird, although he stands as little chance of catching that as he does the real thing.

I'm glad Mum left clear instructions about his meals. Tonight's menu is steamed chicken and rice. I locate a chicken breast in the fridge and carefully poach it while the rice steams. Cooking is not my forte, and I don't want to give him food poisoning on my first evening here.

Humphrey wanders around the kitchen while I work, looking at me hopefully. I tip the rice into a bowl and chop the chicken on top. He places his paws on my chest, and I have to use my free hand to push him away.

'You can't eat it yet. You'll burn your tongue.'

He gives me a blank look, and I sigh. 'Do you have even a shred of common sense? On second thoughts, don't bother. I already know the answer.'

He waits until I think his meal is cool enough, then polishes it off in three swift bites, licks the bowl, and grins up at me.

'I spent ages making that,' I say. 'The least you could have done was to take your time eating it.'

I remember Mum saying this to us when I was small. I finally understand where she was coming from. It must be frustrating to spend all afternoon preparing something that disappears in seconds, knowing you'll have to do the same thing only a few hours later.

My appreciation for her patience is growing by the minute. I resolve again not to make her shoulder the burden of this situation. I'm a grown woman, and I can sort everything out by myself. She has enough on her plate. Unlike Humphrey, who's now looking at me as if he can't remember when he last ate but is reasonably certain it was several days ago.

'Too bad,' I say. 'I'm not having you throwing up in the middle of the night while I'm the only one around to clean it up. Despite what I said to Mum, I have no faith at all in your housekeeping abilities.'

He gives a deep sigh and retires to his basket at the other end of the kitchen to brood over my refusal. He watches with offended eyes as I make myself a grilled cheese sandwich, pour myself a glass of milk and sit at the table.

'We need to set some ground rules so you and I both know where we stand,' I say. 'And rule number one is that I get to eat my meals in peace without being made to feel as though I'm snatching food from the mouths of starving dogs.'

His shoulders slump, and I relent. 'You can have my crusts when I've finished. But not if you sulk.'

He tips his head on one side and surveys me placidly. I'll bet Gran gives him her crusts too. She's besotted with him and thinks nothing is too good for him. I can kind of see why, but there's no way I'm telling him that. He needs to know who's boss right from the start.

I toss him the crusts, then go to the living room to watch something before bed. Humphrey accompanies me and flops down beside the wood burner.

'I'm not sure whether Gran has any wood,' I say. 'And it's too cold to go poking around outside right now. We can check tomorrow morning.'

He pads over to the sofa, climbs up and collapses next to me.

I give him an ineffectual push. 'I don't expect you're allowed up here.'

He closes his eyes and ignores me. There's no point worrying about it tonight.

'You can stay here this evening,' I say. 'But if Gran tells me tomorrow that she never lets you sit up here and you didn't inform me of that fact, you'll be sorrier than a very sorry thing.'

Humphrey shifts himself so he's taking up most of the sofa. I push back, but it's like trying to move the Forth Bridge. I tuck my legs into the tiny space remaining and switch on the television.

I switch it off an hour later. There was nothing good on, and my legs are going to sleep. Humphrey looks perfectly comfortable, sprawled in an untidy heap next to me, his legs twitching occasionally. I hope he's making a better job of catching birds in his dreams than he does in real life. I'm glad there were no other dog-walkers around to witness his ineptitude.

It's been a long day, and I'm exhausted. My main priority should be to get a good night's sleep so I start my stay here rested and refreshed. There's a lot to do if I want to get everything organised and return to London with a clear conscience.

Humphrey appears to be sound asleep. I decide to leave him where he is. He can sleep in the kitchen if he wakes up later. Or he can sleep in Gran's room. Mum said he has a basket by her bed.

I tiptoe out of the room and set off down the hall as quietly as possible. I've only made it as far as the bottom stair when he appears in the doorway.

'I didn't want to wake you,' I tell him.

He trots into the kitchen and waits by the back door.

'Do you need to go outside and do your business?' I ask. 'Better now than in the early hours.'

I open the door, and he shoots out into the night. I hope the garden is secure. I don't fancy the idea of chasing down the street after him in this weather.

He reappears a few minutes later, looking pleased with himself.

'Whatever you've done will have to wait until tomorrow,' I say. 'I'm going to bed. Are you staying down here or sleeping upstairs in your basket?'

He rushes down the hall and takes off up the stairs. I follow as he hurls himself through the guest room door and launches himself onto my bed.

'Wrong room,' I say. 'Your bedroom is down there.'

He rolls over onto his back and starts snoring.

I poke him. 'That has to be fake. No one could snore like that without waking themselves up. Come on, Humphrey. Let me take you to your basket.'

He flops over onto his side, but the snoring continues. I debate whether to pick him up and carry him to Gran's room. But it's no good. He must weigh almost as much as I do. I collect his basket from her bedroom and dump it next to my bed.

'There you go,' I tell Humphrey. 'You can sleep in here if you must, but you'll have to turn down the volume.'

He doesn't move. I lean against him, hoping to push him to the edge of the bed. Nothing happens. I consider sleeping in Gran's room tonight, but I haven't made up the bed, and I'm too exhausted to think about finding clean sheets and wrestling with the quilt cover. I glance over at the basket, wondering how comfortable it is. I could curl up in it, pull a blanket over me and pretend I was camping. I look more closely at the dog hairs and traces of slobber and decide against it.

'You are the most annoying dog I've ever met,' I tell him crossly, but he doesn't stir.

'Last night, I had a lovely double bed all to myself,' I say, climbing in and searching for a space in which to curl up. 'And now here I am, sharing a bed with the world's largest and most ridiculous dog.'

Humphrey shifts enough for me to wedge my legs down beside him. I give him my scariest frown, but without effect. Either he really is asleep or he's very good at pretending to be.

I settle down for the night, thinking about how quickly things have changed. Yesterday, I was battling to make cosmetic products sound new and exciting for all our European customers, and today I'm acting as an unpaid servant for a giant, untrained dog. How the mighty have fallen.

Chapter Five

Humphrey wakes me the next morning by the simple expedient of rolling over and lying on my chest.

I push him as hard as I can. 'Stop it! I'm still asleep.'

He doesn't move. I open my eyes to find him staring at me.

'What?' I say.

He licks my face and sighs deeply.

I sit up. 'That's something that needs to stop right now. I have a perfectly good flannel for when I want to wash my face. Your services won't be required, thank you.'

He sighs again and rolls off the bed, landing with a heavy crash on the floorboards. This house is over one hundred years old and probably has woodworm, dry rot, and goodness knows what else. I close my eyes, half expecting the bed to disappear through the floor and for us both to end up in the living room. When nothing happens, I open them again.

'These pre-war houses were built to last,' I say. 'It stands to reason they must have been if you've been living here for three years, and this one is still standing.'

I swing my legs out of bed and shiver. 'I can't think why you wanted to get up. It's lovely and cosy under the duvet.'

Humphrey ignores me and leads the way downstairs to the kitchen, where he trots over and looks hopefully at the fridge.

'You'll have to move if you want me to find whatever you believe is in there,' I tell him. 'Let's check the instructions Mum left for us.'

I pull the piece of paper off the fridge and study it. 'You're out of luck. You have dried food for breakfast. Did you think you could trick me? That won't work, I'm afraid. I'm not a junior supply teacher.'

Humphrey thumps his tail and watches intently as I reach into the cupboard and measure out his food.

I put the bowl in front of him. 'I should inform you in advance that I intend to do everything by the book while I'm here. Gran will have my guts for garters if I don't. So, if you have any ideas of talking me into doing anything she wouldn't like, forget it.'

Humphrey isn't listening. He demolishes his breakfast in a few quick bites before looking up at me like a Charles Dickens orphan.

I pick up the bowl and dump it in the sink. 'No, you may not have any more! And if you keep asking, I'll send you up the chimney to clean it out.'

I consider his frame. 'Perhaps not. You'd get stuck within the first few feet. Whatever possessed you to grow to this size? Any normal dog would have had the sense to stop long ago. I hope you've finished now. You barely fit in this cottage as it is. If you keep going, Gran will have to extend into next door's garden, and the neighbours are sure to complain.'

I pour myself a bowl of cereal. Ignoring his wistful look, I open the fridge to get myself some milk before realising I ran out last night.

I sigh. 'We'll have to go to the shops before we do anything else this morning. Do they let you go inside, or do I have to tie you to a lamp post?'

He gives me a look that says he would have no difficulty in uprooting any lamp post to which he was tied.

'Perhaps I should go to the shops by myself,' I say. 'I'll have to ask Gran what she does when she has to take you out.'

The letterbox rattles, and Humphrey barks loudly and leaps to his feet. Before I can stop him, he races to the front door and returns a moment later with a mouthful of envelopes, which he drops at my feet. He looks up at me like a dog who knows he's done something clever and hopes for a treat.

I pick up the envelopes and wipe off the slobber as best I can. 'Maybe let me fetch them next time?'

His shoulders sag, and I reach down to pat him. 'Sorry, Humphrey. You did a great job. I'll take you out for a nice, long walk in a minute to say thank you. But first, I need my breakfast.'

Cereal is out, so I make myself a couple of slices of toast and spread them thickly with butter. I ignore his pleading eyes and eat it as I look through the envelopes. None of them seem important – a flyer for a local business, something about local planning permission, and what appears to be a utility bill.

I lay the last one on the counter for later, toss the others into the recycling bin, and run upstairs to prepare for what I suspect will be a busy day. I have a long list of things to do, all arranged in order of importance.

Most pressing is to find someone who can look after Humphrey while Gran is in hospital. Next is to arrange someone to help her at home when she's released. She won't be able to walk Humphrey for a while, and she'll need help with personal care too.

I shower quickly and pull on a pair of jeans and my thickest sweater. It's a chilly morning. A quick look outside tells me it didn't snow in the night, but the sky is thick with greyish-white clouds. I remember being snowed in here one winter as a child. We woke in the morning to find the garden had disappeared under a thick blanket of snow. Most of Bramble Close was invisible too. We'd come down by train, and there was no way to get to the nearest station until the roads were cleared.

Honeywell isn't a huge priority for the local council at the best of times, and Bramble Close is even less so. We couldn't get out for four days, which I found wildly exciting, but Mum told me afterwards she'd been concerned we would run out of food. I make a mental note to check the contents of the larder and the fridge before we go shopping. I could manage on restricted rations for a few days, but Humphrey definitely wouldn't enjoy it.

I put his harness on and make sure I have the front door key before setting off. He joyfully drags me along the lane. Ten minutes later, we arrive at the high street. We would have got here more quickly if Humphrey hadn't insisted on exploring every single hedge and testing the thickness of the ice on every puddle.

'Anyone would think this was the first time you'd been along this street,' I say. 'But I'm sure you and Gran walk along here all the time.'

I march him along to the corner shop. He shows a strong desire to stop at the bakery, but I drag him away.

'You won't be allowed in there. Come on! I want to get us some groceries in case there's a blizzard tonight and the whole village is snowed in until the new year.'

Humphrey doesn't look convinced, but he allows himself to be shepherded to the corner shop. I'm pleased to find he's allowed inside so long as he stays on his lead. That's not a problem as far as I'm concerned. The only time Humphrey is going to come off his lead is in the fields next to the water meadows.

I buy as many groceries as I can carry and load them into my backpack.

'When do you close?' I ask the woman behind the counter. 'I may need to make another run later today. Humphrey here eats as much as a small army.'

She smiles at him. 'We all know Humphrey. He's a lovely boy, aren't you, Humphrey? Are you staying with Mrs Hollis?'

I lift my backpack onto my shoulders. 'She's in hospital with a broken hip. I've come down to look after Humphrey for a few days. I'm her granddaughter, Lucy.'

She looks shocked. 'I'm sorry to hear that. I had no idea. Please give her my love when you see her and tell her I hope she gets better soon. I'm Shirley, by the way.'

'Nice to meet you,' I say. 'I'll pass on your message when I visit this afternoon. You don't know of anyone who could look after Humphrey until Gran gets home, do you?'

'Not off the top of my head. But I'll ask around. Meanwhile, let me know if you need anything. There are plenty of people in the village who would be happy to do whatever they can to help your grandmother.'

Humphrey gives his lead an insistent tug, and I almost overbalance.

'I'm coming,' I tell him. 'I expect you want to go to the bakery, but I've already told you that's not happening.'

'They don't mind,' says Shirley. 'The owners allow dogs to go in as long as they're well behaved.'

I give Humphrey a dubious look. 'I'm not sure I'd go as far as to say he's well behaved.'

She laughs. 'Take him in and say hello. They make excellent coffee, and they may have some suggestions about a dog sitter. Those girls know everyone in the village, and they can be extremely persuasive when they want to be.'

I waver. I could do with a cup of coffee. Mum only got me instant, and I didn't bring a cafetière with me.

'They sell dog biscuits too,' says Shirley. 'I'm sure Humphrey wouldn't say no to a nice biscuit, would you, darling?'

Humphrey gives her a look that says quite clearly he would never say no to a nice anything. He also manages to convey the impression his current caregiver hasn't remembered to feed him since she arrived.

A look outside tells me it's starting to sleet. That does it. There are few things I hate more than sleet. It can't decide whether to be good, honest rain or a magical snowfall, so it compromises on cold, damp sogginess.

'Come on, Humphrey!' I say, tugging on his leash to distract him from the shelf of cereal he's inspecting. 'Let's go and buy you a lovely dog biscuit.'

Chapter Six

Humphrey doesn't need telling twice. He rockets out of the shop and sets off excitedly in the wrong direction. He realises his mistake and turns himself around somewhat in the manner of a giant oil tanker in the middle of the North Sea, with lots of puffing noises and manoeuvrings.

'Finally!' I say when he's facing in the right direction. 'The dog biscuits are this way. And, more importantly, the coffee.'

We walk towards The Sugarloaf Bakery. I hesitate before opening the door. It's all very well for Shirley to say they allow dogs in here, but that description seems a stretch when it comes to Humphrey.

'Excuse me,' says a voice, and I turn to see an elderly woman with a small, curly-haired dog standing behind me.

'I'm sorry,' I apologise. 'We take up a lot of space. Humphrey does, at least. Are you going in here?'

She nods, and I hold the door open for her. The small dog runs inside and jumps up at the counter.

'Now, now, Bernie!' says his owner. 'Sit down nicely, and Lily will give you a biscuit.'

I follow them inside and stand by the door, half expecting an irate staff-member to shoo us out again, sleet or no sleet.

'Hello, Humphrey!' says a pleasant-looking young woman with fair hair, who I assume is Lily. 'We haven't seen you in here for a few days.'

Relieved, I take another step inside and allow the door to close behind me. Humphrey sidles over to the counter and stares up at a basket next to the till. If anyone wanted to hide the dog biscuits, they wouldn't stand a chance with these two dogs around.

'Are you sure he's allowed in here?' I ask.

'Absolutely,' she says. 'You can sit at either of those tables near the door. We reserve those for our canine visitors, don't we, Bernie?'

The small dog, who has wedged himself under one of the two tables, looks up when he hears his name. He grins at us, and the biscuit he's been crunching falls out of his mouth. He stops grinning and makes a dart for it. That may be wise with Humphrey in the vicinity.

I sit down at the second table, hoping Humphrey knows the drill and doesn't disgrace me in front of my new acquaintances. He plumps himself down next to me and heaves an enormous sigh.

'Would you like a biscuit too?' Lily asks him. 'We have some lovely beef ones.'

She hands him a biscuit, and he disposes of it in two mouthfuls.

She laughs. 'That didn't even touch the sides, did it? Is he allowed another one?'

'I'm not sure,' I say. 'What does he usually have when he comes in here?'

'He likes the lamb and herb flavour,' says the elderly woman.

'Thank you,' I say. 'Do you know how many he eats?'

'He has two,' she informs me. 'Bernie is only allowed one, but he's a lot smaller.'

'That's an understatement,' I say, looking at Bernie, who's about one sixth Humphrey's size. 'I hope your dog isn't frightened of Humphrey. I wouldn't blame him if he was.'

'They're good friends,' she says. 'Although Humphrey can be a little overwhelming at times. Bernie's a very sensitive dog, and he prefers to play gently.'

The very sensitive dog looks up at the sound of his name. Noticing Humphrey making a start on his second biscuit, he scrambles to his feet and runs over to join him.

I instinctively tighten my grip on Humphrey's lead. He's clearly fond of his food, and I doubt he'll take kindly to being deprived of it. To my surprise, he drops the rest of the biscuit onto the floor and lets Bernie make a grab for it.

'Now, now, Bernie,' his owner chides him again. 'You know the vet said you shouldn't eat too many biscuits.'

Bernie appears sublimely unconscious of the vet having said any such thing. His expression suggests that he remembers it very differently and that the vet gave strict instructions his blood biscuit-levels should never be allowed to fall too low.

Humphrey flops down next to my chair again, narrowly missing Bernie, who's too preoccupied with the biscuit to notice he's only just escaped being squashed like a bug on a windshield.

'I'm sorry,' I tell his owner. 'Humphrey doesn't seem to realise quite how big he is. But he's very gentle. He wouldn't willingly hurt a fly.'

'We all know him,' says Lily. 'But I don't think we've seen you in here before?'

I explain who I am and what I'm doing in Honeywell. Both she and the elderly woman seem shocked when I tell them about Gran's fall and subsequent operation.

'Anyway, that's why I'm here,' I finish. 'And I'll have to stay until I find someone else to look after Humphrey. I don't suppose either of you has any suggestions?'

'I can't think of anyone right now,' says Lily. 'But I'll ask my mother tonight. She knows everyone around here and may have some ideas.'

'And I'll ask the Silver Surfers,' says the elderly woman. 'Mavis is excellent in a crisis.'

I'm not sure who the Silver Surfers are, but I'm not about to turn down any offer of help. I order a cappuccino and don't take much persuading to try one of the lemon tarts.

'Abby made them an hour ago,' says Lily. 'You're lucky my partner Isabella is out this afternoon, or there wouldn't have been any left for you.'

The elderly woman picks up her bag and prepares to leave. 'I'm Mrs Ogilvie,' she tells me. 'I'll ask around for you.'

'Thank you so much,' I say gratefully. 'I'm Lucy Hollis. Do you have my grandmother's phone number?'

'Mavis will find it. She can find anything.' She nods to Lily, and she and Bernie set off together down the high street.

I catch Lily's eye. 'Who is this Mavis person? She sounds as though she works for MI5.'

'I wouldn't be surprised,' she says. 'She runs the computer club in the village, and she's terrifyingly efficient. I hope you don't have any secrets. She'll dig them out in seconds.'

'None that I can think of,' I say. 'I should be getting home. Humphrey has his lunch at noon, and I don't want to get between him and food. He might eat me instead.'

She ruffles Humphrey's head. 'I think you're safe enough. He's the mildest-mannered dog I've ever met. But don't let Mrs Ogilvie know I said that. She's one of our best customers, and she'd never forgive me. Bernie is the light of her life, and she's convinced he's the best at everything he does.'

'That's how my grandmother feels about Humphrey,' I say, pulling on my coat and hat. 'I can't imagine how she's feeling right now. She won't care about her broken hip, but she'll be desperately worried about Humphrey. I wish I could take him to the hospital so she can see for herself he's fine. But I don't think they would appreciate that. He's a sweet-natured old thing, but even his most fervent admirers would have to admit he's clumsy.'

As if to confirm my statement, Humphrey jumps to his feet, knocking over two chairs and jogging the table so a vase of flowers falls over.

Lily picks it up. 'We all have our faults. To be fair, he's no more clumsy than my business partner. Whenever she catches sight of a fresh batch of cakes, she doesn't allow anything or anyone to get in her way. That's why we always keep plenty of spare cups and plates in stock.'

'That's very sensible,' I say. 'Humphrey kicked his bowl across the floor this morning in his rush to collect the post. I may have to buy some spares myself just in case.'

I look down at Humphrey, who stares back at me with an air of bewildered innocence.

'Let's get you out of here before you do any serious damage,' I say. 'I need to save what little money I have for Christmas presents, not paying for damaged crockery.'

I arrive at the hospital mid-afternoon. Gran is awake and looking more comfortable.

'How's Humphrey?' she asks the moment she sees me.

'Absolutely fine. He's enjoying a well-deserved nap after helping me do the grocery shopping, clean the house, and make lunch.'

I catch her eye and grin. 'When I say helping …'

Her face relaxes. 'That sounds like Humphrey. He does like to be involved with whatever's going on.'

'I expect he'll sleep all afternoon. He needs to recover his energy for this evening's walk. He didn't catch any birds last night, but he's convinced that was just bad luck.'

'I hope he isn't being too much trouble,' she says.

'Not in the slightest. I'm enjoying the break, and Humphrey is wonderful company. I didn't feel at all nervous staying in your cottage by myself last night with such a giant guard dog.'

She smiles. 'The last time he heard a noise in the middle of the night, he hid under the bed until I'd gone to check what it was. Luckily, it was only a squirrel, but he was no use at all.'

'But he looks the part. That's the main thing. If there are any burglars lurking around Honeywell, they'll take one look at him and make a note to avoid your address. By the way, I took him to the village bakery this morning. Or rather, he took me. I met one of his friends. Bernie, I think his name was.'

'I like Bernie,' she says. 'His owner spoils him dreadfully, but it doesn't seem to do him any harm. He's always delighted to see Humphrey when we bump into him on our evening walk.'

'She said she'll ask around to see whether anyone is free to care for Humphrey. And the woman who works in the bakery said she'd do the same.'

'That's so kind,' she says. 'But Humphrey doesn't settle with just anyone.'

'I promise I won't leave him with someone he doesn't love,' I tell her. 'By the way, do you remember mentioning the cookie club yesterday? You were too tired to tell me any details, but I would like to know what you were talking about.'

'It's been going since 1939,' she says proudly. 'Have I never mentioned it to you? My grandmother and her friends founded it at the start of the Second World War.'

'I hadn't heard anything about it until yesterday. It sounds fascinating.'

'There's too much to tell you now,' she says. 'But the club members will tell you all about it at your first meeting.' She closes her eyes.

'Are you alright?' I ask, concerned. 'Shall I get the nurse to bring you some more painkillers?'

'I'm just a little tired, that's all. But I'm so happy to have seen you.'

I tuck the blanket around her. 'I'll leave you to have a sleep. One more thing. You told me yesterday I needed to run this club for you.'

She opens her eyes. 'The first meeting is on Thursday evening at seven o'clock. You need to host it, and you'll need to bake four dozen cookies beforehand.'

'For the club members?' I ask. 'That's a lot of cookies. How many of them will there be?'

'They'll all bring cookies too,' she says. 'Remember, they need to be homemade. No shop-bought cookies.'

'But surely, someone else can –' I begin, but she shakes her head.

'I don't want anyone else to do it. It's a Hollis thing. And you're a Hollis. Please tell me you'll do it.'

It isn't like Gran to be so stubborn about anything. Maybe it's the drugs they're giving her.

I bend down to kiss her cheek. 'I'll do my best if it's so important.'

'It is.'

Her voice is no more than a whisper, but her jaw is set just like Mum's when she won't take no for an answer. That doesn't happen often, but when it does, we all know not to argue with her. It may be the same with Gran. Whatever's going on here is important to her. I resolve not to ask too many questions while she's so vulnerable.

'I'll host it this week,' I promise. 'And I'll feed all your guests. After that, you'll be home and able to host it for yourself.'

'I hope so. Give my love to Humphrey, and tell him to behave himself.'

'I will. Although I can't guarantee he'll take the slightest bit of notice.'

She smiles, and I leave her to sleep. With any luck, all I'll need to do on Thursday is make tea and coffee and hand out cookies, then listen politely while everyone talks about recipes and the war. Even I should be able to manage that.

Chapter Seven

I take Humphrey for a walk the next morning, then settle him into his basket for a well-deserved rest. It takes a lot of energy to chase after rats and other small mammals who heard him coming while he was still several streets away and made their escape long before he reached them.

I dig through Gran's cookery books until I find what looks like a simple recipe for oatmeal and raisin cookies. It sounds as though these club members have enormous appetites. Or maybe it's some sort of cookie-exchange thing. That would make more sense. I'm not sure why they can't eat shop-bought cookies at the meeting, but Gran was adamant, so I'd better do as she told me.

'How difficult can it be?' I ask Humphrey.

He gives me a puzzled frown that makes me laugh, then rolls over onto his back and starts to snore.

'You're no help,' I mutter, assembling my ingredients. It's not too complicated – sugar, butter, eggs, flour, baking powder, oats, and raisins. Gran doesn't appear to have any baking powder, so I improvise with cream of tartar. I can't imagine anyone will tell the difference. I can't find any raisins, but I discover what looks like a packet of currants on the top shelf.

I switch on the oven. Then, feeling rather like the little red hen, I start to mix and stir. The recipe isn't as helpful as it could be. It tells me to cream and fold but not what that means. I do my best and, somewhat to my surprise, the result looks passable. I pick up a couple of teaspoons and attempt to drop the mixture onto the greased baking sheet as the recipe instructs. But the dough isn't keen to comply. It sticks first to one spoon and then to the other. I bang one of them against the sheet, hoping to knock the dough off. Nothing happens.

I try again, then reach into the drawer for a knife and scrape the mixture off with that. Half of it ends up stuck to the knife, but I finally manage to arrange the dough into twelve irregular mounds on the tray. I can claim the size difference is intentional, to make allowance for varying-sized appetites. The oven light has gone out, which should mean it's hot enough.

I cast a quick look at Humphrey to make sure he won't dive for the oven the moment I open it. He's still flat on his back, his legs twitching at intervals. Hopefully, he'll stay that way until the cookies are safely on their cooling tray, well out of his reach.

I slide the tray into the oven, set the timer, and make myself a cup of coffee while the cookies are baking. That didn't go as badly as it might have done, even if they're not as perfectly shaped as the ones in the bakery. I expect they have some sort of machine that turns them out in a uniform size. I make a note to ask about it the next time I go in.

Anyway, I don't want my cookies to look like theirs. The whole point of making them at home is that they're … homemade. And everyone knows homemade cookies aren't all the same as each other. They're quirky and individual, which is why everyone likes them so much.

The timer pings, and I reach for the oven gloves, feeling a pang of anticipation. I open the door, lift out the tray, and inspect my creations with slight dismay. Quirky and individual is one thing, but it doesn't quite describe what I've produced. These cookies seem to have thrown a party while they were in the oven.

They've spread into irregular shapes and are all stuck to each other. To make it worse, they're burned at the edges and still soggy in the middle.

I dump the tray onto the counter-top, suppressing an urge to scream. I followed the recipe to the letter, which means these cookies should look exactly like the ones in the book. That's how cooking is supposed to work. Otherwise, what's the point of having a recipe book at all? It's nothing more than a giant con.

I'll bet the person who wrote this book didn't bother to test the recipes before publishing them. It's the only possible explanation. They're aiming to make quick money from novices such as myself, while all along they have no idea how to cook either. I refuse to allow them to get away with it. I'll write to their publishers to make a formal complaint and request a refund. And a letter of apology.

I pull out my phone to find who publishes this unresearched nonsense. I don't like leaving negative reviews, but in this case I'm happy to make an exception. It serves them right. I tap the name of the so-called chef into the search bar, adding the title of the book. I frown as hundreds of results flash onto my screen. Whoever this Mary Berry person is, she seems to be fairly well known. Which makes it even more annoying that she's allowed to get away with publishing untested recipes.

I scroll through page after page of articles and reviews. No one else seems to have had the same problem. Maybe Gran's book is a misprinted edition. That would explain why the recipes don't work for me, but everyone else thinks they're fine.

I'll have to contact the publishers later, once I've decided what's going on. I have more pressing problems right now. I'm hosting this cookie club tomorrow, and I have to produce something at least partially edible before then. This cookbook isn't the answer. I'll have to find a better recipe online.

This is a more cheering thought. There are millions of free recipes out there. All I have to do is select one that's been well reviewed, and all will be well. I scroll through my phone. As I thought, there are a million and one oatmeal cookie recipes, all apparently more amazing than the last.

I see a name I recognise and click on it. Mum has always sworn by Delia Smith's recipes. She makes her Christmas cake and mince pies every year, and they're delicious. It stands to reason her oatmeal cookies will be too.

I scrape my misshapen, burned cookies into the kitchen bin. Humphrey's nose twitches, but he doesn't move. I wash out the bowl, check I still have enough ingredients, then start again from the beginning, careful not to deviate too much from the recipe. I feel more cheerful as I sift and stir and mix.

I roll the spoonfuls of dough between my hands as instructed, press them lightly with a fork, and put the tray back into the oven, feeling pleased with myself. That wasn't so difficult. The members of the cookie club are bound to be impressed when I hand these around tomorrow, especially when I casually drop into the conversation they're the first cookies I've ever baked. I don't have to mention the failed batch. It wasn't my fault the recipe was faulty.

I finish my coffee and make myself another. Humphrey is still asleep, so I pick up this morning's newspaper and make a start on the crossword. Gran won't mind. She's on powerful painkillers and won't be up to doing crosswords for a few days. I'm so engrossed in four down that I almost jump out of my seat when the timer pings. I lay down my pen and reach for the oven gloves again, giving thanks for actual competent and expert chefs.

I stare at the cookies, stifling a most unprofessional chef-like exclamation. What is wrong with these so-called famous cooks? Why are they invited to do baking shows on the television? More importantly, how are they ever invited back?

These cookies are, if anything, worse than the first batch. They look like something from a horror movie. What were supposed to have been perfectly shaped circles are now oddly shaped blobs that look like a cross between melted snowmen and the Sea of Tranquility. They don't smell right either. Maybe I shouldn't have used that cream of tartar after all, and I probably shouldn't have doubled the amount to help them rise.

These cookies belong in a museum of baking disasters, if there is such a thing. If there isn't, they should open one especially and give my cookies pride of place. Even Humphrey wouldn't want them. Not that I'm giving him the chance. The last thing I need is to explain to a strange vet how I've managed to give my grandmother's dog severe food poisoning.

I settle down to make a third batch of cookies. This time, the recipe doesn't call for baking powder, so I don't have to make any substitutions. I also realise the packet of currants isn't all it seems. I should have noticed the label said Dried Olives. Oh, well. We live and learn.

This batch doesn't look quite as awful as the first two, so I decide to take it with me to the hospital. I've promised to visit Gran at three o'clock. She can take a look and give me some hints about what I can improve before tomorrow evening. How can making cookies be so difficult? You can't watch a holiday movie without stumbling on people merrily whipping up hundreds of batches of perfect cookies whenever they have a spare ten minutes, all iced to professional standards.

I can't let Gran down. This cookie club seems so important to her. Almost as important as Humphrey. I remind myself I'm a modern, capable woman. I can juggle several things at once. Surely, I can look after her precious dog and master the art of combining a few basic ingredients in a way that doesn't send the club members off to join her in the hospital to have their stomachs pumped.

I toy with the idea of writing a feature-length exposé of celebrity chefs. The public ought to know what's going on with these fake experts. I could challenge them to join me in the television studio kitchens and bake one of their stupid recipes, live and without special effects. We could invite real people off the street to sample the results and give their honest opinions, rather than relying on sycophantic TV show hosts to pretend everything is amazing and tastes delicious. If I were one of those hosts, I'd demand danger money before tasting anything produced on my show.

Humphrey is still fast asleep. I pick up the baking tray, cover it with a tea towel, and let myself out of the house. Thankfully, he doesn't wake up and start barking. I hate the thought of him being upset at being left by himself. But I'll be back in a couple of hours, and we can spend the evening together.

We'll go for a nice long walk to his favourite park and play fetch. By which I mean, I can stand in the cold, hurling random sticks as far as possible, while Humphrey races around, forgetting where most of them landed. We all have different ways of enjoying ourselves, and that appears to be his. Who am I to judge?

I walk carefully down the path towards the car. The remains of last night's frost still coats the flagstones, and I don't want to slip and fall. The hospital doesn't need another Hollis woman to care for. I reach out and lift the latch of the garden gate, careful not to catch my sleeve in the privet hedge. It needs a trim, but I know even less about gardening than I do about cooking, so that will have to wait until Gran is home to give me proper instructions.

I balance the tray on my left hip and reach into my pocket with my right hand. My car key is in here somewhere. Unless Humphrey has mistaken it for a dog biscuit and eaten it. I wouldn't put it past him. I find the key and step out onto the pavement.

Something catches my shoulder, spinning me around abruptly. Have I stepped on a patch of ice? A wave of pain shoots down my arm, and I gasp in horror as the tray of cookies flies out of my hands. I can only watch helplessly as they fly into the frosty air, fanning out in a graceful arc. I make a futile grab for one, but it's no good. The entire batch lands on the road in front of me and bursts like a group of shells.

I stare at them in horrified disbelief. I've spent half the day trying to make something fit for human consumption. And now they're scattered across the icy road in tiny pieces.

'I'm so sorry,' says a man's voice. 'I didn't see the gate open. Can I help you pick them up?'

Chapter Eight

It isn't often that I lose my temper. It rarely seems worth it. But I make an exception today.

I inspect the remains of my cookies and turn to glare at the man standing in front of me.

'Why can't you look where you're going?' I demand. 'I spent hours making these, and then you come along and destroy all my hard work in seconds.'

His face shows a mixture of guilt and defensiveness. 'I'm very sorry. You appeared from nowhere. By the time I saw you, the damage was done.'

'You're the one who appeared from nowhere!' I snap. 'You should have been watching where you were going.'

'I was busy looking for the footpath,' he says. 'Someone told me there was a short cut to the fields at the end of this cul-de-sac.'

'That's no excuse for stomping along without looking around you. You must have known I couldn't see around the hedge.'

Is that a look of amusement on his face? It had better not be.

'I didn't know anything of the kind,' he says. 'Mainly because I had no idea there was anyone lurking there. In future, it might be an idea to make some sort of warning noise before appearing unexpectedly – like ships sounding their foghorns in the channel.'

He sees my expression and stops smiling. 'I really am very sorry. Can I help you to … er …?'

He surveys the scattered crumbs. 'On second thoughts, perhaps not. There aren't enough pieces here to make one entire cookie.'

'I know that!' I say. 'Even if I wanted to eat cookies that had been lying in the road.'

'I'm terribly sorry,' he says again. 'Were they for a special occasion?'

'That's none of your business!' I see his lips twitch and add defensively, 'I don't know you.'

'True. But that's easily remedied.' He holds out his hand to me. 'Daniel Chapman.'

I don't take it. 'What's that thing you're holding?'

He glances down at his free hand. 'I'm not sure I should tell you. As you've pointed out, we don't know each other. I think you should tell me your name before I divulge such top-secret information.'

'I'm not interested in whatever it is,' I say, bending to pick up the cookie tray and noticing with annoyance it now has a large dent in the middle. That won't do my future baking attempts much good.

'I'm prepared to throw caution to the winds,' he says. 'I'll risk you being a top-secret spy, living here as a sleeper agent and hoping to set up as my business competitor. It's a drone.'

'I'll take your word for it. Next time you decide to take one of your toys out to play with, I suggest you look where you're going.'

I press the button on my car key, open the passenger door and dump the tray onto the seat. 'I have to go.'

I slam the door and march around to the driver's side. He moves in front of the car and stands there.

I glare at him. 'What are you doing now? I suggest you get out of my way in the next ten seconds or you and your drone will regret it.'

He doesn't move. 'Are you threatening me with the same fate as your cookies? An apt revenge.'

'I'm not threatening anything. I'm telling you I need to leave. I suggest you don't stand in the middle of the road impeding the traffic.'

'An excellent suggestion,' he says. 'We could all benefit from brushing up on the highway code now and then.'

'It's a pity you didn't brush up on it before leaving home,' I say. 'Then you might not have crashed into me.'

'That was on the pavement,' he says. 'Different rules apply there.'

'All I know is that I had a tray of cookies when I left the house. I no longer have any cookies, and this tray has a dent in it.'

'For which I apologise,' he says, sounding surprisingly sincere. 'The least I can do is buy you a new tray.'

'There's no need,' I say. 'The best thing you can do for me now is get out of my way and let me get to my appointment.'

He steps back onto the pavement. 'I didn't mean to hold you up. Can I give you a ride to wherever it is you're going?'

I wave my car keys at him. 'Why would I want a ride?'

'You might be in shock,' he says. 'I'm sure the highway code says you shouldn't drive when you're in shock.'

'I'm not in shock. I'm annoyed. Can't you tell the difference?'

'As you pointed out, I'm a stranger. I haven't had time to learn the full range of your facial expressions.'

I'd like to make a facial expression he won't be able to misinterpret, but I refrain. Gran wouldn't like me lowering the tone of the neighbourhood.

'What about the cookies?' he asks.

'What about them?'

'I assume you need them for this appointment?'

'I'll manage.'

'There's no need,' he says. 'As you say, this was mostly my fault, so I ought to replace your cookies as quickly as possible.'

'It was *all* your fault,' I say, refusing to allow him to blur the edges of the truth and attempt to share the blame. 'And they're irreplaceable.'

His eyebrows shoot up. 'That sounds interesting. Were they coated with gold leaf or just a top-secret family recipe that has now been lost forever?'

I lean against the car and survey him. I'm not sure why I'm bothering to argue. I should climb in and drive away, whether he's standing there or not. Preferably with him standing there. But there's something uniquely annoying about his attitude. He's destroyed several hours of my work, and he doesn't seem as sorry as he ought to be.

'You can make fun of me all you like,' I say. 'But I spent half the morning making those cookies. It's nowhere near as easy as you might think. Those so-called cookery writers have no idea what they're doing. I followed their recipes to the letter, and nothing came out looking anything like the photos in the book.'

'They should all be fired,' he says. 'I'll write a strong letter to the publishers if you like.'

'I'm way ahead of you. But that won't help me right now.'

'If you wait here for five minutes, I'll run up to the bakery and buy you some new ones.'

I give a frustrated sigh. 'Haven't you been listening to a word I've said? They were homemade cookies, not bakery cookies.'

'Would the person receiving them know the difference?' he asks.

'Yes, she would! And so would I. And now I'll have to start all over again and waste more perfectly good ingredients. The Christmas Cookie Club is meeting here at seven o'clock tomorrow.'

'What on earth is a cookie club?' he asks.

'I'm not entirely sure. All I know is that everyone who wants to attend has to bring home-baked cookies. And I have to make some halfway decent ones before then. It doesn't matter why. You wouldn't understand or care.'

'I do care,' he says. 'But I can't help wondering whether you're making this more difficult than it needs to be. They're only cookies.'

He peers at the crumbs lying in the street. 'By the looks of it, they were oatmeal. How difficult can it be to make a batch of oatmeal cookies?'

My temper, which was subsiding, flares up again. 'Extremely difficult! If you knew anything at all about baking, you'd know that. Why don't you try for yourself and then come and tell me how you've done? Even better, go and play with your drone and leave me to get on with my day.'

'I'm sorry to have upset you,' he says. 'Let me know if you change your mind and would like me to replace your cookies. I haven't done much baking, but I'm happy to find a recipe and have a go at making some myself.'

I give a derisive snort. 'I'd give good money to see you make better cookies than mine! It's far more difficult than you might think.'

'I'm sure you're right,' he says. 'Well, you need to get to your appointment. And I should go and … play with my drone. Maybe I'll see you around?'

I switch on the engine and slam the car into gear. 'Not if I see you first,' I mutter.

I ignore his cheerful wave and set off along the street towards the main road, taking great care to avoid the icy patches. I'm sure Daniel would be amused to watch me skid into the verge, and I've embarrassed myself quite enough for one day.

Chapter Nine

Gran is sitting up in bed when I arrive. It's good to see her with some colour in her cheeks. The last couple of times I saw her, she looked as though she could audition for the ghost of Hamlet's father.

I bend to kiss her. 'I'm pleased to see you're looking better. How are you feeling?'

'A lot more chirpy,' she says. 'The doctor saw me this morning and said I should be able to go home within a week as long as I don't do anything stupid in the meantime.'

I smile. 'There goes your plan to organise an inter-ward wheelchair race.'

I sit down next to her bed. 'I meant to bring you some cookies, but I had an … accident.'

I almost mention Daniel and his inexplicable inability to navigate an empty street without crashing into something. But I don't trust myself to describe the incident calmly and without emotion, and I'm determined to be the perfect hospital visitor. It's important not to impede Gran's recovery. Humphrey would never forgive me if I kept the pair of them apart for a moment longer than necessary.

'Do you mean you burned them?' she asks.

'I burned one batch. I'm not sure what happened with the second batch. The third one wasn't too bad. I was bringing the cookies with me so you could offer some expert advice, but I … dropped them on the way to the car.'

'What a pity,' she says. 'What kind of cookies were they?'

'They were meant to be oatmeal and raisin. I'm not great at baking, so I thought I'd start with something simple and foolproof. But they didn't turn out that way.'

'You know Humphrey mustn't eat raisins?' she asks.

'I do. I have a long list of all the things dogs shouldn't eat. Although these turned out to be dried olives, not raisins. Don't worry about Humphrey. I'm taking good care of him, and he isn't going hungry. But that's not the story he'll tell you when you get home. Promise not to listen to a word he says. He's an unreliable narrator.'

Her face relaxes. 'I won't. And I'm not questioning how well you're looking after him. I know he's in excellent hands. I can't thank you enough for dropping everything and coming down here to help out. I feel terribly guilty about it.'

'I haven't dropped anything. I'm enjoying the break. I've always loved Honeywell, so it's no hardship to stay for as long as you need me.'

Her face crumples in distress. 'You mustn't stay for long. As soon as I'm home, we'll find someone to come in and help me each day. The doctor mentioned something about the district nurse, and I'm sure we can get a carer to help me with washing and dressing.'

'There's Humphrey too,' I remind her. 'I don't think carers will be insured for walking him. I'm not sure anyone is. And you're certainly not insured for whatever he may do to them. I'm sure you'd be more comfortable with me than with strangers coming and going, and I know Humphrey would be. You know how he is with new people.'

She doesn't look convinced, but now isn't the time to argue.

'We can talk about all that another time,' I say. 'The more important thing is tomorrow evening. Do you have any special instructions for me?'

'I have a list,' she says, reaching over to the bedside table and rummaging in the drawer.

'How very organised of you. I hope it's not too long. I need to spend every minute from now until tomorrow evening perfecting a basic cookie recipe. Are you sure it wouldn't be better to ask someone else to hold the meeting at their house? The other members are sure to know what you usually do.'

Gran hands me the piece of paper. 'The meetings have always been held at Rose Cottage.'

'This club is very important to you, isn't it?' I ask.

'More than I can say.' She gives me a rueful smile. 'I can tell you think I'm being a fussy old thing, and perhaps I am. But this club has a very special history, and I'm anxious not to break it.'

I fold the paper and put it into my bag. 'How have I not heard about it before?'

'Did your mother never mention it to you?'

'I'm sure she didn't. I have an excellent memory when it comes to the subject of cookies. Eating them, that is, not baking them. I buy all my cookies at the local bakery.'

'Did you never learn to cook?' she asks.

'Mum used to let me decorate the Christmas cookies when I was small, although I usually ended up covered from head to toe in icing. And we never had anywhere nearly as much dough in the bowl as when we started. I've always been partial to raw cookie dough.'

'I remember how much you loved my cookies. I thought your mother would have taught you to bake. I'm surprised she didn't.'

'It wasn't her fault,' I defend Mum. 'I'm sure she would have taught me if I'd asked her to. But I always had my head in a book or I was out with friends. When I left home and went to university, I was living in catered halls. After I started working in

London, I was too busy to learn more than the basics. I can cook baked beans and scrambled eggs, but I haven't got around to anything fancier. I wish now that I had. I don't want to poison the members of your club tomorrow. Maybe I could tell them my cookies are some kind of art installation, and you're supposed to look at them but not taste them.'

Gran doesn't comment, but I'm sure I detect a look of disapproval.

'I can do lots of other things,' I say. 'I can wire a plug and change a tyre and fix a leaking pipe.'

Her face relaxes. 'I'm not criticising you. Your mother was so keen on baking with me when she was a girl that I thought she'd have passed it on to you, that's all. But times change, and we have to change with them. No doubt she thought there were better things to teach you.'

I feel as though I'm swimming into deeper water than I'm comfortable with. And swimming is something else I'm not great at. I can manage a couple of lengths and could keep myself afloat for a few minutes if I accidentally fell into a canal. But I'm not a natural water baby. Still, we all have our strengths and weaknesses. Honeywell is several miles from the sea, so my life-saving abilities are unlikely to be called into play. There's a small river at the far end of the village, into which Humphrey has launched himself thousands of times. But, for a large dog, he's surprisingly buoyant, so I won't lose sleep over the thought of having to dive in and fish him out.

I drag my thoughts away from giant nets and flotation devices to more immediate issues, the chief of which is this cookie club. I hadn't understood at first how important it was to Gran. Now that I do, I feel the weight of responsibility settle on my shoulders. Things are bad enough for her after breaking her hip and being forced to leave her beloved Humphrey. I can't make them worse by ruining her cookie club.

'I have it all in hand,' I tell her. 'I promise you won't have any complaints, even if I have to stay up all night developing my nonexistent culinary skills. And if the worst really comes to the worst, there's always the village bakery.'

Gran shakes her head. 'I told you yesterday they need to be homemade.'

I'm surprised by how definite her tone is, but I remember she isn't herself at the moment. She's had a nasty accident and is still in considerable pain. It's natural she should want to control whatever she can. And if fixating on this club takes her mind off everything else she's going through, that's fine with me.

'Homemade cookies it is,' I tell her. 'It will do me good to learn a new skill. And it makes the kitchen smell delicious, even when the finished product isn't quite what I'd hoped for.'

She sighs. 'You'll have to forgive me. You're doing so much for me, and I'm adding to your burden. I'm sorry, Lucy.'

'You're anxious for everything to go well,' I say. 'And I promise you it will. I meant to ask how this all works. Is it some sort of a cookie exchange?'

'Haven't I explained that?' she asks. 'I thought I'd told you all about it.'

'Only that it was being held on Thursday and you wanted me to host it.'

'No wonder you're confused,' she says. 'I should have explained it to you earlier.'

A hospital porter appears next to the bed. 'Mrs Hollis? I need to take you down for an x-ray before they close.'

'Could I have five minutes?' she asks. 'I need to talk to my granddaughter about something.'

'I'm afraid not. We're running a little late, and the nurse tells me they want it done today.' He pulls up the rails on Gran's bed and unlocks the wheels.

'I'll leave you to it,' I say. 'Humphrey will be ready for his evening walk. He was fast asleep when I left, which means he'll be well rested and eager to explore the muddier parts of the village the minute I get home. It's a good thing I remembered to pack my wellington boots.'

'Give him my love,' says Gran.

'I'll get him to make you a card. I can bring it in with me the next time I see you. I'll go home now and take him for a walk, then cook us both some dinner. I believe he's having steak tonight. That dog eats better than most people.'

I wave goodbye to the nurses and make my way down the now familiar corridors towards the main entrance. I pull the piece of paper out of my bag to check there's nothing important I've missed. It doesn't seem as though I have. Gran has written the time and the date of the meeting, a list of members, and a request to ask someone called Margery about anything I need to know. Her handwriting isn't as clear as usual, which isn't surprising, given what she's been through this week.

Right at the bottom of the sheet is an addendum. Gran has written it in wavering capitals and underlined it twice. It must be important. I look at it more closely and stop dead.

REMEMBER THIS IS A SECRET CLUB. DO NOT MENTION IT TO ANYONE EXCEPT THE CLUB MEMBERS!

I read it again. I'm not sure why. It's perfectly clear. I read it for a third time, hoping the letters will jiggle around before magically resolving themselves into a message saying: MAKE SURE TO SPREAD THE WORD AS FAR AND AS WIDE AS POSSIBLE!

No such luck. The words remain in their original state, their meaning impossible to mistake. Why was this not mentioned before? Everything about this cookie club is important to Gran. But, from what she's written here, the most important thing of all appears to be that it's a secret club. And the first thing I've done is tell a complete stranger all about it.

Chapter Ten

Humphrey is as delighted as ever to see me back. He wouldn't be if he knew what I'd done. Gran gave me one job, and I've spectacularly messed it up. And I've only been in the village for two days.

'Would you like your dinner before I take you for a walk or after?' I ask him.

He gives an enthusiastic bark I have no difficulty interpreting as, 'Both.'

'I only have enough steak for one meal,' I say. 'We'll have to go to the shop tomorrow. Unless I've done the sensible thing and made a run for it by then.'

I look down at Humphrey's trusting face. He gives a thump of his enormous tail. Or do I mean an enormous thump of his tail? Whichever it is, it reminds me I can't run away. He needs me to look after him. No matter what happens, I'll have to stay and face the music.

I have no idea why this club is supposed to be such a secret. It's a club for people to exchange Christmas cookies, not a top-secret summit on the latest developments in germ warfare. But who am I to argue with Gran?

According to her, the first rule of cookie club is very clear – you do not talk about cookie club. Except it's too late for that. I've blabbed the details to a complete stranger. For all I know, Daniel has already sold them to a tabloid newspaper. I may be greeted tomorrow morning by someone parading up and down outside the village shop with a sandwich board saying *Cookie Club Conspiracy Finally Crumbles.*

With my luck, the tabloid will also be the hospital's newspaper of choice, and I'll arrive to find Gran propped up on her pillows, surrounded by nurses, all of them staring reproachfully at me.

I shake off these gloomy meditations. I'll think about this problem later. I clip on Humphrey's harness, and we set off down the garden path together. I peer around the hedge in case Daniel is taking another stroll to give his drone some fresh air and exercise. But the street is empty. Of course, it is. The moment I need to talk to him, he isn't there. Typical man. I cast a quick upward glance in case a drone is hovering above my head, filming my every move.

The sky appears to be clear, so I follow Humphrey down to the field, where he spends forty minutes happily chasing the local bird life with great enthusiasm but no success. Most of the birds barely bother to move as he gallops towards them, chest heaving and tongue hanging out in the excitement of the chase.

'Come on!' I tell him at last. 'It's too dark to see any more birds.'

He reluctantly allows me to lead him back to the cottage, where I cook his steak and he demolishes it in a couple of seconds. He gives me an engaging smile, but I harden my heart.

'I've been given strict instructions about your diet, and I intend to follow them to the best of my ability.'

He gives me a mournful look and collapses into his basket. I open a tin of baked beans, drop a couple of slices of bread into the toaster, and make myself a cup of tea while I wait.

Maybe things aren't as bad as I thought. It's possible Daniel doesn't live in Honeywell. He may have been passing through the village on his way to a drone contest somewhere on the other side of the country. Possibly, his GPS malfunctioned, and he ended up staying here for an hour or two before moving on.

The toast pops up. I butter it and tip the pan of beans over it. It isn't exactly haute cuisine. But after spending such an unsuccessful morning in the kitchen, it's all I'm prepared to do. I can rise to greater culinary heights another night. I may even heat up a frozen pizza.

I dump my plate onto a tray and carry it to the living room. Humphrey follows and climbs onto the sofa next to me, where he surveys my food as though it's a long-lost bird friend and he would like nothing better than to make further acquaintance with it.

I finish my meal before he can get any more ideas about it. We share an apple, then watch University Challenge. Humphrey doesn't get any of the clues. To be fair, neither do I. But it's been a long day for both of us.

My mind drifts back to the problem of Daniel. For all I know, Gran was teasing when she told me it was important to keep the whole thing a secret. It didn't seem as though she was joking, but who knows what effect the regular administration of morphine has on elderly patients?

Assuming she was serious, I should be able to track him down tomorrow. If he lives in the village, someone is bound to know him. It would be impossible to carry drones around in a place like this without someone noticing and asking questions. I'll ask at the corner shop. Shirley seems to know most of the people in the village.

Failing that, I can try the bakery. They make excellent cakes, and it seems impossible that anyone living in the village for any length of time could resist making regular visits. And it will give me an excuse to sample another of their delicious lemon tarts.

Once I have Daniel's address, I can knock on his door and ask him to forget everything I said about the cookie club. I can appeal to his sense of chivalry, if he has one. Or I can tell him I'm suffering from severe concussion as a result of his egregious failure to look where he was going, and I'm considering contacting a lawyer unless he gives me what I want. He wasn't paying attention, so he can't know whether or not I hit my head.

If all else fails, I can contact the police. That would be a little drastic, and I hope it doesn't come to that. But there's bound to be some drone-related law he was breaking, however inadvertently.

I feel much better as I wash my plate and Humphrey's bowl, let him out for his nightly jaunt around the garden, then accompany him upstairs. I go straight to Gran's room and throw myself on her bed.

'What a comfortable bed!' I exclaim. 'I think I'll sleep in here tonight.'

Humphrey gives me a pitying look, trots down the landing, and disappears into my bedroom. I follow to find him spreadeagled across my duvet. There isn't enough room for me to climb into bed. I push hard, but nothing happens.

'You are an ungrateful hound,' I complain. 'I spend all my time cooking for you and cleaning up after you and taking you out to chase birds. The least you could do is allow me into my own bed.'

To my surprise, he rolls over. I jump in beside him before he can change his mind.

'Don't you dare roll over again during the night,' I warn him. 'It would take an entire earthquake rescue team to dig me out, and I'm not sure where the nearest one is located.'

He lays a paw on my leg, looks lovingly up into my face, and licks my hand.

'We've talked about this,' I say. 'I've told you I have a washcloth of my own. Look, but don't lick! It's an excellent motto to live by.'

He heaves a sigh and closes his eyes. Pretty soon, I follow his example. It's been a long day, and tomorrow looks as though it will be even busier.

Chapter Eleven

Humphrey and I walk to the village shop after breakfast the next day. I need to buy him some more chicken, and I've run out of flour and sugar. I'm also low on oats and butter. I try not to think about the huge amounts of ingredients I wasted yesterday in my failed attempts at baking what should have been a simple batch of cookies.

I only have this afternoon to perfect my oatmeal raisin cookies before my guests arrive to sample them. I have no idea what format the evening will take. Presumably, the participants will know. I'm providing the venue and producing refreshments. I can't be expected to do any more at such short notice.

I spend a while in the shop, filling my basket and chatting to Shirley. To my disappointment, she hasn't heard of anyone called Daniel.

'What does he look like?' she asks.

I hesitate. I've built up a picture in my mind of someone with a villainous face covered in scars. I haven't quite given him an eye patch and a wooden leg, but very nearly.

'Medium height,' I say at last. 'About my age. I think he had brown hair, but that might have been a hat.'

She looks amused. 'You'd be useless in a police lineup. They'd never catch the criminal from that description. It could be half the males in Honeywell.'

'It all happened so quickly,' I excuse myself. 'One moment, I was opening the garden gate without a care in the world. The next, my tray of cookies was flying through the air and landing in the street.'

The word flying reminds me of something. 'He was holding a drone.'

She frowns. 'One of those buzzy things?'

'That's right. Quite a large one. I have no idea why anyone would be taking a drone for a walk down the back lanes of Honeywell, but that's what he was doing.'

I remember something else. 'He was wearing red trainers.'

Her look of amusement returns. 'We could get Ivy to make us a sketch like they do on those police programmes. She's very good. She does caricatures at our Easter and summer fetes.'

I muster up the remaining shreds of my dignity. 'Thank you, but there's no need. It doesn't sound as though this man's a local. He must have been passing through.'

I pay for my groceries, ignore a couple of grinning customers who have clearly been listening in to our conversation, and shepherd Humphrey out of the shop before Shirley can make any more suggestions about identity parades.

I should go straight home. I have cookies to bake. If yesterday morning was anything to go by, it may take some time to achieve a passable result. But the lights in the bakery are alluring. I can see a group of women inside. They appear to be playing cards. It seems an odd thing to be doing in a bakery, but each to their own.

Humphrey has stopped too. He pulls me towards the door and whines piteously – the sound of a dog too exhausted to face the five-hundred metre walk home without emergency sustenance. I remember how good the coffee was yesterday and weaken.

'Ten minutes,' I tell him. 'We can't afford to be here any longer than that. And I'll need you to sleep this afternoon. I'll be busy, and I don't want you getting under my feet.'

He gives an excited wag of his tail that I decide to interpret as full agreement.

'And don't sit on that funny little brown dog if you see him,' I add, opening the door.

The bakery smells like a little slice of heaven as we enter. Humphrey makes a dive for the nearest table and curls up beneath it. At least, he would curl if the tables weren't so small and delicate and he wasn't so large. As it is, he looks like a gigantic warship trying to dock at a passenger jetty. Bits of him are sticking out in all directions. I'll have to keep an eye out to make sure no one trips over him.

Does he realise how enormous he is compared to other dogs? If need be, he could carry several small children on his back without even noticing. Not for the first time, I wonder what Gran was thinking when she chose him. According to Mum, it was love at first sight for the pair of them, and I have to admit Humphrey couldn't have hoped for a better home. He's fallen on his size-twenty paws with Gran, and he makes her very happy in return. I resolve to stop complaining about him and appreciate him for what he is rather than what he isn't.

Lily appears behind the counter. 'You're back! I thought you might be. Humphrey rarely allows Mrs Hollis to pass the bakery without popping in.'

'I'd have come in even if he was at home,' I say. 'You make the best coffee I've ever tasted.'

She looks pleased. 'A cappuccino, wasn't it? Coming right up. Would you like something to eat with it?'

I'm about to refuse on the grounds I expect to spend most of the afternoon tasting batches of oatmeal cookies. But I catch sight of some Portuguese tarts in the display and waver. If I eat one of those, I won't have to bother about lunch, which means I'll have more time for baking and tidying up before this evening.

'I'll have a Portuguese tart,' I say. 'And I expect Humphrey would like one of your dog biscuits. He enjoyed the ones he had yesterday.'

Lily hands him a bone-shaped dog biscuit and laughs as he swallows it whole. She offers him a second one. I'm pleased to see he crunches it a couple of times before gulping it down. Is it too much to hope he's learning some manners?

'My partner says we should take a course of dog first-aid classes,' she tells me. 'She's always wanted to perform the Heimlich manoeuvre on someone. None of our customers has given her the opportunity so far. I told her that was a good thing, but I'm not sure she was convinced.'

'Do you hear that?' I say, nudging Humphrey with my foot. 'You're being offered the chance to make medical history.'

He looks at me blankly, stretches out, and goes to sleep.

'I wish I could do that,' says Lily. 'I have two young children, and I'm permanently exhausted. But it still takes me ages to fall asleep each night. Even when I do, I sleep with one ear open in case one of them falls out of bed or decides to take up sleepwalking for a hobby.'

'It's the same with me,' I say. 'Not the sleepwalking bit. Humphrey barely moves when he's asleep. But I'm not sleeping half as well as usual. He's an enormous responsibility – literally! He means everything to my grandmother, and I could never live with myself if anything happened to him.'

'I'm sure it won't,' she says. 'And he obviously likes you. He wouldn't fall asleep like this if he thought there was anything to be afraid of.'

I'm not sure she's right, but I hope she is. Does Humphrey see me as his protector while Gran is in the hospital? Or does he believe he's protecting me? Anyone seeing me with such an enormous dog ought to think twice before trying anything. On the other hand, anyone seeing his uncoordinated attempts to decimate the local bird population would be forgiven for thinking they had nothing to worry about. I put all this out of my mind while I drink my coffee and eat my tart. As I expected, it's excellent.

'Please tell whoever does your baking that these are amazing,' I tell Lily as she passes my table on her way to serve a large plate of cakes to the card players.

'You can tell her yourself,' she says, pointing to a woman emerging from the kitchen carrying a tray of rolls. 'This is Abby. Abby, this is Lucy. She's Mrs Hollis' granddaughter. She's staying in her cottage and looking after Humphrey while Mrs Hollis is in the hospital.'

'I heard about that,' says Abby. 'Your mum was in this morning, Lily, and she told me about the accident. She's popping into the hospital this afternoon.'

'That's so kind of her,' I tell Lily.

'Mum keeps an eye on everyone in the village,' she says. 'It's a pretty friendly place, and most people here know everyone else.'

'Which reminds me,' I say. 'I'm trying to track down someone called Daniel. I wondered whether you might be able to help me?'

'Can you narrow it down a little?' asks Abby.

I launch into my rather less than detailed account again, refraining from adding any interesting details like a bright red beard or a skull tattoo on his forehead. If this man lives in the village, I'd like to find him as quickly as possible. A sinister description, although fun, won't speed things up.

'I can't think of anyone matching that description,' says Lily. 'Has he lived here for long?'

'He may not live here at all. But if he does, there's something I need to discuss with him.'

'Intriguing,' she says, and I flush.

'I know it sounds weird, but I can't give you any more details.'

She and Abby glance at each other, but neither of them pursues the matter.

'I'll ask my mum when I see her this evening,' says Lily. 'If this man is a resident rather than a visitor, she's bound to know all about him. Don't even think of committing a crime while you're here, Lucy. My mum would track you down in seconds.'

'I wasn't planning on any felonies while I'm here,' I say. 'And I'll do my best to ensure Humphrey remains on the right side of the law. That may not be so easy.'

He opens an eye and looks enquiringly at me.

I laugh. 'Are your ears burning? They say listeners hear no good of themselves. We should get going. We have a lot to do before tonight.'

'What's happening tonight?' asks Lily.

What is wrong with me? All I have to do is refrain from mentioning the cookie club, yet that seems to be the one thing I can't manage. Time to go before I crack and spill my guts, giving them the precise details and location of the club and ending by inviting them both to come along and bring a friend.

'I'm having a couple of my neighbours over for a cup of tea,' I say.

'That's nice,' says Lily. 'Have fun. I'll ask Mum whether she has any idea who this mystery man of yours might be.'

'He's not mine,' I say before she or Abby can get any ideas.

I'm worried she may think I see myself as the heroine of a romantic novel, who's met a complete stranger, lost her heart to him, and is now chasing all over the village to find out where he lives so she can engineer another meeting. That would be humiliating, but there's nothing I can do about it now. Better for her to think that than realise how badly I've let my grandmother down.

'Come on, Humphrey,' I say. He rises reluctantly to his feet and follows me towards the door.

'Have a lovely evening,' says Lily as we go.

'Thanks,' I say. 'You, too.'

Humphrey and I set off together down the high street. A pigeon settles on the barber shop sign and gives Humphrey a contemptuous look. He stops dead and stares up at it.

'Come on!' I say, pulling at his lead. 'I hate to break it to you, but if you're thinking about pigeon pie for lunch, you have no chance. You'll be far better off coming home with me and allowing me to cook you some chicken. It's the only bird you're likely to get anywhere near today.'

Chapter Twelve

I make three more batches of cookies before I'm happy to consider serving them to anyone. I'm not sure why this has been such a steep learning curve. It's only a case of throwing a few ingredients into a bowl and stirring them together before sticking them into the oven. But there seems to be some weird extra alchemy involved, and I haven't yet tracked it down. Maybe some people are born with the baking gene, and some aren't. If that's the case, I'm forced to admit I'm not a natural-born cookie-whisperer.

It's not that I dislike cookies. I'm as happy as the next person to get stuck into a plate of them. But I've never felt the urge to be involved in the production side of the business. My view has always been that everyone should play to their own strengths, and this clearly isn't mine. I should just appreciate them as a consumer and leave it at that.

But fate has intervened, so here I am, standing in Gran's kitchen, trying not to trip over a gigantic dog, frantically stirring and mixing and attempting to calculate the difference between the Fahrenheit temperature the recipe calls for and the centigrade dial on Gran's oven. Life is full of surprises.

Still, I've achieved my goal. Admittedly, I've set myself a low bar – to produce something edible that won't make me the laughingstock of the cookie club. But I've managed to do it without suffering more than a couple of burned fingers and several wasted batches of cookies.

The local birds have benefited from them, which is a good thing. It's been a bitterly cold week, and they must be struggling. The sudden miraculous appearance on Gran's lawn of dozens of delicious, albeit slightly scorched, cookies must have felt like a Christmas miracle to the local starlings and robins and blackbirds.

I slide the final batch onto a cooling tray. They can stay there until the club members arrive. I'm not risking anything happening to them.

I can't imagine what horrors could befall them. But I had no idea when I set out for the hospital yesterday afternoon that a strange man would materialise and send my cookies flying into the street, crushing them to powder beneath his hobnailed boots.

'Fine, he was wearing trainers,' I tell Humphrey, who has been watching my every movement. 'And he may not have stamped exactly, but the cookies were still ruined.'

He tilts his head on one side and looks up at me with soulful eyes.

'They were!' I insist. 'They burst into tiny pieces when they landed, which shows he must have knocked the tray out of my hands at a terrific speed. Cookies don't usually turn to powder the moment they hit the ground.'

I put the last cookie onto the tray. 'Sorry, Humphrey. You aren't allowed raisins. But I'll make you something nice after your walk. We'd better get going if we want to be back on time. It's all very well Gran running a secret club, but it would be taking it too far if you and I weren't here at all.'

We set off on our usual walk. I don't notice Humphrey has turned off up an unfamiliar path until it's too late. I tug at his lead, but he ignores me.

'Not today, Humphrey!' I protest. 'We're on a tight schedule. I can't afford to get lost in the middle of nowhere. We have to be home in time for me to host the club.'

He continues to ignore me and ploughs along the path at breakneck speed, with me panting along behind.

'I won't have time to make your dinner,' I warn him, but he isn't listening.

Where is he taking me? Is there a house down here I don't know about? Maybe one of Gran's friends lives there, and Humphrey is accustomed to visiting. I peer through the fading light, but there are no signs of a dwelling. Not even a house made of gingerbread with a beautifully iced roof. It's a pity. I could have broken off something unimportant, like a windowsill, and impressed the members of the cookie club with it.

Humphrey abruptly dives off the path. Has he seen a bird lurking in the undergrowth? There's no mad flapping of wings, and no sign of pheasants whirring into the air. What, then – a rat? I very much hope not. Rats are all very well in their place, but I prefer that place to be several miles away from me.

He lurches out of sight, almost tugging my arm off and causing me to drop the lead. There's a loud squelching sound, then silence. A wave of panic sweeps over me. Has he disappeared into a patch of quicksand? If so, how will I get him out again?

I crash through the undergrowth after him, trying to remember everything I've read about quicksand. I know the best thing is to stay calm and not struggle, but I'll never be able to explain that to Humphrey. All I can hope for is to find a solid patch of ground, lie down on it, and support him under his shoulders until either someone comes along or I freeze into a lump of ice. Why didn't I bring a coil of rope with me? And a megaphone. And a thermos flask. Perhaps even a small emergency tent. Those things should be basic precautions when setting off for a walk in a strange place. I can't believe I've been so woefully unprepared.

'I'm coming, Humphrey!' I shout, then stop as I see him sitting there, beaming up at me. There's no sign of the quicksand for which the New Forest may or may not be famous. But there's most definitely a massive patch of mud. And right in the centre of it is an enormous dog, coated in it from head to paw and looking delighted with himself.

'Did you know this was here?' I demand. 'Or was it a lucky coincidence?'

Humphrey scratches his ear, then collapses sideways into the mud.

'Stop it!' I tell him. 'You aren't at a spa. I wish to goodness you were. Someone else could clean you up. But I suppose it will have to be me. You're an infuriating dog!'

He flickers his eyes towards me, looking apprehensive. I remember his background and relent, kneeling down next to him and slipping my arms under his shoulders.

'I know you didn't mean to cause any trouble. Let's get you home and clean you up before anyone arrives.'

I haul him to his feet and pat his mud-coated head. I'm almost as muddy as he is, so there's no point in being stand-offish. He licks my hand, and I pick up his lead.

'There should be enough hot water for both of us to have a quick shower.'

I fix him with a stern look. 'But don't get your hopes up too much. I have no intention of giving you a seaweed wrap or an aromatherapy massage.'

Chapter Thirteen

Half an hour later, I finish rubbing Humphrey dry, check the cooling tray, and breathe a sigh of relief. These may not be the most exciting cookies in the world, but at least they're edible. And they're roughly the right shape, size, and colour. At this moment, I'll take what I can get.

I look at my watch. Half past six. I just have time for a quick shower before taking up my position by the front door, all ready to play the gracious hostess. I'm making a joke of it, but I don't want to let Gran down. This club is important to her, and she isn't here to run it herself. I'm determined to make sure it runs smoothly for her and is still in one piece when she returns.

I'm not sure what I could do in a single evening to destroy something so stable and long running, but I'm not prepared to take any risks. I've come to Honeywell to look after things for her while she's incapacitated, and look after them I will.

I check that Humphrey is dozing in his basket and not likely to leap around the house causing havoc in the few brief minutes I'm in the shower. Then I run upstairs and undress. I pull on Gran's dressing gown, snatch up my wash bag from my bedside table, and run back downstairs. It would have been more comfortable if the bathroom was upstairs instead of tacked onto the back of the house behind the kitchen, but it's better than no bathroom at all.

I should count myself lucky that, sometime between the end of the war and today, one of the owners of this cottage dug their heels in and refused to visit the outhouse at the bottom of the garden on a freezing winter's night. Humphrey still has to do that, but he doesn't seem to mind. He appears to see it as a positive thing to prance around the lawn on a bitter winter evening, leaving footprints and goodness knows what else in the frost, and checking out likely places where birds might be perching.

Still, beggars can't be choosers, and the house is warm enough this evening. I put the central heating on after lunch, and I lit the fire in the living room an hour ago. I don't know who's coming tonight, or whether they're all Gran's age. But if they are, they may feel the cold.

I switch on the shower and pull off the dressing gown, shivering in the sudden blast of chill air. Whoever built this bathroom didn't get as far as insulating it. They must have been of the tougher generation who believed in cold showers and general spartan living.

I'm from the more recent generation that is less convinced cold showers and frost on the windowsills each morning is a guarantee of mental strength in future life. What would my great-great-grandfather Simon think if he could see the coffee machine in my kitchen at home? Or, for that matter, the seat warmers in my car.

I take a deep breath, ready to demonstrate both my mental and physical toughness, when the doorbell rings. I utter an exclamation of annoyance. Who can that be? Surely, not a member of the cookie club? Their generation is always punctual – neither fashionably early nor fashionably late. Maybe it's someone here to read the meter. In which case, they're on their own. I have no idea where the meters are located. Great-great-grandfather Simon probably hid them at the far end of the garden, hoping to induce stamina and perseverance in the poor person who was sent to check them.

It can't really be a meter reader at this time of night. They'd have to pay them overtime, which is unlikely. Although it might explain the size of everyone's energy bills. I pull on the dressing gown and pad along the hallway, grumbling under my breath. If it's someone trying to sell us double glazing, I plan to give them short shrift.

I slide back the latch and tug open the door. I remember what Mum always used to say to me when I was young and pestering her to do something right *now*.

'I only have one pair of hands,' I mutter, opening the door a crack and assuming the sort of neutral expression that can be adapted into a welcoming smile or a forbidding scowl depending on who might be standing there.

'Good evening,' says a man's voice.

I push back my shower cap, which has slipped over one eye, obscuring my vision. His voice is familiar, but I can't see his face. The porch light is supposed to come on automatically when someone comes up the path. I remember Dad fitting it a couple of years ago and telling Gran the motion sensor would frighten off burglars.

'Hello?' I say cautiously.

I don't want to be rude in case he's here to tell me Gran has won a million pounds on the premium bonds, and the small print says the prize will be withdrawn if the recipient doesn't greet the messenger warmly and invite them in for coffee.

'Have I got the right house?' asks the man.

'That depends. Which house were you looking for?'

This strikes the correct tone. Not too welcoming if he's trying to sell me something, but not too repressive if he's the bearer of glad tidings.

'Can I come in?' he asks.

He's holding what looks like a tray. It's covered with a cloth, so I can't see what's on it. He can't belong to the cookie club. He's far too young. And male. He must be selling something.

'I'm afraid I'm rather busy right now,' I say. 'You'll have to come back another time.'

Why did I say that? As Mum always says, give these people an inch, and they'll take a mile.

'On second thoughts,' I add, 'I'm sure we aren't interested. I'm sorry to have wasted your time. Have a good evening.'

I start to close the door. The man sticks his foot in it, and I gasp in outrage. Who does he think he is?

'Move your foot this minute!' I say in an icy tone. 'Or I'll call the police.'

'But you invited me,' he says.

'I did no such thing! Move your foot or I'll slam the door on it, and it will be your own fault if you can't walk for months.'

'Yes, you did,' he insists. 'You invited me yesterday afternoon.'

I'm too taken aback to carry through with my foot-slamming threat. 'Yesterday afternoon?'

He shifts his foot out of the danger zone. 'That's right. You dropped your cookies, remember?'

'Of course, I remember. Some stupid passer-by was walking along without looking where he was going, and he sent them flying everywhere.'

I look at his face more closely, and he grins back at me. 'Would you call me a stupid passer-by, precisely?'

'Yes, I would. I didn't recognise you at first. Especially wearing that hat.'

'I bought it at the stupid passer-by shop,' he says. 'They like us to wear distinctive hats so people can tell at a glance we're likely to do ridiculous things like knocking people's cookies into the road.'

I feel an urge to smile but suppress it. 'So, why weren't you wearing it yesterday? Was it at the dry cleaners after you'd caused some other catastrophe?'

'I didn't know I'd need it,' he says. 'I was only walking a few hundred metres, and this street seemed deserted. I wasn't expecting someone to burst out of their front gate waving trays of cookies at me.'

'Only the one tray. And no one informed me I was supposed to give formal notice before walking down the front path to my car. What do you expect people to do – carry a bell and ring it at three second intervals?'

'That's up to you,' he says. 'A bell, a buzzer, a siren. Your choice. Any or all of them work for the members of the stupid passer-by club.'

'None of which explains what you're doing on my doorstep this evening. Are you here to apologise? If so, there's no need. It happened, and that's all there is to it. So, you can be on your way.'

He doesn't move. 'I'm not here to apologise. I did that to the best of my ability yesterday. I even offered to make reparation in the form of a fresh batch of cookies from the village bakery. But you were having none of it, so I gave up.'

'So, why are you here?' I ask. 'Whatever the reason, it's terrible timing. I have a –'

I break off, remembering I've been wanting to talk to this man. 'That thing I told you about the cookie club yesterday. It was supposed to be a huge secret. I'd be grateful if you didn't pass it on to anyone else.'

'So, the ad I took out in the free local newspaper this morning was a bad idea?' he asks.

'You didn't!' I catch his eye and see he's grinning at me. 'Very funny. But I'm serious about the club. I didn't realise when I met you yesterday that I wasn't supposed to tell anyone about it. I'm still not sure why that is, but that doesn't matter. If you want to apologise to me, the best way of doing it is to forget I ever mentioned it. And now, if you'll excuse me, I have to –'

He doesn't take the hint. 'That doesn't alter the fact you invited me to attend this top-secret event.'

'Have you been listening to a word I've said? I've told you this event is private.'

'You said secret,' he reminds me. 'They're two very different things.'

'Who cares? It's both private and a secret. Which means you're doubly not welcome here.'

He holds out his tray. 'That's not what you said yesterday. You said, "I'd love to see you do any better than I did."'

'I remember saying something of the kind. But it was a figure of speech. It didn't mean I was inviting you here tonight.'

'Then I've wasted my entire afternoon,' he complains. 'I could have been striding through the snow being a stupid passer-by. Instead, I was chained to the kitchen, perfecting my chocolate chip cookies.'

'I'm sorry you misinterpreted my words,' I say as politely as possible. 'Hopefully, you can find someone to enjoy the cookies. It shouldn't be too difficult. Most people love cookies. If yours are any good, you're bound to find some takers.'

He shakes his head. 'All my friends are gluten-intolerant.'

I don't mention how unlikely it is that no one in his entire social circle can tolerate wheat. The glint in his eye tells me that conversation wouldn't go well. He seems the sort of man who has an answer to everything. I'd usually be up for the challenge, but time is running out as fast as the warm air pouring through the open front door into the frosty garden.

'That's a shame,' I say. 'But it isn't my problem. I'm afraid you'll have to go now. You can leave your cookies here if you like. I'm sure my visitors won't suffer from the same digestive problems as your friends.'

'I can't,' he says. 'This cookie tray is a family heirloom. It's been passed down through generations of Chapmans. My father gave it to me a few years back and made me promise with his final breath never to let it out of my sight, even for a second.'

'I'm sorry your father died,' I say. 'But –'

'He didn't die,' says Daniel. 'It was after a strenuous squash game. I beat him hands down, and he bequeathed me the tray in recognition that the elder had been bested by the younger.'

Why am I continuing this ridiculous argument? I should have told him the minute he appeared on my doorstep that there had been some mistake and he would have to go.

'I get the message,' he says. 'Your invitation wasn't as clear cut as I believed. I will acknowledge defeat and leave with my tail between my legs.'

Like Humphrey, I think. As if in acknowledgment of this unspoken thought, the dog himself appears in the hall at this exact moment, probably summoned by the smell of the cookies Daniel is waving around.

Chapter Fourteen

'Hello,' says Daniel, holding out his hand to Humphrey. 'It's a pleasure to meet you. I'm the stupid passer-by who bumped into your owner yesterday and deprived you of your cookies.'

'They weren't for him,' I say. 'They were for my grandmother.'

'Then please pass on my apologies to your grandmother.'

He gives Humphrey's head a pat. 'Nice to meet you, but I have to be going.'

Humphrey stares up at him for another moment. Then, without giving me time to prepare, he slips past Daniel and charges down the garden path at top speed.

'Stop him!' I shout, but it's too late. Daniel hasn't closed the gate properly. Humphrey rushes through it and keeps going.

'Move!' I yell, shoving Daniel aside and setting off up the street as fast as I can. Humphrey is almost out of sight already and making excellent speed. I don't know where he's going, but he seems to have a plan in mind. All I can do is follow as closely as possible and hope to catch up with him before he disappears completely.

I'm not a good runner at the best of times, but I seem to be slower than usual tonight. I glance down at my feet and realise I'm still wearing my slippers. This is all Daniel's fault. He knows perfectly well I didn't invite him over this evening, yet he chose to come anyway. He seems determined to annoy me. I'm not sure why, but I don't have time to think about it now. I'm too busy concentrating on not losing my balance and ending up sprawled full-length in the frosty street in Gran's dressing gown, revealing far more than is usual in a quiet country village. That's the last time I answer the front door in anything other than full formal attire – preferably including a fur-lined coat and knee-length boots.

I hear footsteps behind me and glance over my shoulder to see Daniel racing along the street. He's gaining on me quickly, which is no surprise. He's wearing jeans and trainers, so it's hardly a fair contest.

'Which way did he go?' he gasps as he catches up with me.

I'm too winded to answer, so I point.

'I'm on it!' He increases his speed, rounds the corner, and is soon out of sight.

I slow to a painful walk, clutching my side. I could run as fast as Daniel if I were dressed for it. I'd like to see him keep up with me if I was the one wearing running shoes and he was hampered by a knee-length pink dressing gown with nothing on underneath.

I give an involuntary shiver and pull the thin wisp of material around me, wishing I'd had the presence of mind to don some sort of thick bathing costume for my shower. I've seen pictures of Victorian matrons descending from their bathing machines into the sea, swathed from head to foot in black bombazine ruffles. I've always felt sorry for those women, but I'm starting to see the benefits of it. You might not be able to swim one hundred metres in fifty seconds, but it would be far easier to sprint down the street on an icy winter's night in pursuit of the most badly-behaved dog in living memory.

People say that those who don't learn from history are doomed to repeat it. Maybe that works in reverse too. Those who refuse to repeat history are doomed to run half-clad marathons in sub-zero temperatures and die from hypothermia only metres from their own front door.

I refuse to have that happen to me tonight. There's nothing I can do about Humphrey right now. Daniel is in hot pursuit, and I'm in freezing cold non-pursuit. I should go home and get dressed before the guests arrive. I've given up any idea of getting a shower. Judging by the way this evening has gone so far, I'd step into it just as the village earthquake alarm went off, and I'd end up outside wearing even less than I am now, soaking wet, and chilled to the bone. If further calamities befall us tonight, I intend to meet them decently clad and with a hot drink in my hand, preferably laced with something alcoholic.

I turn and retrace my steps to the cottage. Presumably, Daniel won't give up the chase and return without Humphrey. I know almost nothing about him, but he doesn't seem the type to do something like that. And he must realise that, yet again, this is his fault. I was careful to latch the gate when Humphrey and I returned from our muddy walk this evening.

It isn't my fault Daniel didn't know the trick of it and left it to swing open, but he had no business being on my property at all. I seem to remember there's some legal maxim stating ignorance is no defence. If anything has happened to Humphrey, I'll sue Daniel for everything he's got.

That would be of no comfort to Gran. Humphrey is her entire world, and nothing would ever compensate her for his loss. That goes for me too. I've always been fond of Humphrey, but now that I'm responsible for his well-being, I realise it's more than that. Until Gran is home and able to take over again, Humphrey is the only thing that matters to me.

And he's running around – goodness knows where – in the pitch dark, wondering where I am. Even worse, he may be looking for Gran. As far as he's concerned, she left without saying goodbye or explaining where she was going. After which, I arrived and turned out to be an extremely poor substitute. No wonder he's set off into the night to find his real caregiver. And he hasn't the faintest chance of doing so.

A small sob escapes me as I imagine what it must be like to be Humphrey at this moment – lost and distressed and feeling abandoned by the one person in the world who truly loves him. A tear rolls down my cheek and I wipe my eyes on my dressing gown sleeve, choking back the flood of further tears that threatens to overwhelm me. I can't do this right now. Humphrey needs me to stay calm and be ready to run to his side at a moment's notice.

It occurs to me that even if Daniel catches up with him, he has no way of letting me know. We haven't got to the phone number-exchanging stage yet, and we probably never will. So far, all we've reached is the insult-exchanging stage on my side and the amused smile on his. I swallow hard and take several deep breaths. The only way to cope with an emergency is one step at a time. And step one is to get some clothes on so that I'm prepared for whatever step two turns out to be.

I'm about to open the gate when I hear a noise. Is that a bark or am I so desperate for a sign of Humphrey that my ears are shaping stray sounds into what I want them to be? I look back along the road and my heart almost falls out of my chest as I see two figures walking towards me. There's enough light from the nearest streetlamp for me to see it's Daniel and Humphrey.

I give a gasp of relief and set off back towards them, completely forgetting my exposed flesh from the knees down. Humphrey catches sight of me and gives an enormous bound, almost dragging Daniel over. He recovers his balance and breaks into a run, still holding onto Humphrey's lead. No, not his lead. That's on the table next to the front door. I squint through the gloom but can't make out what's tied to his collar. I don't care.

'Humphrey!' I gasp, flinging my arms around him and bursting into tears.

He sits back on his haunches, giving me a puzzled look. He doesn't seem like a dog who's been breaking his heart for his lost mistress and vowing never to eat or sleep again until he finds her. In fact, he looks more than usually pleased with himself.

I raise my head to look at Daniel, who grins down at me. 'Sorry you had such a fright. He's a fast runner, isn't he?'

'Where did you catch up with him?'

'At the far edge of the field. It looked as though he was carrying on down to the water meadows.'

'Humphrey!' I say. 'What did we say about staying away from wet and muddy places?'

Humphrey scratches his ear and gives me an innocent look, as if to say he doesn't remember us ever discussing the subject.

I climb stiffly to my feet, attempting to cover myself as much as possible.

'That's why I was about to have a shower when you arrived,' I explain to Daniel. 'Humphrey and I went for a walk earlier this evening.'

His eyebrows lift. 'And you thought you'd roll around in the mud for a while? Far be it from me to judge, but I'm not sure that would have been my preferred activity on a cold winter's night. Still, each to his own. It takes all kinds to make a world, and all that.'

I choke back a giggle. 'Humphrey rolled in the mud, and I got covered in it trying to haul him out. He had the first shower. I left him to dry off in his basket while I jumped into the shower and cleaned myself up. But then you rang the doorbell and –'

My grievance returns. 'You didn't even bother to check the gate was shut. This is all your fault.'

'Again?' he says.

I take Humphrey's lead from him. 'You do seem to be a bit of a disaster magnet, don't you?'

My eyes fall to the piece of fabric I'm holding. 'This isn't a lead.'

Daniel looks embarrassed. 'I had to improvise. I caught him by the collar, but I didn't trust him not to break free again. He's very strong.'

I inspect the fabric more closely. 'Is this a sock?'

'Several socks. We passed a washing line during our evening jog. I'm not sure what the laundry was doing out on a night like this, but I wasn't about to complain. I grabbed the four nearest socks and tied them together. Luckily, they were knee length or I don't know what I'd have done.'

'I hope you plan to return them before the resident realises and calls the police,' I say self-righteously.

'Of course,' he says. 'I have no wish to become known as the Honeywell Clothesline Bandit.'

We reach the garden gate, and I notice Daniel's cookies scattered along the path.

'I'm sorry about your cookies,' I say. 'I didn't mean that to happen.'

'You mean it wasn't in retaliation for what I did yesterday?'

'Of course not! That would be petty.'

'It would,' he agrees. 'I apologise for the insensitive suggestion. How can I ever make it up to you?'

'You can leave,' I suggest. 'Before you do any more damage.'

'Don't you need to shower?'

'I don't have time now. Even if I did, I don't need anyone's help with that. I've been taking showers since I was a child.'

'But surely you need someone to watch Humphrey for you while you get yourself ready?' he asks.

'Humphrey will be fine in his basket.'

'How did that work out the last time you said that?'

'He only escaped because I had to open the front door to you.'

'Exactly,' he says. 'And you've told me you're expecting a load of guests any minute now. Won't someone have to open the front door for them while you're getting dressed? Otherwise, they might all go away again.'

I waver. I want to get Daniel out of here before the club members arrive. But I also need to get dressed. And he's right. The way tonight has been going, I wouldn't put it past Humphrey to slip past one of my guests if I leave the door unlatched for them. He may end up in the next county before I've pulled on my jeans.

'You can stay for five minutes while I get ready,' I say. 'But if anyone arrives, please don't tell them who you are. Make up some story or other, then get yourself out of here as quickly as possible.'

Chapter Fifteen

Humphrey pulls himself free of my grip and sets off to the kitchen, a purposeful look in his eyes. A moment later, I hear him hurl himself against the back door.

'He needs to go outside,' I say. 'Could you let him into the back garden and stay with him while he does his business?'

'I'll watch him like a hawk,' Daniel promises. 'I assume there isn't a back gate with a broken lock?'

'The front gate doesn't have a broken lock,' I tell him. 'It just needs closing properly.'

'So you've mentioned several times. I promise to check it carefully next time.'

I want to point out that there won't be a next time. But it's getting late, and I don't want to waste precious minutes arguing about the precise mechanism of Gran's gate latch.

I unlock the back door, and Humphrey surges out into the garden.

'Do you need a torch?' I ask Daniel.

'Not if you leave the kitchen blinds open until we return. Go and get ready, and I'll keep an eye on him.'

Humphrey is scrabbling at a patch of grass and shows no sign of wanting to escape for a second time.

'Watch out for birds,' I warn Daniel as I turn to leave.

'What sort of birds?'

'Night birds,' I say nonchalantly, trying to hide the fact I have no idea. Why should I be expected to be an ornithological expert? I can just about identify robins, blackbirds, and sparrows.

He gives a snort of laughter. 'Night birds? What species is that?'

'Plenty of birds fly around at night. I thought everyone knew that. Snowy owls, for instance.'

'Snowy owls?' he asks incredulously.

'That's right. And bats. I know they aren't birds, but they flap around the garden, and Humphrey won't know the difference. He loses his head and runs after anything that flies. I'm telling you to watch him carefully.'

Daniel gives me a mock salute. 'Understood. I'll be on the alert for anything airborne. It's a good thing I don't have any drones with me today. They're surprisingly expensive. I'd hate Humphrey to mistake one for a snowy owl and launch a ground-to-air assault on it.'

'I think he prefers real things to toys,' I say. 'Anyway, it's only for a couple of minutes. I'll be back as quickly as possible. If anyone turns up, can you tell them you're the plumber?'

'The plumber?' he repeats.

'Or the dog walker or the electrician. Use your ingenuity. How hard can it be to come up with a plausible reason for you being here? The important thing is that you leave without raising suspicion.'

I don't wait for him to argue further but run up to my room, where I pull on a pair of jeans and a thick roll-neck sweater. I'd been planning to wear my one and only skirt in honour of this occasion because I have no idea how formal the club meetings may be. But a glance in the mirror shows several streaks of dried mud on my neck. There may be others I can't see in this dim light.

It's best to be safe and cover as much of myself as possible. I'd prefer the story of tonight's escape to stay a secret between the three of us. It would only upset Gran if one of the club members contacted her to tell her about it.

Secrets seem to be the watchword of this club. It can't harm for me to add one more. I give my hair a quick brush and run downstairs as the doorbell rings. There's no sign of Daniel and Humphrey. They must still be hunting for owls in the garden. With any luck, I can greet whoever this is before slipping away and letting Daniel out through the back gate. No one need ever know he was here.

I compose my face into a welcoming smile – the expression of a calm and experienced hostess who has everything under control and has never heard of such a thing as a runaway dog, let alone anyone pelting along the street dressed in nothing but a flimsy dressing gown and slippers.

A woman is standing on the doorstep holding a box of what I assume must be cookies. She doesn't wait for me to greet her but steps past me into the hall and pulls off her coat.

'It's cold out there,' she says, handing it to me. 'Hello, I'm Margery Townsend.'

I glance over her shoulder before closing the door. The front gate appears to be shut. Humphrey is in the back garden, but I don't want to take any chances. Any minute now, he may break free from Daniel's inexperienced grasp, crash through the back door, and appear in the hallway, all ready for his third expedition to the local mud pit.

'I'm Lucy,' I say, looking around for somewhere to hang up the coat.

'I know you are. You're Lavender's granddaughter. She sent me a message to say you'd be hosting us tonight.'

I hope this hasn't offended her. For all I know, several members of the club have offered to hold tonight's meeting at their house, and Gran has refused. It's common knowledge what these village institutions are like, with their petty jealousies and feuds. Entire generations of families are always falling out with each other, with Shakespearean consequences. This one act of perceived nepotism on Gran's part may rend the village asunder and result in one half of it no longer speaking to the other for decades to come. Civil wars have started with less provocation.

To my relief, this woman doesn't look as though she plans to return home to fetch her pitchfork. She walks towards the kitchen as though she owns the place. It isn't surprising. If she's a long-standing member of the club, she'll have visited this house more often than I have.

'I'm not sure whether we've met before,' I say, following her into the kitchen.

She dumps her box of cookies onto the counter and turns to look at me. 'Several times. But you'd be forgiven for not remembering much about it. Your mother used to wheel you around the village in your pram when you were a baby.'

'I'm afraid I don't remember that,' I say. 'Have we met again since I was a little older?'

'Not often. I think your family usually spent Christmas in Coventry, and Lavender and Ed came to you.'

'Until she got Humphrey,' I say. 'He doesn't travel well, so Gran decided to stay here with him instead. We were going to come down last year, but my father had an accident.'

I don't elaborate. If she's one of Gran's friends, she'll know all about it, and it isn't a subject I enjoy discussing.

'I heard about that,' she says. 'A terrible business. But I hear he's going on a little better. Perhaps we'll see him down here this Christmas?'

'It isn't likely. Dad has made a better recovery than we expected when it first happened, but I don't think he'd be able to travel this far. I'm not sure what will happen this Christmas. Even if Humphrey didn't suffer from travel sickness, I doubt Gran will be going much further than the sofa.'

'I'm sure you'll work something out,' she says.

The back door opens, and Humphrey bounces in. If possible, he looks even more full of beans than usual.

Margery holds up her hand. 'Don't even think about it! I don't want mud all over my clean skirt.'

To my amazement, Humphrey abandons his evident intention of hurling himself at her. He sidles over and sits next to her, looking the picture of injured innocence.

She scratches his head. 'Good boy. You know I love you. Neither of us needs to cover each other in mud to prove it.'

She notices Daniel. 'I didn't realise you had company.'

'Not company!' I say, taking the makeshift lead from Daniel and giving him a speaking look. 'He's here to …'

I trail off, trying to remember whether Daniel and I settled on a cover story to explain his presence. Why couldn't this woman have arrived a few minutes later? I could have bundled him out of the back gate, and he would have been halfway home by now.

He holds out his hand to her. 'My name's Daniel. I'm the plumber.'

'The plumber?' she asks. 'At this time of night?'

'That's right. Lucy called me earlier this evening and asked me to stop by on my way home. It's very nice to meet you, Ms – '

He glances over at me, and I frown back at him. Why does a plumber need to know the names of all the visitors to this house? Shouldn't he be concentrating on doing the job for which he's being paid? I remember he isn't an actual plumber and bite my lip.

Margery breaks the silence. 'I'm Margery Townsend. Nice to meet you.'

'I'm afraid he has to get going,' I say. 'He mentioned earlier that he has a big event tonight. I'm sure he's looking forward to it. I'm sorry to have called you out at such short notice, Daniel, but I know my grandmother will appreciate it.'

The doorbell rings again. I hesitate, not wanting to leave Daniel alone with Margery. Goodness knows what he'll say to her while I'm gone. The one thing I'm sure of is that it will end up embarrassing me further. But neither of them moves, so I have no choice.

Three more women are standing on the doorstep, all carrying boxes. They introduce themselves as Irene Henshaw, Phyllis Meadows, and June Parker.

I take their coats and point them to the kitchen. 'Margery is here already. She's talking to the plumber, but he's about to leave.'

'The plumber?' asks Irene. 'Do you mean Steve Wately?'

'He didn't mention his full name,' I say, trying to play it safe.

Phyllis gives me a quizzical look. 'Then how did you know it was the plumber?'

'I … er … called the number, and he turned up.'

'And you didn't ask for any ID? Even I know better than that.'

She walks down the hall to the kitchen, and I follow, hoping Daniel has taken the chance to leave by the back door. What am I thinking? Of course, he hasn't. He's sitting at the kitchen table, talking to Margery. I frown at him, but he doesn't appear to notice.

'You aren't Steve Wately!' Phyllis greets him.

'You're quite correct,' he says. 'Is there any reason I should be?'

'Lucy here told me she'd called the plumber in. Who do you work for?'

'I work with someone called Marcus Turner,' he says.

'I've never heard of him. Where are you based?'

'All over the place. We go wherever we're needed.'

She looks doubtful. 'What's wrong with Steve Wately?'

'I have no idea,' says Daniel. 'This is the first time I've heard of him.'

'How can you not have heard of Steve Wately?' demands June. 'I thought all you tradespeople knew each other.'

'Not yet,' says Daniel. 'I'm new around here. But I look forward to making his acquaintance very soon.'

June glances at Margery, then at me. 'How did you get this man's number, Lucy?'

'From the local newspaper Gran has delivered each week,' I say, just as Daniel says, 'We have an online ad.'

'That's right,' I say. 'I meant to say it was an advert in the online newspaper.'

June doesn't look convinced. 'And why did you say he was here?'

I rack my brain for a plausible sounding plumbing emergency. 'I thought one of the pipes had burst. But it turned out it hadn't.'

'Interesting,' says Margery. 'This man told me he'd been called out to unblock a toilet.'

I glare at Daniel, who looks as though he's trying not to laugh.

'It was the pipe that leads to the toilet,' I say. 'I thought it was blocked.'

'You said burst,' Margery reminds me.

'That's right. I thought it had burst because it was blocked. But Daniel told me it was just frozen.'

'He told me it was one of the worst blockages he'd ever come across,' she says.

She turns to Daniel. 'I'd like you to sit right there and keep your hands on the table where we can all see them while I call the police. They'll soon find out what you're up to. Have you been doing this all around the area? I suppose you thought a place like Honeywell was the perfect place for your scam because there are so many elderly people living here. Well, you're about to find out you're mistaken. We may not be as young as we were, but we're capable of dealing with someone like you. Keep an eye on him, ladies!'

This is terrible. While I don't have any general objection to Daniel being made to leave the house, I can't let it be in the back of a police car.

'There's no need to call the police,' I say. 'Daniel isn't a plumber.'

'No kidding!' says Margery. 'I wasn't born yesterday. He clearly doesn't know one end of a waste pipe from another. He's heard your grandmother is in hospital, and he thought he'd con his way in and see whether there was anything worth stealing.'

'No, he didn't,' I say, ignoring Daniel's snort of laughter. 'I invited him in.'

'You shouldn't have done that,' says June. 'It's exactly the sort of thing our Neighbourhood Watch group is always warning us about. You ought to know better, Lucy.'

I'm tempted to agree with her that Daniel is a dangerous criminal who needs to be hauled before the local magistrates, but I get the better of myself.

'I mean I'm the reason he's here,' I explain. 'I asked him to come in and watch Humphrey for me while I got dressed.'

'You mean he's your boyfriend?' asks Phyllis.

'Absolutely not! I barely know him. At least, I know him well enough to trust him with Humphrey, but –'

I break off and glance at Daniel. 'You aren't being much help. Can you please explain who you are and what you're doing here?'

'I'm not sure I can,' he says. 'I've lost track. One moment I'm a dog sitter, and the next I'm a plumber. It's all very confusing.'

'You were lucky,' I say. 'My first idea was to tell them you were a member of the local history society, here to inspect the beams in the walls.'

'Inspect them for what?' he asks. 'Dry rot? Wouldn't you be better off calling a surveyor for that?'

'I'm not sure,' I admit. 'Carbon dating, maybe?'

'It sounds a lot more fun than being a plumber,' he says. 'Is it too late to change our story?'

'I think that ship has well and truly sailed. The best thing you can do is to come clean, tell everyone who you are, then leave before they call the police on you.'

Margery looks from me to Daniel, then back again. 'I think you'd better both sit down and tell us what's going on.'

Chapter Sixteen

I look at Daniel and see he's grinning again. This annoys me even more than everything else he does.

'I'm not sure what you find so amusing,' I tell him. 'This was your idea, so you can do the talking.'

He gives me a pained look. 'As far as I'm concerned, this is all on you. I'll admit I knocked your cookies into the street yesterday afternoon. I tried to put that right, but you wouldn't let me. It was your idea to invite me to this club. I turned up tonight, ready to do whatever I was asked, but first you threw my cookies all over the path, and then you sent me off on a muddy rescue expedition in the cold and dark with no thought for my safety.'

He glances around at the interested faces, warming to his theme. 'I co-own a drone company. We're in the area doing some work for the local council. I've only been staying in this village for a few weeks. I haven't had time to explore any of the local beauty spots or make a mental map of all the dangerous places in the area. Lucy's very lucky this didn't end up as a Hound of the Baskervilles situation, with me as the innocent entomologist meeting an untimely death in the Grimpen Mire.'

'He wasn't innocent!' I almost shout.

Humphrey looks anxious at the sound of raised voices.

Daniel leans down to stroke his ears. 'Sorry, old man. No one is angry with you. Quite the contrary. We could cast you as the lead in the next village play. You'd make a wonderful Hound of the Baskervilles.'

'Humphrey would hate that,' I say. 'He doesn't like crowds and loud noises. Crowds, in particular. I'm sure he feels there are too many people in his kitchen as it is.'

'I know a hint when I hear one,' says Daniel.

'Not so much a hint as an instruction,' I say. 'This meeting is about to start. I'm sorry you were confused and thought you'd been invited to attend, but it doesn't make any difference now. This is a cookie club, and you no longer have any cookies, so –'

'Not so fast!' says Irene. 'We've established Daniel isn't a plumber. And you've told us he isn't your boyfriend.'

'Or a member of the local historical society,' adds Phyllis.

'Should I have told them I was delivering your Christmas tree?' Daniel asks me.

'No. Everyone would have asked me where it was. And I'm tired of making up stupid stories you can't even be bothered to corroborate.'

'You could tell them the truth,' he says.

'I'm quite keen to hear the fiction,' says Margery. 'Did you consider telling us he was here to sweep your chimneys, Lucy?'

'That one didn't occur to me. But Daniel is welcome to crawl around inside the chimney if he likes.'

'I don't like,' he says.

I sigh. 'The truth is that Daniel and I bumped into each other by chance, and I told him about this club. I didn't realise it was a secret when I first heard about it. Gran only mentioned that when I visited her in the hospital later on. Anyway, one thing led to another, and Daniel somehow got the impression I'd invited him to attend this evening.'

'Lucy issued a challenge,' says Daniel. 'And honour compelled me to rise to it.'

'It wasn't a challenge!' I say. 'Daniel knocked my cookies into the street, and I told him how long it had taken me to make them. He seemed to think baking cookies was easy. I said it wasn't, and he couldn't do any better than me. The rest is unfortunately history.'

'Every time Lucy tells that story, I come out of it looking a little worse,' says Daniel. 'But I don't want to set her off again, so I'll leave it there.'

'You told him about our club?' Irene asks me.

I hang my head. 'I'm very sorry.'

'The one that's been kept a closely guarded secret for decades?' says Phyllis, looking equally horrified.

'I didn't know that when I told him about it.'

Margery frowns. 'I can't imagine what your grandmother will say when she hears about this.'

'Do you have to tell her?' I say with sudden hope. 'Could we swear Daniel to secrecy and threaten him with something awful if he ever tells anyone?'

'I'm right here,' says Daniel.

'That's the problem,' I say. 'You shouldn't be.'

'Don't put all the blame on him,' Margery tells me. 'From what you say, you were the one who told him our closely guarded secret.'

'And let the cat out of the bag,' agrees June.

This is awful. They're all looking at me as though I've committed an actual crime.

'I've already told you how sorry I am,' I plead. 'It was an honest mistake.'

'I'm surprised you're able to let yourself off the hook so easily,' says June.

'Just what I was thinking,' agrees Irene. 'It's all very well for you to brush it off like this, Lucy, but the rest of us see it as a horrible betrayal.'

I dart a look at Daniel, who's grinning again. I look from him to Margery and see her shoulders are shaking.

'Are you winding me up?' I ask her.

She gives a splutter of laughter. 'You could say that.'

'But why?'

'I'm sorry. You looked so terrified when you said you'd given away our secret.'

'I *was* terrified!' I say. 'I've been dreading you finding out what I did. Isn't it a secret after all?'

Phyllis pours herself another cup of tea. 'That's the thing. It is, and it isn't. How much do you know about the history of this club?'

'Almost nothing. Gran told me it's a village institution, and it was important I took over for her – as a Hollis woman. She didn't mention that I shouldn't tell anyone about it until it was too late. I had no idea it was a secret.'

'It started off that way,' she says. 'The club was founded by your great-grandmother Sylvia during the second world war. Honeywell took in a lot of evacuee children. Sylvia and several of her friends decided it would be a nice idea to make Christmas special for the children while they were away from their parents. So, they came up with the idea of this cookie club. They met once a week in the run-up to Christmas, and they all brought a batch of cookies. They made them into parcels and secretly delivered them to each of the households who'd taken in an evacuee.'

'Like a Secret Santa?' I ask.

'Exactly. The children would come down in the morning and find the cookies on their doorstep, and no one would know where they'd come from.'

'That's a lovely idea,' I say. 'What happened when they went back to their parents at the end of the war?'

'Sylvia and her friends kept up the tradition. They'd never told anyone who they were, and they decided it would be fun to continue like that. Each year, they baked cookies, parcelled them up, and dropped them off at various houses around the village. During rationing, they delivered the cookies to those people who were less well off. They thought it would be nice to do something to make their Christmas more fun. As time went on, those club members with daughters passed on the baton to them. Occasionally, someone else would be invited to join. By the nineteen-seventies, the club was delivering cookies to every house in the village that had children living there.'

'That's a lot of cookies,' says Daniel.

'There are around a hundred and fifty houses in Honeywell with children,' she says. 'Irene makes a spreadsheet to make sure no one gets missed out. We all bake fifty cookies each week and bring them here. We sort them into parcels of ten, and Irene tells us which houses will be getting cookies that week. It's a lot of work, but it's worth it.'

'Is it no longer a secret?' I ask.

'As I said, it is, and it isn't. The children love the tradition. They look forward to it all year. Everyone goes out of their way to make sure they don't find out who's behind it. We try to keep it a secret from the adults too. I'm sure several of them have a reasonable idea who's involved, but no one ever mentions it.'

'It's a lovely idea,' I say. 'I'm so sorry I mentioned it to Daniel.'

'Which brings us back to where we started,' says Margery.

'What are we going to do about this?' she asks the others. 'Should we retire to another room to consider our verdict?'

'There's only the living room,' I say. 'And Humphrey seems to have retired there already to get away from things. I'm not saying he won't budge up to make room for a couple of you on the sofa, but I wouldn't bet next week's salary on it.'

'He does love his home comforts,' says June.

'I don't want to hurry you,' I say. 'But time's getting on, and the rest of the members will be arriving at any moment. Would someone like to administer the oath of silence to Daniel, and then we can get on with our evening?'

'We don't have an oath of silence,' says Margery.

'If that's your only problem, I can knock one up for you in no time at all. I can even translate it into German if you like.'

She smiles. 'I don't think we need anything too formal.'

'I agree,' I say. 'Just give him a stern warning and throw him outside before it starts to snow. Hopefully, there will be a blizzard later that will hide his footsteps. No one will know he was here.'

I turn to Daniel. 'Please remember to latch the front gate properly. I don't want a repeat of this evening's performance.'

He pushes back his chair and stands. 'The people have spoken. I'll say goodbye to Humphrey and be on my way.'

'I'll show you out,' I say. 'I'd hate you to get lost in the hall and fail to find your way out.'

'Not so fast!' says Margery, and I sigh. We were so nearly there.

Daniel stops dead, and I cannon into him. 'Ouch!'

'Sorry,' he says. 'But Margery seems to have something to say. It would only be polite for us to hear her out.'

I glance at my watch. 'Fine. But it's getting late, and you're still here.'

'You have the floor,' he tells Margery.

She glances at the other three. 'The members of the Honeywell Christmas Cookie Club would like to invite Daniel to become an honorary member. For this year only,' she adds, seeing my horrified expression.

I'm not sure how that makes anything better. I'm only here this year because Gran had an accident. I'm not likely to be back here again next year. If Daniel becomes a member of the club, it may as well be permanent.

'I disagree,' I say as calmly as possible. 'For one thing, this is a women-only club, and Daniel is definitely not a woman.'

'Technically, this isn't a women-only club,' says Phyllis. 'It's always been that way because it was started by a group of women, and they passed it on to their daughters and female friends. But there's nothing in the constitution saying it has to remain that way.'

'I didn't like to say anything,' says Daniel, his face straight, but his eyes dancing. 'But it is the twenty-first century, and there are certain laws pertaining to the equality of the sexes …'

'That's irrelevant!' I say. 'This isn't a place of employment. It's a meeting that takes place in a private home. My grandmother is free to invite whomever she likes to her house.'

I turn to face the rest of the women. 'Don't let Daniel tell you that you're breaking the law if you don't admit men. It's absolute nonsense. I vote we ask him to leave at once.'

'But who are we to argue with the club members?' says Daniel. 'I'm prepared to bow to greater authority here. I'm surprised you're not.'

'This is your club,' I tell the women. 'It's up to you. I accept your ruling.'

'How delightfully formal,' murmurs Daniel. He raises his voice. 'I too accept the ruling of the court. I don't have a gavel to hand. But if I did, consider it banged.'

'That shows what you know about court proceedings,' I mutter.

'Have you two finished bickering?' asks Margery.

'Certainly, your honour,' says Daniel. 'My fellow defendant and I would like to offer our apologies for having wasted the court's time.'

She waits for a moment to see whether I'm going to speak. When she's satisfied I'm not, she picks up a teaspoon and taps it sharply on the kitchen table.

'The ruling stands. Both Lucy and Daniel are henceforth admitted to the sacred chapter of our organisation. Let the eighty-fifth annual meeting of the Honeywell Christmas Cookie Club come to order!'

Chapter Seventeen

I close the door with a sigh of relief after the final guest has left. This evening was more fun than I expected, despite the unwelcome addition of Daniel. But I'm exhausted, and I still need to clear up before I go to bed. The rest of the club members turned up shortly after Daniel and I were formally admitted, which meant an extraordinary amount of tea and coffee making.

Humphrey nudges my ankle and looks up at me with pleading eyes.

'I haven't forgotten you,' I tell him, leading the way back to the kitchen. 'But don't try to look as though you haven't eaten since yesterday. I saw you polish off that piece of shortbread that fell on the floor. You thought no one was looking, but I was. I'm learning that someone needs to have their eye on you twenty-four hours a day. That's normally Gran's job, but she isn't here right now, so you're stuck with me.'

Humphrey isn't listening. He's standing next to the larder door. I consult the list on the fridge.

'How did you know you were getting liver snaps tonight? A lucky guess, I suppose.'

I pick up his bowl and pour the pieces into it. 'Mum said I should only fill it up to the line, so don't try telling me I've got it wrong. I don't expect you have much of an appetite if you've been eating cookies.'

I'm wrong. He finishes the liver snaps in four gulps and coughs.

'Serves you right for eating too fast,' I say unsympathetically. 'Would you like to go outside while I wash the rest of these dishes?'

I unlock the door, and he catapults joyfully past me and into the garden. I check to make sure Daniel didn't attempt to open the back gate. He and Humphrey came back into the house through the kitchen, so I doubt he did. But it's as well to be sure.

I think back over the evening as I wash the dishes. How did Daniel manage to worm his way into the club? He can't have planned it all in advance. Too many unpredictable things have happened this evening for him to have done that. He might have left the front gate open on purpose, but he couldn't have predicted Humphrey would then break free and pelt down the road at top speed. Nor did he know about Humphrey's deep and unshakeable love for mud or that I would be hampered by running in my grandmother's dressing gown.

Forget Hansel and Gretel. This evening had far stronger overtones of Little Red Riding Hood. Except that my grandmother wasn't lying upstairs in bed. And Daniel, for all his annoying qualities, is hardly cut out for the part of the big, bad wolf. The most he can be accused of is clumsiness – and a propensity to appear at times and places where he's least welcome.

He certainly got what he wanted tonight. He came here with a plan to gate-crash the cookie club, and that's what he did. I'm not sure he expected to become a fully-fledged member, but that's what happened all the same. What is it with elderly women? A halfway personable man flashes them a smile and turns on the charm, and they're putty in his hands.

That's not entirely fair. I've seldom encountered a group of women less likely to do something they don't want to, or more capable of reducing those around them to stunned silence. Which must mean they knew what they were doing when they invited him to join their exclusive club, and it had nothing whatsoever to do with his smile. I'm glad because I hate to see anyone manipulated.

Objectively speaking, Daniel does have a very nice smile, but that's just a matter of genetics and no credit to him. The fact his eyes crinkle when he laughs is also irrelevant to whether he's a good person. It's the way his face is structured, and he'd better not try to use it to bamboozle people. Any hint of that at future club meetings, and I'll be forced to step in and put him in his place.

I have to admit he didn't behave too badly this evening. He let Humphrey out, but he did everything he could to rectify that mistake. He found him again, improvised a lead, and brought him safely home. And I did spoil his cookies. To my mind, that was poetic justice, and I was prepared to argue my case if Daniel complained. But he didn't, so there was no need.

Humphrey appears at the door and slinks past me, throwing himself into his basket with a gusty sigh and starting to snore.

'All finished?' I ask him. 'I see it's started snowing. I'll have to brave the cold and dark and go outside to clean up after you. I'm not digging through six feet of snow tomorrow morning to see what you've left for me.'

Humphrey's snores grow louder.

'You're faking it,' I tell him, pulling on my coat. 'You don't want to clear up after yourself, so you're pretending to be asleep.'

He rolls over and buries his face in his cushion. I sigh, open the back door, and step out into the falling snow.

I wake the following morning filled with a determination to beat Daniel at his own game. If he's so determined to be a member of this club, he can work for it. I know it's not a competition, but there's nothing to stop me competing with him privately. He doesn't even need to know about it. Nor does anyone else.

'It will just be our little secret,' I tell Humphrey. 'You want me to beat him, don't you?'

Humphrey yawns, stretches, then climbs off the bed by simply rolling sideways with his eyes shut until he crashes onto the floor. He picks himself up with a look of surprise and sidles over to the door. That's not the right word for a dog his size. It's less of a sidle and more of a crash.

He looks at the doorway with a puzzled expression, as though it's some devious obstacle I've set up during the night to confuse him. He negotiates it with care before running down the landing. I wait until the usual set of crashes and bumps tell me he's arrived downstairs, then follow at a more sedate pace. I'm too old to throw myself down the stairs and hope for the best.

My friends and I used to slide down the stairs on a tea tray when our parents were out. There must be some obscure saint dedicated to preserving small children on tea trays because none of us ever broke any of our limbs. Maybe I should give Humphrey a tea tray to use while Gran is away. I'm not sure where I'd find one big enough, but that's the beauty of the internet. There's a website for everything.

I measure out his breakfast and drop some bread into the toaster. While I'm waiting for it to brown, I leaf through the pages of Gran's baking book, hoping to find a recipe that's both simple to follow and stunning to look at. Annoyingly, the writer has forgotten to include anything matching this description, and my opinion of professional cookery writers falls even lower. How difficult would it be for them to create a gourmet recipe that only uses three ingredients and takes less than ten minutes to make?

I find Humphrey's harness and check it several times before opening the front door. We don't want a repeat of yesterday's jailbreak. I almost expect to find Daniel lurking behind the hedge as I step onto the pavement and latch the gate closed behind me. But a quick glance up and down the street shows it's refreshingly

Daniel-free. Our first stop today is the bakery. Maybe I'll walk in and discover him sipping a cappuccino, but it isn't likely. According to him, he runs his own company, so he must have to work sometimes. Hopefully, this morning is one of those times.

I can't imagine what sort of things he uses his drones for. He mentioned his company was doing some work for the town council, but he didn't say what it was. Maybe they use the drones to inspect the drains. It would be a great pity if one of them got stuck and Daniel had to climb into the sewer to rescue it. If it were me, I'd be inclined to leave the drone where it was and write it off against tax.

Humphrey skips ahead of me, tugging at his lead. It's even colder than yesterday. It snowed a little in the night, but not enough for a snowball fight.

'Sorry, Humphrey, I tell him. 'Maybe tomorrow. In the meantime, you'll have to make do with a couple of dog biscuits.'

The bakery door opens, and Humphrey makes a dart for it, almost knocking over an elderly woman carrying several paper bags. She looks very like Mrs Ogilvie, except for the brightly dyed hair.

'Careful, young man!' she tells him. 'If you damage my plum slices, you'll find yourself on the wrong end of a lawsuit.'

'I'm so sorry,' I say. 'I'd like to say my dog isn't usually like this, but I was brought up to tell the truth.'

She gives a loud laugh. 'I understand. My sister and I have a badly behaved dog at home. You can't imagine how I suffer. These things are sent to try us. In fact, I wanted to change the dog's name to *Tryus*, but he refused to answer to it. It's lucky for him I have the patience of a saint.'

She gives me an amiable smile and sets off down the street at a surprisingly brisk pace.

'Did you hear that?' I ask Humphrey. 'I'm allowed to change your name if you don't behave.'

He grins up at me and thumps his tail.

'Fine,' I tell him. 'We'll go in and get your biscuits. But I need you to be on your best behaviour, or I'm changing your name to Biscuit Bandit, and there's absolutely nothing you or Gran can do about it.'

Chapter Eighteen

Humphrey and I have fallen into a routine of waking bright and early each morning. It would be nice to think the fresh country air and simple living is having a beneficial effect on me and encouraging me to embrace a more healthy and productive lifestyle. The truth is that Humphrey, despite being the size of a small to medium-sized lion, possesses one of the smallest bladders known to mankind – or dogkind.

I have to make sure he doesn't drink too much before we go to bed or my nights become a series of trips downstairs. I stand by the back door, shivering, as Humphrey gallops merrily around the garden, searching for the perfect spot in which to relieve himself. I grit my teeth as he lifts a leg and stares around before heaving an audible sigh and bounding off in search of an even more ideal location.

I have no idea what goes through his head at these times. I'm not sure I want to. Humphrey's thought processes are a mystery known only to himself. Judging by the blank expression on his face during these midnight trips, he may not even be aware of what he's doing.

But I don't intend to make a habit of standing around in the snow, however educational these nocturnal garden visits may be. Even David Attenborough would draw the line at standing shivering in his pyjamas while Humphrey makes a careful study of the local flora of south Honeywell.

I groan and roll over on Sunday morning when I feel his nose pushing into the small of my back.

'It's not even light yet,' I tell him in my sternest voice. 'You're confusing your time zones. You aren't in Asia. You're in Honeywell in December, and this isn't a time for any self-respecting dog to be awake.'

I roll away from him and close my eyes, hoping he'll take my words to heart and see the error of his ways. He nudges me again and whines.

'Half an hour?' I plead.

He yawns and waves his legs as though practising for the next canine Olympics. I'm not sure which event – possibly the heavyweight butterfly-swimming relay. He slithers off the bed and lands with a thud on the floor. Maybe he plans to take a nap there. This mattress is softer than I'd like. Humphrey may have come to the same conclusion and fears for the future health of his spine. Very sensible of him.

He heaves himself to his feet and sets off towards the bedroom door. A moment later, I hear him crash down the stairs. I sigh and swing my legs out of bed. I don't want to start my day clearing up one of Humphrey's accidents, with him staring at me as though he's wondering why I don't just kick some soil over it and wander off.

A blast of arctic air greets me the moment I open the back door. I shiver and pull my cardigan more tightly around me. Humphrey, who wears a thick woollen coat at all times, is unbothered by the cold. He dashes out, joyfully kicking up clouds of snow and barking at the top of his voice. I hope Gran's neighbour either sleeps at the front of her house or is afflicted with deafness. If she wasn't deaf when she moved in, I expect she is now.

We walk to the village after breakfast. Humphrey stops to greet everyone we pass. Most of them seem to know him by name, and they all ask me how my grandmother is doing. News travels fast in a place like this. I try to memorise all the messages people ask me to pass on to Gran when I next visit her, but it's impossible. Maybe I should carry a notebook and pen with me when I come out shopping. Or attach a small recording device to Humphrey's collar. But he'd probably try to eat it.

I pop into the bakery to pick up some cherry slices for Gran. I remember her baking them when I was small. Hopefully, the ones here will be as good.

The moment we're through the door, Humphrey flings himself under a table and closes his eyes.

'We're not staying,' I tell him. 'We're just buying something for Gran.'

He doesn't move.

'If you're playing dead, it won't work,' I say. 'I can see your ribs moving. And your leg is twitching.'

'He wouldn't win any games of musical statues, would he?' says Lily, who's watching in amusement. 'By the way, did you find that man you were looking for?'

'Not exactly looking for,' I say, keen to squash any ideas she may have got about me and Daniel.

'I thought you wanted to find out who he was.'

I give her a cool smile. 'In a sense, I suppose I did.'

She looks confused. 'In what sense?'

'In the sense of trying to ascertain his identity,' I say, sounding like a police officer giving a press conference. 'But not in the sense of being interested in him as a person.'

'A fine distinction,' she says.

'But an important one. As it happens, we did bump into each other again.'

'Is he a local, after all?'

'Temporarily. He's working down here for a few weeks.'

She waits for me to elaborate, but I don't want to mention the circumstances under which I met Daniel or tell her the reason why I needed to talk to him so urgently. I've learned my lesson about the cookie club, and I don't plan to mention it to anyone unless I know they're already a member.

'I can't stay for too long,' I say. 'I'm popping over to the hospital this afternoon.'

'How is your grandmother today?' asks Lily.

'When I called the ward this morning, they said she'd had a good night. They're hoping she'll be well enough to come home quite soon.'

'That's wonderful. She and Humphrey must be missing each other so much. Does that mean you'll be leaving us?'

'I'm not sure how long I'll be here. Gran can't stay at home by herself. She can't climb the stairs, for one thing. And she won't be able to take Humphrey for his walks. I expect I'll be around for a while longer.'

'That's nice,' she says. 'Honeywell is lovely at this time of year. Have you visited the Christmas fair yet?'

'I didn't think it was Humphrey's kind of thing. Or rather, I was worried it might be too much his kind of thing.'

'It can get crowded,' she says. 'And Humphrey is quite a large dog.'

'If he gets any bigger, he'll be a whole other species. Maybe I'll pop along one evening after Gran gets home.'

'Are you here for anything special today?' she asks.

'Apparently, I'm here to buy Humphrey some biscuits. I also wanted to pick up some cherry slices for Gran. I don't know how she's getting on with the hospital food, but it can't hurt to take her a few extras. I remember her baking them for me when I was a child.'

'Abby made a batch this morning,' she says. 'I'll pop a few into a bag for you. No charge. Tell Mrs Hollis everyone at The Sugarloaf Bakery is thinking of her.'

'That's kind of you,' I say. 'But there's no need. I can pay for them.'

She waves my offer away. 'It's only what we'd do for any of our regular customers. I'll put a couple of biscuits in for Humphrey to take his mind off being away from your Gran. Not that you aren't doing an amazing job with him.'

'I'm doing my best, but I'm a poor substitute. He'll be delighted when Gran gets back.'

Humphrey ambles over to sniff the bag. I hold it out of his reach. 'You can have one now and another if you can walk all the way home without diving into any muddy ditches.'

Gran is sitting up in bed knitting when I arrive at the hospital. She looks up and smiles when she sees me.

'I see they've put you to work,' I say, dropping the bag of cherry slices onto the bedside table.

'I've been finding it rather dull in here,' she says. 'I'm not used to sitting around doing nothing, and I've finished my book. Angela Carson says she'll drop by later and bring me the next one in the series.'

'Was it she who brought you the needles and wool?'

'Yes. She knows I enjoy knitting, and she had some spare balls of wool. I'm making Humphrey a sweater.'

'How much spare wool did she have?' I ask, and Gran laughs.

'He isn't that big. I made him one last year, and I only used three large balls.'

'Why does he need a new one? Is he fashion-conscious? Does he refuse to wear last season's styles?'

'I'm afraid last year's jumper didn't last for long,' she says. 'It was my fault. Humphrey discovered it before I could explain to him what it was. He thought it was a toy.'

'And played with it very, very gently?'

'He doesn't always know his own strength,' she defends him. 'He had a little chew, and it fell apart.'

'You mean he ate it?'

'Not all of it. Just the front half.'

I push the bag towards her. 'Your vet must have her hands full with Humphrey. What did she say when you told her what he'd done?'

'I'm not sure whether I mentioned it. Humphrey has eaten things like that before. The vet usually tells me to keep an eye on him and let her know if he's in any discomfort.'

'Or coughs up the world's largest hairball,' I say. 'It's lucky you're so patient with him.'

She helps herself to a cherry slice and offers the bag to me. 'He's an easy dog to be patient with. He's so loving and gentle.'

'He's a very friendly dog,' I agree. 'And he wouldn't hurt a fly. Although I can't say the same for birds. Luckily, he's too big to be very agile. He's like one of those cargo ships. They travel fast once they're underway, but they take a while to pick up speed. Any bird in the vicinity is long gone before he can reach them.'

'I think they just interest him,' says Gran. 'He's a naturally curious dog.'

'Poor Humphrey. It must be hard living among such standoffish birds.'

'Are you sure you don't want one of these?' she asks. 'They're delicious. Did you make them?'

'I wish! They came from The Sugarloaf Bakery, with their compliments and best wishes. And they're all for you. I thought you might be getting bored with the hospital food.'

'It's not too bad,' she says. 'Although nothing beats a nice cherry slice.'

'I remember you baking them when I was small. They were my favourites. Maybe you can teach me how to make them when you get home.'

'How did the cookie club go?' she asks.

'Very well, I think.' I clear my throat and speak in an artificially bright tone. 'We have a new member this year.'

She looks interested. 'Who's that? Did Irene bring her niece along? I know she was thinking about inviting her to join.'

'Not Irene's niece. He isn't related to Irene at all. I just meant –'

'He?' asks Gran. 'You mean a man?'

'That's right. His name is Daniel. He's staying in the village for a few weeks.'

'He's a friend of yours?'

'Not at all!' I say with unnecessary emphasis, remembering my cookies lying crushed in the street.

Gran looks even more confused. 'Then, why was he at the club? Who invited him?'

'He sort of invited himself.'

I tell her the whole story, starting with the destruction of my first batch of halfway decent cookies and ending with Daniel's admission to the club as a temporary member. I skate over Humphrey's break for freedom as quickly as possible. Gran doesn't look anywhere near as annoyed as I'd expected. I'm surprised to see she's laughing by the end of my story.

'It sounds as though you had an exciting evening,' she says. 'And don't worry about Daniel. If the members decided to invite him to join, that's good enough for me.'

'They didn't have a lot of choice,' I say. 'He'd already heard all your club secrets.'

She gives me an embarrassed smile. 'It must seem rather ridiculous to you. But the ritual and tradition of our club has been a great comfort to me, particularly after your grandfather's death.'

'Daniel has been sworn to secrecy,' I assure her. 'I'm not sure how much notice he'd have taken of me, but Margery, Phyllis and June made it clear to him he wasn't to mention it to a soul. They're scary women. I doubt he'll risk upsetting them.'

'Margery takes no nonsense from anyone,' she says. 'But she's been a good friend to me over the years. I must say I rather like the sound of this Daniel. It's about time we had some men join the club. Everyone nowadays is talking about equality, so we're keeping up with modern ideas.'

'I'm not sure men suffer from too much inequality,' I say. 'If you want to keep your club for women only, go right ahead.'

'We have to move with the times,' she chides me. 'My great-grandmother knew that. She was the first in our family to keep her own name when she married. And the rest of us have followed suit. As long as this Daniel of yours is a nice man, that's enough for me. Is he nice?'

This question takes me by surprise. I've spent most of my brief acquaintance with Daniel either shouting at him or sending him chasing off into the night in pursuit of an errant dog. I haven't had time to consider what he's like as a person.

'He seems pleasant enough,' I say. 'When he isn't hurling my cookies into the street. He was quite helpful with Humphrey.'

'Is he good looking?' she asks with a roguish smile.

'Handsome is as handsome does,' I say darkly.

She laughs. 'I look forward to meeting him and deciding for myself.'

'Aren't we supposed to assess people by their personality?' I tease her.

'Of course,' she agrees. 'But a handsome face never hurts.'

I reach for my bag. 'Your generation never ceases to shock me. I should let you get some rest. Angela Carson will be dropping by later with that book you mentioned. I don't even want to know what it's about. It will only shock me more.'

She squeezes my hand. 'Thank you for everything you've done, Lucy. Give my love to Humphrey.'

'I will. He'll be so excited to see you when you come home.'

'I can't wait to see him too. The doctor says there's a chance I may be allowed home this week if all goes well.'

'That's wonderful!' I say. 'You'll be pleased to be back in your own house after all this time.'

'I'll be delighted,' she says. 'I'm looking forward to catching up with everything I've missed since I've been away.'

She shoots me a sidelong glance. 'And I'll be most interested to meet this Daniel.'

Chapter Nineteen

I'm determined to do better at this week's meeting of the cookie club. I can't risk Daniel turning up on the doorstep bearing a plate of *langues de chat*, while all I have to show for my week is a batch of scorched shortbread.

I've finally realised where I've been going wrong. The secret is to ignore everything celebrity chefs tell me to do and use the simplest recipes I can find. I can always add my individual touches once I'm sure I've mastered the basic recipe.

With any luck, Gran will be home this week, and I may be able to withdraw gracefully from the baking part of the club. I'm only standing in for her while she's away. I'm not a proper member, which means there's no real reason I should continue to take part. I could be more usefully employed in making the tea and keeping an eye on Humphrey.

If so, will the club members suggest to Daniel that he withdraws too? They voted him in as an honorary member because they had no choice. The alternative would have been to kick him out and risk him spreading the story all over the village. He only wanted to join the club to annoy me. If I'm no longer taking part, that won't be necessary. He can go and play with his drones and forget all about baking cookies.

It's a nice thought, and I almost convince myself that's how it will play out. But I don't dare take the risk. For this week at least, I should be prepared to crush him – literally if need be. I scroll through various baking sites until I come across a recipe for cinnamon cookies. They look simple yet elegant. Maybe I could accessorise them with glitter to make them more seasonal. Do I mean accessorise? These baking terms are all so complicated. Decorate! That's the word. I can decorate them with edible glitter.

I get out the mixing bowl and prepare for action. Humphrey has been lying in his basket half asleep for the past hour, but at the first sound of me opening the larder door, he opens his eyes.

'Go back to sleep,' I tell him. 'This isn't for you. It's for the cookie club.'

I prop my phone on the counter and study the recipe. 'Take two cups of flour.' I frown at the screen. What is that supposed to mean? What sort of cups? I run an eye along the shelf above the kettle. There are several flowered teacups, two drinking glasses, and an enormous china mug saying *Best Dog Owner.*

Which one should I use? The flowered ones fit the technical definition of a cup. But the mug is much larger, so it ought to produce more cookies, which can only be a good thing. I pick up a teacup and dip it into the container of flour, then empty it out and replace it. I can't take the risk of its being the wrong size.

I read through the recipe again. One cup of butter and three quarters of a cup of sugar. This chef appears to be obsessed with the subject of cups. Perhaps their hobby is collecting rare drinking receptacles from all over the world. Fair enough, but why use them for cooking instead of keeping them in a glass display case like other obsessive collectors?

I click through the recipes again until I find one that gives actual weights. That's more like it. I measure the ingredients into the bowl and stir them together. It takes a while because the butter is almost frozen solid. I make a mental note to melt it in the microwave next time and continue mixing. My arms start to ache, but I persevere. If I keep baking, I'll develop enormous biceps and be the envy of everyone at the gym. I'd have to join one first, but it would be worth it just to see all the admiring looks.

I'm sliding the finished tray into the oven when the doorbell rings. Humphrey leaps from his basket and surges down the hall, barking loudly.

'Stop it!' I tell him without much hope. Once he starts, he takes a while to wind down, rather like a music box.

'Just a minute!' I call through the door, pulling the latch across before turning the handle. I have no intention of joining Humphrey in a brisk jog up the street today, no matter how aerobically beneficial it may be.

When I'm sure there's no chance of him escaping, I open the door a crack. If this is someone trying to sell me new guttering or persuade me to join some weird cult, they'll be sorry.

'Hello there,' says a familiar voice, and I sigh.

'What are you doing here?'

'I've come to collect Humphrey and take him round to your neighbour's house to apologise for stealing their laundry.'

'That was nothing to do with Humphrey!' I say. 'It was all your idea, and I won't have you blaming him for it. You can apologise to whomever you like, but you're not dragging Humphrey into it.'

'It was the other way around,' says Daniel. 'He was dragging me. That's why I had to improvise a makeshift lead.'

'You're wasting your time,' I tell him. 'He's staying here with me. If that's all –'

'I'm also here to see you,' he says. 'I won't stick my foot in the door again because I'm sure you'd slam it shut. But I'm hoping you'll let me in for a few minutes.'

Humphrey gives a delighted bark and scrabbles at the door.

'Traitor!' I tell him. I unlatch the door and open it a little further. 'What do you really want?'

'To see how Humphrey is after his adventure.'

'As you can see, he's fine. But I don't want him getting cold, so I'll have to close the door now.'

'And to talk to you,' he says.

I'm about to refuse when I realise this is the perfect opportunity for us to have a reasonable discussion, during which I can inform him of my resolution to withdraw from the club the minute Gran gets home and suggest he does the same.

I open the door just far enough for him to squeeze inside without Humphrey escaping. 'I'm busy right now, but you can come in for five minutes if you must. You'll have to leave any drones outside.'

He laughs. 'I don't have any with me. Do you think I take them for an afternoon walk every day?'

'That's what you were doing the first time I met you.'

'I was taking it down to the field for a test flight,' he says. 'Not showing it all the local sights.'

Once inside, he pulls off his coat and grins at me. 'Do you always welcome your neighbours with such enthusiasm and display of rural hospitality?'

'Only the annoying ones. You can hang your coat on that peg.'

He follows me down the hall to the kitchen. 'How are you?'

'Busy.'

'I won't take up too much of your valuable time,' he says.

'I'm sorry. I was making some cookies when you arrived, and I was finding the whole thing rather frustrating.'

I catch his eye and flush. 'I don't mean it's particularly difficult. But it's one more thing to do on top of everything else.'

'The first time we met, you told me baking was one of the most difficult things in the world,' he says.

'I was having a bad day. It's quite simple, really. I'm surprised you would think otherwise.'

The corners of his mouth twitch. 'I bow to your superior knowledge. Anyway, I'm not here to exchange baking tips. My landlady told me she'd heard your grandmother may be coming home this week. I wondered whether you needed any help getting the house ready for her?'

'You mean cleaning?' I ask.

'More like fitting a grab rail for her in the shower – things like that.'

I'm taken aback by this thoughtful gesture. 'That's very kind of you. I'd really appreciate that. One of the nurses mentioned she might need some adaptations. I was planning to call a handyman.'

'No need,' he says. 'I'm good at that sort of thing. And diagnosing blocked pipes just by looking at them.'

I laugh as I remember our club meeting. 'I don't think I'd trust you with anything plumbing-related. You're definitely no Steve Wately. But the shower thing would be good. Thanks, Daniel.'

'And I'm happy to stay with Humphrey whenever you go to collect your grandmother,' he says. 'It may take longer than you expect. I picked up a friend after his operation last year and had to sit in the waiting room for hours while they waited for all the right people to sign the forms and the doctors to check him over before he left. Then we had to stop by the pharmacy and pick up his meds.'

I waver. It's true that Humphrey has been fine by himself when I've visited Gran, but I've never been gone for more than an hour or two. If I end up stuck at the hospital for the entire afternoon, who knows what Humphrey might get up to all by himself? He may escape from the house somehow and end up in the mud-hole again, and I'll arrive home to find him wearing Gran's pink dressing gown.

'I could take him for a walk,' offers Daniel. 'I know where his favourite field is, and I could use a proper lead this time.'

'Would you like a cup of tea?' I ask to give myself time to think.

'I thought you'd never ask. I'll make it. I know where everything is. I've been here before, remember?'

'I'm not likely to forget.'

'I had a great time at the cookie club,' he says. 'Who would have thought there would be secret societies and goings-on in such a sleepy little village as Honeywell? It's like something out of Agatha Christie.'

'Except that no one was murdered.'

'You said that with a little too much regret. Did you mind me being there?'

I'm about to say yes, but it strikes me I'm being ridiculous. He gate-crashed a cookie club, not the secret society to promote cyber-warfare across the entire New Forest area. Technically, he didn't even gate-crash it. Our initial meeting was accidental, and I was the one who told him all about the club. If I hadn't overreacted in the way I did, he wouldn't have taken my words as some sort of ridiculous challenge and turned up at the house the following day. I only have myself to blame.

'It's fine,' I say. 'I told Gran all about it when I visited her. I thought she'd be upset, but she appeared to find the whole situation amusing.'

'I'm glad to hear it,' he says. 'I look forward to meeting her.'

Humphrey has been taking a well-earned nap in his basket. He opens one eye and looks at Daniel.

'He seems to like the idea of me looking after him for a while,' says Daniel.

'Fine, you can watch him if you want.' I hear how ungracious this sounds and add a belated, 'Thank you.'

'I'll look forward to it,' he says. 'I've often wished I could have a dog, but I move around so much it wouldn't be fair.'

'What kind of dog would you have?'

'One exactly like Humphrey.'

'There are no dogs exactly like Humphrey. He's one of a kind. I've always thought that was a good thing. I never imagined anyone would want to duplicate him.'

'I doubt I'll ever own somewhere large enough for a dog his size,' he says.

'This is a tiny cottage, but Gran seems to make it work. I'm starting to doubt your commitment to this whole dog thing.'

'He's obviously very happy here. But I may stick to a slightly smaller breed when I get a dog of my own.'

I look at Humphrey, sprawled half in and half out of his basket, his legs all going in different directions. I'm never sure how he does that. It looks as though he has several destinations in mind and can't quite decide which one to pursue first, so he's keeping all his options open.

'I'm not sure Humphrey counts as any kind of breed,' I say. 'My personal theory is that he's the original dog designed by a committee. No one could agree on the essential features, and they ended up with this.'

Daniel bends down to pat Humphrey's head. 'I think the committee did a great job. They may have gone overboard a bit on the size, but I expect that was a mixture of enthusiasm and inexperience. They got it just right with the rest of him.'

'Gran certainly thinks so. She's besotted with him. I won't say he's a substitute for my grandfather. No one could be that. But he's the perfect companion for her. She told me once he gave her a reason to get up in the morning after Grandpa Ed's death. After a while, it became a habit, and now she wakes up excited to face the day and discover what Humphrey will find for them to do.'

'No wonder he's so precious to her,' he says. 'I promise to look after him and keep him out of trouble. No more running off to search for mud.'

'And for goodness' sake use his proper harness and lead,' I warn him. 'Gran will suffer a relapse if she sees you walking him around the garden using one of her torn up sheets as a lead.'

'Why are her sheets torn up?' he asks.

'They're not.'

'Then, why …?'

'I'm talking about you tearing them up, as you very well know. And I'm telling you not to.'

He reaches into his pocket and pulls out a pen. 'Do you have a piece of paper I could use to note all this down? It's all too much for me to remember by myself.'

'How difficult is it to remember to keep Humphrey safely away from the water meadows and not to use various pieces of clothing or bedding instead of his lead?'

Daniel drops the pen back into his pocket. 'When you put it like that, it doesn't sound too bad. But I can't give you any absolute guarantees.'

Chapter Twenty

The kettle switches itself off, and he picks up the container of tea. 'How strong do you like it?'

'Medium. The milk's in the fridge.'

He reaches up to the shelf for a couple of cups and frowns. 'This one appears to have flour on it.'

'I don't think so. It's … dust.'

He inspects the cup more closely. 'It's an odd colour for dust.'

'What colour is dust supposed to be?'

'Greyish, in my experience. This is white.'

'Dust goes white when it's old,' I say, adopting an air of expertise, although why anyone would want to claim to know all the facts about dust, I have no idea. I'm not likely to appear on Mastermind any time soon. 'This is Lucy Hollis. She lives in London and works as a translator. Her special subject tonight is the history and evolution of dust – both local and foreign. Lucy, your two minutes start now!'

'That must be a countryside thing,' he says. 'In the city, it stays the same colour for years. Believe me, I know. I had a flatmate once who refused to clean his room because he was convinced that clean surfaces attract dust faster, which forces people to do more housework. His theory was that by leaving it well alone, it stops increasing and disappears entirely.'

'A self-cleaning house?' I say. 'That's the dream. Did it work?'

'Not even close. All that happened was he developed asthma and had to move out.'

'Couldn't he just have cleaned his room?' I ask.

'I suggested it several times, but he refused to accept the connection. He hinted at one point that I was in the pay of Big Cleaning.'

'Interesting,' I say. 'How do I know you aren't? You may have offered to look after Humphrey to give yourself the opportunity to snoop around the house, looking for ways to sell me your products.'

'I doubt anyone has made one to deal with persistent white dust. It's a real gap in the market.'

He pours me a cup of tea and hands me the milk. 'You don't take sugar, do you?'

'No, but there's a bowl of sugar lumps in the pantry if you do. Gran has two lumps in her tea. She doesn't like to use regular sugar. She says it makes her tea taste funny.'

'Aren't sugar lumps just compressed sugar?' he asks.

'I think so. But she insists she can tell the difference, so she continues to buy lumps. Grandpa Ed used to sneak me a few after dinner when Mum wasn't looking. We'd take them out to his shed and share them while he showed me whatever he'd been making that day. He was very good with his hands. He and Gran never threw anything away. He was always mending and repairing things.'

I point to a kitchen chair. 'I helped him fix that one. Someone had left it on the street for anyone who wanted it. Not surprisingly, no one did. It only had two legs, and the back strut was missing. Grandpa Ed and I spent a day in his shed mending it. He showed me how to use his lathe to make new legs and round them off. I remember how proud I was when it was finished and we took it in to show everyone. It must have been sat on thousands of times, even by Humphrey when he gets the chance. He likes to climb onto anything that will bear his weight – and several things that don't.'

'If you can construct something that can withstand Humphrey, you're clearly a skilled craftswoman,' he says.

'I was mostly in charge of the gluing,' I admit. 'But I finished this leg off on the lathe. That's why it's not as smooth as the others. But it does the job, and everyone kindly pretended not to notice. How about you? I suppose you must be quite technically minded if you fly drones for a living.'

'I don't build them from scratch,' he says. 'I just operate the controls.'

'That's disappointing. You're missing out on the satisfaction of creating something all by yourself – like me and that chair leg. Grandpa was right when he said all the traditional skills are dying out.'

'I'm not sure building a drone counts as a traditional skill,' he says. 'It isn't something that's been handed down through the generations by our forefathers.'

'Grandpa would have enjoyed it. He loved learning new things. The first thing he did when he and Gran bought a computer was to take it apart to see how it worked.'

'And how did that go?' he asks, taking a sip of his tea.

'Not well,' I admit. 'He had to take it in to be repaired. At first, they told him it was under warranty, and he should just return it. That was before they saw what he'd done to it. But Grandpa told me the quickest way to learn something new is to strip it down and see what's inside it.'

'I'm glad he never got his hands on one of our drones,' says Daniel. 'With high-end cameras, some of them can cost fifty thousand pounds.'

'That can't be true!' I protest. 'You could buy a car for that. Possibly, more than one.'

'I'm afraid it is. It's why it took us so long to build the business. We had to expand fairly slowly and pay off one loan at a time. But it was what we wanted to do, so it was worth it.'

'I've always wanted to translate novels,' I say. 'But that sort of thing is difficult to break into. It can be a precarious life until you build up a reputation.'

'You could do it in your spare time,' he suggests. 'Plenty of people start off a new career that way. Marcus and I used to spend hours flying drones for fun before we decided to turn it into a full-time business.'

'Maybe. But I don't have much spare time. I work long hours, and I'm permanently exhausted.'

He nods towards Humphrey, who, for some reason, is lying on his back with his legs in the air, peddling furiously. 'Looking after him must be hard work too.'

'Looking after Humphrey doesn't take much time,' I say. 'Except when he decides to visit the spa for a mud facial.'

'And you have to bake cookies for the club,' he says.

'That's simply a case of mixing the ingredients together and putting them into the oven.'

'I'd forgotten what a skilled baker you were,' he apologises.

'I'm a Hollis. It's in my genes. Don't forget my great-grandmother was the founder of this club.'

He looks interested. 'I didn't know that sort of thing was passed down the generations. I always thought genes controlled things like blue eyes or short-sightedness.'

'Talent can be passed down as well,' I assure him. 'Haven't you ever heard of someone having a natural talent for something? Where do you think that comes from?'

'Chance?' he suggests.

'Genes. Ask any scientist.'

'So, my talent for flying drones is a genetic legacy? How does that work? They only started being available commercially in the past twenty years.'

'It's the principle of the thing,' I explain. 'Maybe one of your ancestors was a fighter pilot.'

'Not that anyone has ever mentioned.'

'Then maybe you shouldn't be unleashed on the unsuspecting local citizens.'

'Speaking of unsuspecting local citizens,' he says, 'Humphrey is begging to be unleashed on them.'

I turn to look at Humphrey, who has picked up his lead and brought it over to me. He stares up at me hopefully, the lead dangling from his mouth. His meaning couldn't be any more clear.

'Just a short walk,' I tell him. 'We'll take a longer one this evening.'

'I'll come with you if you like,' says Daniel. 'Even if you don't want Humphrey to accompany me to apologise for the sock theft, you can show me exactly how you like him to be walked.'

'On his lead,' I say. 'And not in anyone else's garden. Otherwise, you'll be fine.'

He pulls on his coat. 'It wasn't snowing when I walked here, but the sky was grey, so it might start again at any moment. Does Humphrey wear a coat and little bootees? Perhaps you could shop at the same store London Zoo uses? *Giant Pets R Us* has been supplying the zoo by royal charter for more than two hundred years. You should pop in one day and ask for the baby elephant section. It's where they keep all their Dumbo-themed clothes. They should suit Humphrey very well. And you could buy him an out-sized tuxedo for special occasions.'

'I don't think he's invited to many special occasions,' I say.

'After witnessing his performance last night, I'm not surprised. However, with the right wardrobe, all that may change.'

I clip on Humphrey's harness and attach his lead, which I hand to Daniel. 'If you're planning to walk him at some point, you may as well get used to each other now.'

He takes the lead and winds it around his hand a couple of times. 'Once bitten, twice shy. You won't be getting away from me today, young man.'

'Either that or you'll end up in the emergency room with a sprained wrist,' I say.

'That would be convenient for you. You could visit me when you've finished visiting your grandmother.'

'Not a hope,' I say. 'Have you seen how much they charge for hospital parking these days? I'm in and out as quickly as possible. I don't have time for detours.'

'That's a shame. I was hoping you'd bring me some cookies while I was waiting to be assessed.'

He sniffs. 'Speaking of cookies, didn't you say you were making some before I arrived? Shouldn't they be ready by now?'

I'd forgotten about the cookies. I wonder why the timer hasn't pinged. I snatch up the oven gloves and bend down to look. To my horror, I realise that not only did I forget to set the timer, I forgot to turn the oven on. But there's no way I'm telling Daniel that.

I straighten up and drop the gloves back onto the countertop. 'They're fine.'

'You didn't open the oven door to check.'

'I didn't need to. I'd forgotten they need a couple of hours to ...' I cast around for something that sounds like a proper culinary term and remember Delia's cookbook. 'To prove!' I say triumphantly.

'Isn't that something to do with bread?' he asks.

'We generally use that term when we're talking about bread making. But it's also a technique that chefs use for certain types of cookies.'

'How fascinating,' he says. 'May I ask which type you're making today?'

I don't dare name a variety of cookie, not without knowing what the word prove means. I'd be sure to give myself away.

'I can't tell you,' I say. 'I'll be baking them for this week's cookie club, and you know they're supposed to be a surprise.'

He twists Humphrey's lead even more tightly around his hand. 'Of course. I'm sorry I asked. I look forward to trying them at the meeting if there are any extras.'

I follow him down the hall towards the front door, noticing he has no difficulty keeping Humphrey in check.

'Are you sure you don't mind me coming with you?' he asks. 'It would be good to get some practise with him and pick up some tips.'

'Not at all,' I say. 'But it will have to be a short walk. I have a lot to do today.'

'We can stay out for just as long as it takes your cookies to prove,' he says, holding open the door for me. 'I know how important timings are when you're baking. You'll want to switch the oven on at just the right moment to avoid them collapsing.'

That does it! I'm walking up to The Sugarloaf Bakery first thing tomorrow morning and asking Abby for cookery lessons.

Chapter Twenty-One

Humphrey and I walk up to the village after breakfast the following day. As usual, he stops to sniff every single blade of grass and plant on the way. He last sniffed them twelve hours ago. What does he expect to have changed in the meantime? I'd like to ask him, but there's no point. Even if he could speak, I doubt I would understand his reasons.

He and I are very different. When it's this cold, I have an overwhelming desire to stay at home next to the fire and watch the snowflakes fall from inside a warm and cosy living room. Whereas Humphrey would spend all his time outside if he could, crashing around the neighbourhood making friends with the unsuspecting local wildlife. If his genetic makeup is ever examined, I suspect he'll turn out to be equal part wolf and teddy bear.

The high street is almost deserted, which doesn't surprise me. I wouldn't be out on a day like this unless necessity demanded it.

Lily greets me with a cheerful smile when I walk into the bakery. 'Hello, Lucy. Hello, Humphrey. What can I get for you both today?'

I order a coffee and an apricot Danish while Humphrey looks up at her imploringly.

'Will he be having his usual?' she asks.

I smile down at him as he shifts from foot to foot in his anxiety to know what flavour this morning's biscuits will be. 'I'll let you choose for him.'

She brings my coffee over a few minutes later, and I ask whether Abby is working today.

'She's here until two o'clock,' she says. 'Did you want to see her?'

'I was hoping to ask her something. Maybe I could ask you instead.'

She sits down at my table. Humphrey is busy with his second biscuit and doesn't look up. She strokes his ears and smiles at me. 'How can I help you?'

'I was wondering whether Abby might be prepared to give me a couple of cookery lessons. I know she doesn't have much time, but I'm desperate.'

I hadn't intended to say that. The last thing I want is for Daniel to hear about this. I've told him how professionally I can cook, so he would be well within his rights to wonder why such an experienced chef would need any extra help.

'As a matter of fact, she does give lessons,' says Lily. 'We sometimes hold evening classes at the bakery, although not in the run up to Christmas. I don't know whether she'll have time at the moment, but we can ask her. She's due for a break soon. I'll tell her you were asking.'

Abby appears ten minutes later and comes over to my table carrying a cup of coffee. 'Lily said you wanted to talk to me.'

'Not to complain about anything,' I say before she can get the wrong idea. 'This apricot Danish is delicious.'

She looks amused. 'So, you just wanted to compliment the chef?'

'Not exactly. I wanted to ask whether you might be free sometime to give me a cookery lesson. But not if you're too busy. It was just an idea.'

'Do you want to learn anything special?' she asks.

'I need to bake some cookies.'

'Any cookies in particular?'

'Fancy cookies,' I say, and she laughs.

'Can you be more specific?'

I'd like to tell her I want to wipe the floor with Daniel, to crush him beyond hope of recovery, and to make him wish he'd never heard of the Honeywell Christmas Cookie Club. But I refrain. To an outsider, that may sound a little extreme. So, I content myself with saying, 'I'd like to bake the sort of things you might find in Harrods or Fortnum and Mason.'

She raises an eyebrow. 'Is there a specific reason why you need to become a pastry chef overnight? Do you have a YouTube channel or are you some kind of influencer?'

'Not at all. I can't even influence Humphrey not to dive into every puddle he sees. I could try to go viral with videos of him chasing birds, but I'm not sure it would catch on. I'm afraid I can't tell you exactly why I need to learn to bake, but I'd be everlastingly grateful if you could help me learn a few techniques. I have no idea what I'm doing. I can't even figure out how my grandmother's oven works.'

'I don't have a lot of spare time,' she says. 'But I could squeeze you in for an hour or two tomorrow evening. How would five thirty work for you?'

'That would be perfect!' I say. 'Thank you so much.'

'Is there anything specific you'd like to start with?' she asks.

'I'm not too sure. I was hoping you might suggest something exotic.'

She considers this. 'In my experience, making a simple recipe extremely well can be more effective than attempting something too complicated and doing it poorly.'

'I expect you're right,' I say. 'But not too simple. I need to make something eye-catching.'

'I'll think about it and try to come up with a recipe that looks good but is fairly foolproof,' she says.

'I'm sorry I can't tell you more about why I want to do this. I know how busy you must be. I wouldn't ask if it wasn't important.'

'Don't worry about it,' she says. 'I always enjoy helping people learn to bake. I often give private lessons. Sometimes, I combine them if there's more than one person wanting to learn. It keeps the price down.'

'That sounds good,' I say. 'But I'm happy to pay whatever it costs. I wasn't sure you'd have the time.'

'I never have enough time for all the things I want to do,' she says. 'But somehow, it all gets done. I like to keep busy, which is lucky working in a place like this. And now I have to get back to the kitchen. Those mince pies won't bake themselves.'

I look out of the window as I finish my coffee. A few more people have appeared on the high street, heads down against the freezing wind. It's started to snow again. The flakes swirl and eddy around their heads. From inside the cosy bakery, it's the perfect Christmas scene, although I doubt that thought has crossed the shoppers' minds.

I nudge Humphrey with my toe. 'Time to go. Don't look at me like that. I know you'd like to stay here all day eating biscuits, and so would I. But we have a lot to do before Gran comes home, and I'd like you to start by hoovering out the spare room.'

Chapter Twenty-Two

When I leave the house the following evening, Humphrey is sprawled out on the sofa and barely stirs when I say goodbye. I gave him an extra-long walk this afternoon, so I'm hoping he'll sleep until I get back from my cookery lesson. I'd like to think he'll guard the house for me, but I have to admit no security outfit would recruit him as a guard dog. He's noisy enough, but I've never met such an uncoordinated animal. Any burglars would be halfway home before he'd untangled himself enough to chase after them.

It often seems as though he's a much smaller dog trapped inside a large dog costume. His real legs have a good idea of what they want to do, but the rest of him doesn't always respond. Still, Gran didn't adopt him as a guard dog. She adopted him because she fell in love with him, and he with her. So, it isn't important that he'll never rival Kevin Costner in the bodyguard stakes.

I walk quickly up to the village. It's been a cloudy day, so it hasn't been as chilly as the last few days. But the sky has cleared now, and the temperature has dropped. It's a beautiful evening, but I hardly notice it as I pick up the pace and almost run towards the high street. The bakery is always lovely and warm and smells of cinnamon and vanilla. I wonder what Abby will teach me to bake. We may not start with cookies. She may decide to teach me something Christmassy like stollen or panettone.

'I'm afraid we're closed,' says Lily, who's busy wiping down the table nearest to the counter. She looks up and realises who it is. 'Sorry, Lucy. I'd forgotten you were coming. Abby said you should go through as soon as you arrived.'

I find Abby sitting in the kitchen drinking a cup of coffee and leafing through a binder. She jumps up when she sees me. 'Hi, Lucy. Right on time.'

'I didn't want to keep you waiting. I'm so grateful you agreed to do this at all.'

'It's fine,' she says. 'My partner is working late this evening. He's picking me up later, and we're going to the Christmas fair before meeting some friends for dinner. Have you visited it yet?'

'I haven't been anywhere except the field near the water meadows and the streets around our house. I'm not sure Humphrey would be welcome at the fair.'

'They allow dogs if they're kept on their leads,' she says.

'That's true of a lot of places. But I doubt it really applies to dogs like Humphrey. He has a large helping of carthorse in his genes.'

'I see your point,' she says. 'I know Bernie's owners always take him, but he's only small.'

'I can just imagine the scene,' I say. 'The stalls would go down like dominoes, leaving Humphrey sitting in the middle of the wreckage with that puzzled look he always wears when he's sat on something and broken it.'

The shop door jangles, and I hear the sound of voices.

'That will be my other pupil,' says Abby. 'Did Lily mention I'd found someone else who wants a cookery lesson? I hope that's alright with you. It will keep the costs down.'

'Someone else wants to learn to bake?' I ask, surprised.

'It was a bit of a coincidence, but this is the time of year for baking. He seemed very nice, and he was anxious to start at once.'

'He?' I say, a flicker of suspicion curling around my brain.

The kitchen door opens, and I turn to find my worst fears confirmed.

'Hello, Lucy,' says Daniel pleasantly. 'What a surprise to see you here today.'

'Do you know each other?' Abby asks me.

'You could say that.'

'I've always said what a small world it is,' says Daniel.

I roll my eyes. 'Everyone says that. You're not the first person to come up with the phrase. It's a massive cliché.'

Abby looks from me to Daniel. 'I hope neither of you minds me booking a double lesson. It seemed the best thing to do.'

'I'm delighted,' says Daniel. 'I'm just a little surprised. Lucy is such an accomplished cook, I didn't think she had anything more to learn.'

'Only arrogant people think they have nothing to learn,' I say.

Abby looks puzzled. 'I thought you hadn't done any baking before, Lucy?'

'I said not much,' I correct her. 'Obviously, I know the basics.'

Too late, I remember telling her I wasn't even sure how to switch the oven on.

'How about you?' I ask Daniel. 'What brings you here this evening?'

'The same as you, I imagine. It's an arrogant chef who thinks they know everything.'

'But you both seemed in such a hurry for this lesson,' says Abby. 'I thought you were complete beginners. Perhaps I should revise what I was planning to do with you today.'

'No!' Daniel and I say simultaneously.

'There's no need for that,' I add. 'It never hurts to go over the basics. There's always something new you can learn.'

'Exactly,' agrees Daniel. 'It's how all the great chefs work. Isn't that right, Abby?'

'Most people like to move on once they've mastered the basics,' she says.

'Obviously, Lucy and I approach the whole thing differently,' he says. 'She and I are perfectionists. I thought the first time we met how similar we were, and this only goes to prove it.'

'That's great,' says Abby. 'Shall we get on with the lesson?'

'Certainly,' he says. 'We can discuss our similarities another time. Perhaps over a drink at The Red Lion when we finish here?'

'I have to get home to Humphrey,' I say.

'Then, let's make a start,' says Abby. 'The recipe I've chosen combines several different techniques you may find useful.'

She points to the sink and tells us to wash our hands.

'It's like being back at school,' says Daniel. 'I remember washing my hands each day after playing in the sand pit.'

'I assume that would have been at secondary school?' I say.

'That's right. I took a GCSE in advanced sand sculpture.'

I reach for the towel and dry my hands. 'How did you do?'

'Not well, I'm afraid. I think the sand was too dry or something.'

'All set?' asks Abby. 'I thought we could start by finding out what you do and don't know.'

'Lucy knows everything there is to know about cookery,' says Daniel. 'She told me so herself the last time I saw her.'

'And Daniel is an experienced baker,' I say. 'He couldn't stop talking about it.'

'Why don't you both tell me what you're hoping to achieve in this lesson?' she asks. 'And I'll do my best to provide it.'

Daniel and I glance at each other. I'm fairly sure we're thinking the same thing. If we're not careful, either Abby will decide there's nothing she can teach us or she'll realise we've been lying to her and fail us on the spot. Is that a thing with cookery lessons or only sand sculpture examinations?

'There's no harm in refreshing the basics,' I say hoping Abby won't mention how desperate I was when I begged her to help me.

She points to a table at the far end of the kitchen. 'I've set up over there. Let's start with the basic ingredients and take it from there.'

She hands us both aprons, and we put them on.

Shall we make a start?' she asks.

'I'm ready,' I say.

Daniel smooths down his apron and gives me an irritating smile. 'Me too. Let the contest begin!'

'This is a bakery lesson, not the Hunger Games,' I say under my breath.

'I've weighed out all the ingredients to save time,' says Abby. 'I assume neither of you has any trouble with the concept of scales or weights?'

'I expect Daniel does,' I say. 'You've heard him boasting about his failed exams. I wouldn't be surprised if he had to repeat his reception year several times.'

'Miss Bright gave us an excellent grounding in weights and volume,' says Daniel. 'I was top of the class in pouring water from a large container into a smaller one and proving it couldn't be done. I was very good at fetching a cloth to wipe up afterwards too.'

'A simple yes or no will suffice,' says Abby.

'I'm sorry,' I apologise. 'I didn't mean to waste your time by talking about irrelevant things. Neither did Daniel.'

'Let's start by adding the butter and flour into the bowl and rubbing them into breadcrumbs,' she says.

I tip the cubes of butter into my bowl and add what I assume is the flour. It's a fine white powder, which means it's either flour, icing sugar, or baking powder. I'm a little hazy about the purpose of baking powder, but I don't remember any of the recipes I've made so far calling for more than a couple of teaspoons of it. I don't dare ask Abby in front of Daniel. I want to appear like someone who's very much at home in the baking arena but who recognises there's always room for improvement and isn't too proud to pick up tips from an expert.

'Mission successfully completed,' says Daniel. 'Where are the breadcrumbs?'

Abby smiles. 'I'm never sure when you're being serious.'

It seems safe for me to smile too. I'm not sure why she thinks he isn't serious, but it's always good to hedge your bets.

'You said something about breadcrumbs,' says Daniel. 'I don't seem to have any here. How about you, Lucy?'

I'm almost sure this is a trick question, but I'm not sure why. And I don't want to make a fool of myself by falling into whatever trap he's set for me.

'I'm not talking about real breadcrumbs,' says Abby. 'I'm talking about the baking technique where you rub the butter and flour between your fingertips until they combine and look like breadcrumbs.'

I'm glad I didn't say anything to incriminate myself. This way, I can maintain my pretence of culinary expertise a little longer.

'I'm surprised you've never heard of that,' I tell Daniel. 'It's a fairly basic technique.'

'Is that right?' he says. 'Would you mind demonstrating so I can get the hang of it?'

'Perhaps it would be better for Abby to do it while we both watch. I know how I usually rub the breadcrumbs into … I mean the butter … how I do it. But she may have something up her sleeve to speed up the process.'

'Not really,' says Abby. 'I'm sorry, but I've just realised the slow-rise dough is ready for kneading. It would be great to get a jump on that for tomorrow morning. Do you mind if I sort that out while you two make a start on this?'

'Not at all,' says Daniel. 'Take all the time you need. I'll watch Lucy and copy what she does.'

'Thanks. I'll only be a couple of minutes.' She walks over to a machine and switches it on.

Daniel gives me an expectant smile. 'Over to you, Lucy!'

'You don't need me to show you how to do something as simple as this,' I say. 'You heard what Abby said – you rub the breadcrumbs together until they're ready.'

'I'm not sure that's what she said, but I bow to your superior knowledge.'

He folds his arms and leans back against a pillar to watch me. There's nothing for it. Maybe if I assume an air of competence, the rest will follow.

I take a deep breath and plunge my hands into the mixing bowl. It feels revolting. The butter is cold and slimy. I move it around a bit to collect the flour, but nothing happens. I pinch my fingers together, and the butter slides through them and shoots towards the other side of the bowl.

I retrieve it and roll it in the flour again before giving it another good pinch. This time, a chunk of butter flies out of the bowl, skids across the table, and lands on the floor. I can't use it in the cookies now. It may have picked up all sorts of dirt. I'm fairly sure you aren't supposed to throw your ingredients all over the floor before returning them to your bowl and carrying on as though nothing has happened.

I drop the piece of butter into a nearby bin and return to the table.

Daniel looks from me to the mixing bowl. 'What now?'

'What do you mean?' I plunge my hands back in, trying not to shudder at the feel of the slimy paste beneath my fingers.

'Aren't you going to replace the butter you sent flying?'

'It fell on the floor, remember?'

He grins. 'Fell is rather a passive word. I'd prefer to say it flew through the air like the latest military jet plane, crash-landing three metres away from the launch site.'

'I'm still not using it in my dough,' I tell him.

'Don't you need to replace it with the same amount of butter?'

'That won't be necessary. This isn't a chemistry lesson where the exact proportions are of vital importance. Cookery is an art, not a science.'

'Fascinating,' he says. 'It's great to get an insight into a new subject from someone as qualified as you.'

I grab another chunk of butter, careful to squeeze it more gently this time. I don't want Abby to return to find all the ingredients she's carefully weighed and chopped are lying on her kitchen floor. She might slip on them and go flying. How would I explain to Lily I'd only been here for five minutes before hospitalising her pastry chef with a severe concussion?

I could blame the whole thing on Daniel. He and I are the only two witnesses, so it would be his word against mine. I glance around the kitchen but don't see any CCTV cameras. Why would there be? It's unlikely there's much risk of burglary in a village bakery. But they might be using them as a live stream for a reality TV cookery programme. If so, I'm in trouble. The entire nation will have seen me dropping the deadly butter trail into Abby's path. I'll never be able to pin the blame onto Daniel.

'Everything alright over here?' asks Abby, switching off the mixer and walking towards us.

'Mind the floor!' I say. 'I dropped some butter. If you give me a cloth, I'll wipe it up before anyone slips on it.'

'I'll do that for you,' offers Daniel. 'I'd hate to break your rhythm with the breadcrumbs. I'm learning so much.'

Abby hands him a cloth, and he kneels down to clean the floor.

'It's as though a giant, buttery snail has gone past,' he says chattily, giving it one final wipe.

'That looks almost as much fun as playing in a sandpit,' I tell him.

He straightens up and grins at me. 'You're right. I'm having a lot of fun this evening.'

I'm glad one of us is. This lesson isn't turning out as I expected. I saw myself spending an hour in a cosy kitchen with

Abby, while she imparted a few little-known yet stunningly effective techniques that would enable me to knock the socks off everyone at the cookie club, and Daniel in particular.

Instead, I've ended up having to share a lesson with my arch-nemesis. To add insult to injury, I'm making a complete fool of myself in front of him. Not for the first time. There are some people who bring out the worst in me for no discernible reason, and Daniel appears to be one of them. The only thing to do is stay away from them. I'd love to follow this advice, but it's a little difficult at this precise moment.

'Let's have a look how you're doing,' says Abby. She peers into my mixing bowl. To my annoyance, I see her lips twitch.

'I haven't finished,' I say. 'I was delayed by dropping that piece of butter, so I'm not quite at the breadcrumb stage yet. But I'm almost there.'

'I'm finding this entire process quite fascinating,' says Daniel. 'I can't wait for that magical moment when it all comes together and turns into breadcrumbs. It's like an experiment when you combine two chemicals and they react with each other to produce the desired result.'

He claps his hand to his forehead. 'That's a ridiculous analogy. I'd forgotten that cookery is more of an art than a science.'

'Is it?' asks Abby.

'Lucy thinks so. She was explaining the concept to me while you were busy with the dough.'

'I was simplifying it for you,' I say. 'Obviously, there's a certain amount of science in it too.'

'I would say cookery is more of a science when you're a beginner,' says Abby. 'It's important to follow the recipes until you've got the hang of basic cooking techniques and understand why they're written as they are and how the ingredients combine to produce the correct results. After that, it's fine to deviate from them in small ways and be creative. That's when cookery becomes more of an art, and a chef can start to produce signature dishes.'

'Lucy told me the proportions don't matter,' says Daniel.

'I'm afraid that's not quite true when you're making pastry,' says Abby. 'The proportions are very important.'

'That's not quite what I said,' I tell her, shooting a baleful look at Daniel. 'All I meant was that it was only a small piece of butter, and it wouldn't make much difference.'

'It was about a quarter of the butter in your bowl,' says Daniel. 'But you spilled quite a bit of flour while you were working the mixture into breadcrumbs, so I expect you thought it would all balance out.'

'You have lost a fair amount of flour,' says Abby. 'What happened?'

'I wasn't concentrating as hard as I should have been,' I say. 'Daniel was distracting me with irrelevant chatter.'

'Not to worry,' she says. 'Perhaps I'll just …'

She drops another cube of butter into my bowl, plunges in her hands, and does something mysterious for a few seconds. She tips up the bowl to show us the result. 'Breadcrumbs!'

I have no idea what she's done, but the slimy chunks of butter have disappeared, and so has the flour. In their place are tiny grains of what do actually look like breadcrumbs.

'That was going to be my next step,' I say. 'I was about to demonstrate the technique to Daniel when I lost that piece of butter.'

'You can demonstrate it with my ingredients if you like,' he offers.

'I'll bet you were the pupil always asking others to do your homework for you,' I say.

'You're quite right. I offered to pay Simon Peterson to sit my GCSE sand sculpture exams for me. Unfortunately, he was sick on the day of the final exam, which rather left me in the lurch. It's amazing how tiny things can change the course of your future forever. If it hadn't been for that, I might now have been one of the country's leading beach artisans.'

'I hate to rush you,' says Abby. 'But Chris is picking me up soon, and we haven't got as far as I'd hoped. Would you like me to finish this part for you, and then we can move on?'

'It might be best,' says Daniel. 'I can watch you and learn how to do it for next time. Lucy doesn't need to see this part. She already has her breadcrumb technique sorted.'

I don't answer but watch as Abby reaches for Daniel's bowl and deftly rubs the chunks of butter into the flour. It takes almost no time at all until she has his ingredients under control.

She hands him back his bowl. 'You see? It's very easy when you know how. The next thing is to add water to bind it together. Iced water is best. That isn't difficult at this time of year. Chris and I live in fear of the water freezing in our pipes. We live in an old flat that needs some serious re-plumbing, which we can't afford.'

She points to the jug of water on the table. 'That's nice and cold. I keep it in the fridge all day.'

Now is the time to redeem my shaky start and show I know what I'm doing. I pour a generous amount of water into my bowl, then pick up a spoon and start mixing, wondering whether there's some special technique I ought to be using – stirring anti-clockwise, for instance, or flicking my wrist to incorporate air.

'What are you doing?' Abby asks.

'Binding the pastry together,' I say, pleased to have remembered the technical term she's just used.

Daniel leans over to look. 'It's quite … runny, isn't it?'

I give it another brisk stir. 'The water soaks into the flour, and the mixture will thicken in the oven like a sauce.'

Abby is watching as though she can't believe her eyes. 'No, it won't. Have you never made pastry before?'

I stop stirring and try to look thoughtful. 'Pastry? As in pie crust?'

'As in basic pastry,' she says.

I look down at my bowl. The so-called breadcrumbs have disappeared. In their place is a sloppy, stringy mess. On the face of it, I have to admit this doesn't seem like something that might turn into a crisp golden sheet of pastry. But it hasn't been in the oven yet.

'It looks like the glue we used in primary school,' says Daniel.

I notice Abby staring at the floor, her left cheek twitching uncontrollably. Is she ill? Maybe she's angry at the waste of good ingredients. I don't know her well enough to tell.

I glance into my bowl again, hoping the flour will have performed its magic and done whatever it is that flour does – swelled, maybe – and turned into a nice, neat ball of pastry, all ready to be rolled out and formed into pastry shells. It hasn't. The contents of the bowl are as glue-like as ever. Daniel's right. It looks like the paste we used at school to stick cut-out shapes onto sugar paper.

I feel a brief flicker of hope there may be something wrong with the flour Abby gave us. That hope dies almost immediately. I've tasted some of the cakes that come out of this kitchen, and there's no way they were created using substandard ingredients. I have to face it. I'm a useless cook. I don't have a shred of natural talent, and I'm unable to follow even the simplest of instructions.

I push away the bowl and sit down at the table, burying my face in my arms.

'I give up,' I say. 'There's no point in pretending any further. I have no clue how to bake, and I doubt anyone could ever teach me.'

Chapter Twenty-Three

Neither of them speaks for a moment. I raise my head to see Daniel's lips are tightly pressed together, and his shoulders are shaking. Abby is staring at the floor. She looks up at last and meets my gaze, and I stare back at her. A small sound escapes her. Is she choking on something? It can't be my so-called pastry. It's too runny to block even the smallest windpipe.

Daniel makes a stifled noise, which seems to set her off. She starts to laugh – soundlessly at first, but increasing in volume as her entire body joins in. Her face turns red, and tears run down her cheeks.

I try to feel annoyed, but one look at the gluey mess in my bowl is enough to set me off. I laugh too, the tensions of the past week flowing out of me. It feels good. I hadn't realised how worried I've been about everything – Gran, my job, Humphrey, having to organise her beloved cookie club.

I laugh until the tears stream down my face, hardly aware of the others. I laugh until there's no energy in my body for anything else. At last, my shoulders relax, and I give a final, hiccupping sob.

Abby wipes her eyes. 'I'm sorry, Lucy. I couldn't help it. All those things you came out with about the mixture thickening in the oven were just too much. Especially when I saw what was in your bowl.'

'I'm glad to have amused you,' I say. 'I'm sorry about the wasted ingredients. I'll pay for them, of course.'

'I should pay you,' she says. 'I haven't laughed that hard in a long time.'

'I don't understand,' says Daniel. 'Are you telling me all Lucy's advice was worthless, when I've been hanging on her every word and treasuring it all up for future reference?'

'Give it up,' I advise him. 'You're not fooling anyone. It's obvious you and I have no idea what we're doing. I know why I was pretending, but I'm not sure why you were.'

'Because you're so competitive and have such a low opinion of my capabilities,' he says. 'How about you?'

Various explanations flit through my mind. But what's the point? I'm a terrible liar, and Daniel seems to read me like a book.

'Because I find you intensely annoying,' I say.

'I'd kind of picked that up. It's hard to say how. Tiny hints and vibes that would have gone over the head of a less sensitive person. No matter how hard you tried to hide it –'

'I didn't try to hide it at all.'

'That would have been why. Either way, it doesn't come as a huge surprise.'

I smile at him. 'I expect a lot of people tell you how annoying you are.'

'Daniel seems very likeable to me,' says Abby.

'That's because you don't know him,' I say. 'He can keep up the façade for a little while, but his true self always shines through in the end.'

She doesn't react in the way she should to this information. She looks more amused than horrified. 'How bad can he be?'

'How long do you have?'

'I'm right here,' says Daniel plaintively.

'You're always right there. And not in a good way, like when someone says, "I'm there for you." In your case, it's more like –' I break off, trying to think of an analogy.

'An annoying rash?' he suggests.

'Exactly. Or a mosquito.'

'In December?' asks Abby.

Daniel shakes his head. 'That's a terrible example, Lucy. You can't have been paying attention during your school biology lessons.'

'I meant in Australia,' I say. 'It's the middle of summer there.'

I'm half expecting him to look impressed at my Antipodean knowledge, but he only shakes his head again. 'Pathetic try.'

'Is that all?' asks Abby. 'Daniel is always there?'

'But it's the manner in which he's always there,' I explain. 'The first time I met him, he crashed into me because he wasn't looking where he was going, and he knocked a tray of cookies out of my hands.'

I see her eyes dart from my face to the bowl on the table. She doesn't say anything, but I'm sure I know what she's thinking.

'Today was a one-off,' I defend myself. 'The cookies Daniel destroyed were actually very good.'

'We'll never know that for sure,' says Daniel. 'For all we know, I may have done the world a favour. GPs are massively overstretched at this time of year without having to deal with cases of mass food poisoning.'

'I was taking them to my grandmother in the hospital,' I say.

'Even worse. The hospital owes me a letter of thanks. So, that's one of your objections disposed of.'

'In your opinion. But then you turned up at my house the following day.'

Abby stops smiling. 'That's not good.'

I feel a pang of guilt at having made Daniel sound like a crazed stalker. 'He kind of had a reason.'

I stop, unable to think of a convincing explanation for his presence that doesn't involve mentioning the existence of the cookie club.

'I was bringing her some replacement cookies,' says Daniel. 'As a peace offering, you might say.'

Abby's face relaxes. 'That was nice of you.'

'Wasn't it?' he agrees. 'But it was no good. Lucy hurled them all over the path.'

'That was an accident, as you very well know!' I protest.

'You told me it was. But it was difficult not to take it personally. However, being the bigger person, I rose above it and stepped in to help with your dog emergency.'

'Humphrey?' asks Abby. 'Is he alright?'

'He's fine,' I say. 'But that's another example of what I'm talking about. When Daniel arrived with his so-called replacement cookies, he left the garden gate open, and Humphrey made a break for it.'

'I rescued him,' Daniel defends himself.

'He wouldn't have needed rescuing if you hadn't let him escape. You can't cause a problem, then claim to be a hero for fixing it.'

'Hero?' says Daniel. 'That's a big word, but perhaps you're right. Let's go with that.'

'I'm so sorry,' I tell Abby. 'I can't tell you how terrible I feel about all this. I know how busy you must be at the moment. I've wasted your time after you were kind enough to offer me a lesson.'

'She's right,' says Daniel. 'I'd like to apologise too.'

Abby surveys us both. 'You'd better come with me.'

She walks towards the bakery, and we follow her. Is she about to open the door and throw us out into the snow like the little match girl? I've left my bag in the kitchen along with my phone and front door key. Daniel will have to cause a distraction while I run back to fetch it. Something tells me he won't have any trouble coming up with a hundred different ways to achieve that.

I walk over to the coat rack and reach up for my jacket.

'What are you doing?' asks Abby.

'It's snowing. I don't want to walk home without my coat.'

'We still have half an hour left of our lesson.'

'I know. I'm very sorry. Please add whatever you like to the bill.' I glance at Daniel. 'That's only fair, isn't it?'

'More than fair,' he says.

'Don't be ridiculous,' says Abby, and I'm relieved to see she's smiling. 'I haven't enjoyed myself so much for a long time.'

She opens a paper bag and picks up the tongs. 'Do you like Bakewell tarts?'

'I love them,' I say.

She drops several tarts into the bag and hands it to me.

'How about you?' she asks Daniel.

'I love them too.'

She hands him his bag. 'These are to inspire you. This is what we would have been making tonight if circumstances – by which I mean the pair of you – hadn't got in the way.'

'This is more than generous of you,' I say. 'Please add something to the bill and send it to Daniel.'

'Fine with me,' he says. 'This entire lesson ought to be on me. If it hadn't been for me distracting her, Lucy wouldn't have thrown her butter all over the floor, and none of this would have happened.'

'Some people aren't meant to become bakers,' I tell Abby. 'Obviously, I'm one of them. In the future, I'll stick to translation, and Daniel can stick to bothering the local inhabitants by zooming his cameras over their heads and invading their privacy.'

'I'm afraid I can't spare any more evenings before Christmas,' she says. 'Or I would insist you both came back until you'd learned at least some basic skills. In the meantime, I suggest you watch some YouTube videos. They're great for teaching new techniques step by step. Good luck!'

'I'll give it a go,' I say doubtfully. 'Although I can't guarantee it will work.'

'And now you can help me clean up before Chris arrives,' she says. 'That's one of the most basic kitchen skills of all – don't leave any trace behind when you finish cooking.'

She marches us back into the kitchen and hands us both a cloth.

'It's like being in the boy scouts again,' says Daniel. 'Akela taught me how to stay downwind when I was tracking animals and never to leave any indication I'd been there.'

'Are you telling me they took the cub scouts hunting?' I ask. 'That doesn't sound likely.'

He gives me a pitying look. 'It was for my photography badge. We did lots of litter picking too, which has prepared me for the task ahead of us. Cleaning up your buttery mess holds no terrors for the man who once took a picture of a fox's back leg disappearing into the undergrowth.'

'There's something I want to know,' I tell him. 'If you're as bad at baking as I am, how did you make the cookies you brought over to my house?'

He grins. 'My landlady made them for me.'

I'm about to accuse him of cheating when I remember Abby doesn't know about the cookie club and stop myself.

The shop bell jangles. A second later, the kitchen door opens, and a man puts his head around.

'How's it going in here?' he asks.

'We're finishing a little early today,' says Abby. 'Chris, this is Daniel and Lucy.'

He gives us a friendly smile. 'Nice to meet you both. How did the lesson go?'

'Abby was just saying I was tonight's star pupil,' says Daniel. 'Lucy did very well, but her heart didn't seem in it. Maybe next time.'

Chris looks around the kitchen. 'What did you make tonight? I can't smell anything.'

'That's because we haven't started the baking part of our journey,' says Daniel. 'Tonight was all about the theory. Abby insists on her pupils getting a grasp on the basics before she allows them anywhere near an actual oven. She bases her approach on the abstract rather than the practical method. It can be a little frustrating, but her pupils always thank her in the end.'

Chris glances at Abby, who shakes her head. 'I'll explain later.'

'I've only touched on the idea of her system,' says Daniel. 'Abby will explain it all to you in far more detail. It will give you something to talk about during your meal.'

Chris looks at his watch. 'We'd better get going if we want to visit the fair first.'

'Don't let us hold you up,' says Daniel. 'Lucy and I can look after ourselves. Have a lovely evening.'

'If I were you,' I tell Chris. 'I'd start by buying Abby a very large drink. And then I'd follow it up with several more.'

Abby locks up the bakery, and we watch them walk off in the direction of the Christmas fair.

'Speaking of very large drinks,' says Daniel, 'The Red Lion is just down the street. I think we should drink a toast to our successful lesson.'

'You and I have very different ideas about success,' I say. 'I really shouldn't. I can't leave Humphrey alone for too long.'

'I wasn't suggesting making an evening of it. But it feels important to mark the occasion somehow, and my landlady tells me their mulled wine is excellent. Just one glass?'

I waver. It's a bitterly cold night, and the thought of mulled wine is tempting.

'I'll walk you home afterwards and make sure you don't end up in the mud,' says Daniel.

'If your tracking skills are anything like your cookery skills, I'd be safer navigating home by myself. Fine, I'll come for one quick drink. And then I'm going home to see how Humphrey's doing.'

'Wonderful!' he says. 'It's important to celebrate the small victories in life. If you wait for the big victories, you miss out along the way. The Red Lion is down there by the crossroads. We should memorise the colour of each other's coats in case a blizzard hits and we can't see each other.'

'If a blizzard hits, I'll follow the sound of your voice,' I say. 'I can't imagine even the most violent snowstorm would stop you talking for long.'

Chapter Twenty-Four

The Red Lion is crowded when we enter. I expect it usually is. It's a lovely country pub with a welcoming atmosphere. There's a huge fire at one end with a couple of sofas next to it.

Daniel points. 'There's a table about to come free if you hurry. That couple is leaving. Why don't you grab that while I get our drinks?'

'Because I haven't yet told you whether I like mulled wine?'

'You want to argue with me while our only chance at getting a table slips away? You'd prefer to stand outside in the garden sipping your mulled wine and freezing to death?'

I consider telling him I never touch mulled wine, and all I want is a glass of mineral water. But there's no point in cutting off my nose to spite my face. I've always loved mulled wine.

'Fine,' I say. 'See you in a minute.'

He appears to read my mind. 'Text me if you really can't bear for me to be right about the best drink for a snowy night.'

I'm about to say I don't have his number when I notice a man eyeing the table Daniel pointed out. I push my way through the crowds and arrive a second before he does.

'Are you about to leave?' I ask the couple with a bright smile.

The woman finishes buttoning her coat. 'That's right. Would you like to sit here?'

'That's so kind of you,' I say, sinking into the chair she indicates and not meeting the hovering man's eye.

Daniel joins me a minute later with two glasses of steaming mulled wine.

'That was impressive,' he says, handing me a glass. 'It obviously wasn't your first attempt at snatching a seat from under a rival's nose. You did it so professionally.'

'I've had a lot of practice,' I tell him. 'Management cutbacks at work mean we're all hot-desking. We operate on a first-come, first-served basis, and the losers end up sitting on the floor. They tried to sell it to us as collaboration and space-efficiency, but it's just meanness.'

'You haven't told me much about your job,' he says. 'Until recently, I'd have hazarded a guess you worked as a professional chef, but I have to admit certain doubts have set in.'

'I'm a translator,' I say. 'I studied modern languages at university. I spent a year in Berlin after I graduated, then took a job for a cosmetics company based in London. I translate all our ad copy and brochures and promotional material into German for them.'

'You don't translate recipes in your spare time?' he asks.

'What spare time? I work for a woman who believes any of her employees who show the faintest sign of having a personal life should go on a watch list and be first in line for the next round of redundancies.'

'Aren't you working remotely at the moment?' he asks. 'How can she monitor your personal life from a distance?'

'No one in our department works remotely. Some of the other departments are more flexible, but not ours. Caroline believes that unless every one of her direct reports is physically in the office for at least ten hours a day, they'll be at home building blanket forts or writing the next great British novel.'

'Hasn't she heard of videoconferencing?'

'She has, but she doesn't approve of it. She thinks it can be nobbled to show her staff is online when they're actually creating an indoor obstacle course for their new puppy.'

'That's the sign of a bad manager,' he says. 'You have to show some faith in your staff if you want them to show faith in your company.'

'Caroline doesn't think so. Her motto is to keep your enemies close but your staff even closer.'

'I'm glad she has at least some humanity and allowed you to take emergency leave when you needed it.'

'She doesn't have any humane instincts,' I say. 'Left to herself, she would never have allowed me to come here.'

'Did you have to go to HR instead?'

'In our company, HR stands for Horrible Regulations. They're worse than Caroline.'

I take a sip of the mulled wine and feel a shot of warmth course through my veins. At this moment, Caroline feels pleasantly far away.

'I hate to be intrusive,' says Daniel. 'But I'm curious to know how you persuaded her that Humphrey was more important than their bottom line. Did you cite some little known ancient Germanic law? The Canine Companionship Act, perhaps?'

'I walked out.'

There's a brief pause.

'You walked out?' he asks. 'Literally?'

I take another sip of my wine. 'That's right. I picked up my bag when Mum called me, and I left the office.'

'And how did that go down with this Caroline woman?'

'Not well,' I confess. 'I called her as soon as I got home and told her what had happened and that I hadn't had the chance to talk to her before I left. You can imagine her reaction.'

'I'm imagining it now,' he says.

'I don't know what got into me. I was having a terrible day. I'd worked right through the weekend, and I was exhausted. People kept sending me documents and hounding me to finish them within the next hour. I hadn't eaten lunch, and then my computer packed up. The IT department only turns up if you're management, so I had no idea how long it would take to get it fixed. Then Mum called, and something inside me snapped.'

I turn back to Daniel. 'All I could think of was that my mother spends every day doing something important, even if she doesn't get much recognition for it. But I spend every day doing something I hate, simply to make money for a huge corporation. I could have asked Caroline for a few days of annual leave, but I was sure what her answer would be. I didn't want to listen to her explaining for the hundredth time that plenty of people are lining up to do my job and how important it is for us to hit our deadlines for the good of the company. For her good, she means. People at her level get huge productivity bonuses. None of which are passed on to menial employees like me, no matter how much overtime we've been forced to do.'

I pause for breath. That felt good. I haven't said that out loud to anyone before. There's no point complaining to my flatmates each night. They all have similar jobs and troubles of their own. And there's no way I'd ever mention it to Mum and Dad. They were so pleased and proud when I got this job, and they're both so anxious for me to keep it. I suspect the reason is that they don't want Dad's accident to have ruined my life too.

Daniel is different. He and I don't know the first thing about each other, or nothing personal. I know he doesn't look where he's going when he walks down the street. I know he can't bake and doesn't take anything seriously. I also know he's resourceful when it comes to fashioning a dog lead out of a couple of pairs of socks, and that he has an unexpectedly kind and thoughtful side. But that isn't the same as knowing him well. The point is, he's enough of a stranger for me to unload some of my troubles, but I'm not worried about him spreading it further.

'Good for you,' he surprises me. 'I'd have done exactly the same thing in your shoes.'

'How can you say that? I've just told you I walked out on my job with no notice during one of our busiest periods.'

'You had a good reason.'

'I did, but even I can't defend not taking it to my manager and trying to persuade her to let me take some leave rather than just walking out.'

'Any manager who needs persuading that family comes first isn't one worth working for.'

Something inside me unknots a little. I've been putting a brave face on it, but I've been worried about my actions. I called Caroline from home instead of talking to her in the office because I was sure she would refuse to give me any leave if I asked her face to face, and I might have said something I'd regret. But she has every right to be angry with me for being so unprofessional.

Daniel's reaction is comforting. It gives me hope that I've been worrying for nothing. It's Christmas, after all – the season of goodwill to all people. Maybe Caroline will not only allow me to take my leave but refuse to count it towards my annual vacation.

If Scrooge could see the error of his ways and start looking after his employees, there's still hope for me that Caroline will do the same. She may go to sleep tonight and be visited by the ghost of performance reviews past, the ghost of employee retention present, and the ghost of client satisfaction future. She'll wake tomorrow and realise how badly she's treated me and start working on plans for my immediate promotion. Hopefully, that will include a brand-new computer, a hotline to the IT department, and a company account at the nearest decent coffee shop.

Chapter Twenty-Five

The pub is filling up fast. It's a good thing we arrived when we did. People are standing at the bar chatting while they wait for a table to open up. I don't catch anyone's eye. I have no intention of moving until I'm ready. I'm exhausted after my day with Humphrey and a less than successful cookery lesson. I'd like to sit here all evening, sipping this delicious mulled wine and letting the stresses of the day flow out of me. But I can't do that because I need to get back to Humphrey. However, I can allow myself another twenty minutes before venturing out into the cold again.

'I've told you about my job,' I tell Daniel. 'But you haven't told me much about yours.'

'Yes, I have. I co-own a drone company. I've already mentioned that.'

'I wasn't sure whether to believe you. I never am.'

'That's a terrible thing to say. I'm as open and honest as a –'

'Politician at a truth-telling contest?' I suggest.

'Your words, not mine. Ask me anything you like. Nothing is off limits.'

'All I want right now is a brief history of what you do, and how you came to do it.'

'That's easy enough. I graduated from Leeds University six years ago with a degree in Environmental Science and got a job working in Urban Planning in Cardiff. I was there for two years, but I wasn't enjoying it, so I left to start my own company with my friend Marcus. We were both mad keen on drones, and we decided to use that in a positive way. We're still building the business up, but we're doing pretty well. We have more work than we can handle, so we're expanding as fast as possible.'

'You're very lucky to have found something that combines your skills and your passions,' I say. 'What sort of positive ways are you talking about?'

'It varies. At the moment, we're working for the local town council doing a roof survey. Sometimes we're hired by farmers to help with their crops. My favourite job was a couple of summers ago when a local historical society asked us to help them survey a site where they were sure there had been a Roman Villa. It was easy enough to see the changes in vegetation from the air and tell them where to excavate. You may have read about it. It was a little place in Shropshire, not far from Ludlow. They said it was one of the most important finds of the past century.'

'That sounds a lot more useful than what I do,' I say.

'Don't say that! You may be the means of improving complexions all across Europe. But only if you translate the ingredients properly. Otherwise, your company will find itself on the wrong side of a class action lawsuit.'

'I wouldn't lose much sleep over that. It might do them some good.'

'It may be none of my business,' he says. 'But why are you working there if you hate it so much?'

'Don't think I haven't asked myself the same thing a hundred times over the past year. It's complicated. Translation work can be difficult to get into when you're newly qualified. And my current job is a permanent position.'

'That makes a difference,' he agrees. 'Have you thought of moving into something else?'

'I've always wanted to be self-employed. I told you the other day that I'd love to translate novels for a living, but that wouldn't be as secure as my current job.'

'Too much of a risk?' he asks.

'Kind of.' I finish my drink and stare at the bottom of the glass.

'Can I get you another one,' he asks.

I pick up both our glasses. 'It's my turn, but this will have to be the last one. I can't leave Humphrey on his own for much longer.'

I return a few minutes later and hand him his wine. 'I should have sent you, after all. I had to fight my way to the bar, and I never learned to play rugby at school. We learned much less useful sports like tennis and badminton.'

'I was terrible at rugby,' he says. 'But I could have used my scouting skills to figure out the quickest way to the front of the queue. Thanks for this. Should we drink to something?'

I take a gulp of my wine. 'I already am – as fast as I can. I don't need a specific reason.'

'I can see that. I hope you aren't drowning your sorrows. Take it from me, that never works.'

'Not exactly,' I say. 'More like taking them for a quick swim.'

'You're welcome to talk to me any time if they bob back up to the surface.'

'That's kind of you, but I wouldn't know where to begin.'

'That sounds serious,' he says.

'Things aren't that bad. They're just more complicated than I'd like.'

He doesn't speak, which surprises me. He usually has so much to say for himself.

'It's my dad,' I say suddenly. 'He had an accident last year.'

To my surprise, I find myself telling him about the drunk driver and the weeks Dad spent in hospital when none of us knew how well he would recover. I tell him about the months of recuperation and the complete annihilation of all my parents' plans for retirement.

'I know we're luckier than a lot of people,' I finish. 'Things could have been far worse. But it's difficult to feel lucky when you see one of your favourite people in the world confined to a wheelchair and needing round-the-clock nursing care because some idiot decided to drink six pints of beer before climbing into his car and driving home.'

He nods. 'I can't imagine what you've all been through.'

'My parents more than me. My mum is amazing. She looks after him without a word of complaint. She held everything together when it first happened, and she's still doing that. She and Dad were so delighted when I got this job. They thought it would offer me some stability while I was starting out, and it would give me some great experience. I'd only been working there for a few months when Dad had his accident. I wanted to move back home to Coventry to help out, but they were both terribly upset when I suggested it. Dad said it would make things much harder for him if he thought his accident had changed my plans. I tried to tell him it was no such thing, but he and Mum were adamant. I know they feel a lot more secure knowing I'm in steady employment. It's not a boat I'm prepared to rock. Not for a while, anyway.'

'I get that,' he says. 'I hope your manager doesn't give you a hard time when she sees you again.'

'Me too. I wish I hadn't walked out like that, but I did. All I can do is hope for the best and that I get away with a written warning.'

'Meanwhile, there's no point in worrying about it,' he says. 'Are you working remotely while you're here?'

'I suggested that when I called Caroline, but she wasn't having any of it. She told me she was disappointed with my lack of professionalism and would have to think about what to do next and contact me with her decision. I haven't heard from her since.'

'It sounds as though she's the victim of her own lack of flexibility,' he says. 'I suggest you forget about her for now and concentrate on the important things in life.'

'Such as?'

'How can you ask? I'm talking about the cookie club.'

'I'm glad you're taking it so seriously,' I say. 'But it shouldn't take up too much of my time. If I do as Abby says and watch some videos, I should be able to make a passable batch of cookies for the next couple of weeks, which is all I need to do.'

'I can't believe what I'm hearing! Is that really your attitude? What happened to the woman who was so desperate to beat me that she booked herself a private lesson with a professional chef?'

'She was exposed as a fraud,' I say. 'And now she's drunk two glasses of mulled wine and doesn't care about anything at all.'

'That will pass,' he assures me. 'I'd put good money on it you'll wake up tomorrow morning and start thinking of ways to get the better of me again.'

'I'm more likely to be thinking of ways to pay my bills in the new year if I'm performance managed out of my job.'

'There's nothing you can do about that,' he says. 'But there's plenty you can do about the cookie club. I should warn you I'm in this thing to win it. If you can't be bothered to compete, it will make things much easier for me.'

'Compete in what way?'

'Any way you like. You're the one who turned this into a competition. What do you suggest?'

'You want to figure out a way to decide which of us makes the best cookies each week?' I ask.

'Exactly. You're all talk about your cookery skills. I want to see you put your money where your mouth is.'

'I don't have any money. And what little I have may need to last me a long time.'

'I don't mean literally,' he says. 'But where's your competitive spirit?'

'Why don't we ask the club members to vote each week?' I suggest.

'That wouldn't work. They'd just refuse to be a part of it. It isn't what the club was set up to do.'

'True. You come up with something then.'

He stares around at the crowd for a minute. 'Instagram!'

'What about it?' I ask.

'Do you have an account?'

'I think so. I rarely use it though.'

'Neither do I,' he says. 'But I set one up when we first started the business.'

'That's fascinating,' I say. 'Could you get to the point? Humphrey will be wanting his evening walk.'

'That is the point,' he says. 'We'll each post our cookies on Instagram and see which of us gets the most likes for them. We'll add them all up in the final week, and the person whose cookies are the most popular wins.'

I open my mouth to tell him how ridiculous this suggestion is, then close it again. I'm not sure whether it's the two glasses of wine in quick succession or something else, but this could work.

'You're on!' I say.

He holds out his hand. 'It's a deal.'

'Wait a moment. Is this a trick? Do you have ten million followers or something?'

'I doubt I even have one hundred. You?'

'About the same. It's been years since I checked.'

'There you go,' he says. 'We're both hopeless social media losers. So, we'll start on an equal footing.'

I reach over and shake his hand. 'I'm sure I'll regret this in the morning, but we have a deal. And now I have to go and see what Humphrey has been up to while I've been away. The last time I left him alone, he tried to sit on the back of the sofa. It will never be the same again. I can't imagine what Gran will say when she gets home.'

'Tell her I did it,' says Daniel.

'That's a great idea. I can say you're a social media addict, and you were posting a video for likes. She can send you the bill.'

'She won't know where to send it,' he says. He opens his wallet and pulls out a card. 'Maybe you should give her this. It has my company name on it and a number where I can be reached at any time.'

'Thanks,' I say, tucking it into my jacket pocket. 'This should be useful if she chooses to file a lawsuit. I have to go now. You know how it is – dogs to walk, world-class products to bake. I'll see you on Thursday with a box of what you believe passes for Christmas cookies.'

Chapter Twenty-Six

I spend the next morning watching cookery videos. I alternate between despair at what the amateur chefs so effortlessly produce and daydreams of the sort of thing I might produce for this week's cookie club.

I finally switch off Junior MasterChef and make us both some lunch. It snowed again during the night. I try to persuade Humphrey he doesn't really want to get his paws wet and cold by going outside, but he's having none of it. So, I stack the plates in the sink and button up my coat.

'I wonder whether they make winter coats large enough for dogs like you,' I tell Humphrey as I pull on my boots. 'You'd look lovely in a nice gilet.'

Evidently, he doesn't care about the finer points of canine fashion. He tugs impatiently at his lead until I open the front door, then sets off to the village at a brisk pace.

Lily beams at me when we walk in. 'How lovely to see you! It's been remarkably quiet in here today. I thought all our regular customers had been put off by the snow.'

I hadn't thought of myself as a regular customer until now, but I suppose I am. She leans down to pat Humphrey, and I realise she's talking about him. I'm just a temporary passer-through. I'm surprised by how much I wish that weren't the case. London isn't the friendliest place, and I've barely got to know anyone while I've been living there. It would be nice to have some local shops where everyone greeted you and knew all about you. Humphrey doesn't know how lucky he is.

'What can I get you?' asks Lily. 'Abby's been making macarons, if you like those. I can recommend the orange spice ones.'

'That sounds great,' I say. 'And a cappuccino please.'

She smiles at Humphrey. 'Would sir like his usual order?'

Again, I feel a pang at the thought of being a local and having a usual order.

'I was hoping for a quick word with Abby if she has a free moment at some point,' I say.

The corners of Lily's mouth twitch as she reaches for the cake tongs. 'Of course. May I tell her what this is with regard to?'

'I take it she's told you about last night.'

She switches on the coffee machine. 'She may have mentioned it in passing.'

'It was a bit of a disaster. Mostly due to Daniel, but a tiny bit to me.'

'I hear you didn't actually bake anything,' she says.

'I went home with some lovely Bakewell tarts. I had one for breakfast this morning.'

'I noticed several of them were missing when I came in this morning,' she says.'

'It was very kind of Abby after the shocking way Daniel behaved.'

She hands me my mug of coffee and smiles at Humphrey. 'I haven't forgotten you. Here you are.'

He grabs the biscuit she gives him and tries unsuccessfully to cram himself behind my chair while he eats it.

'There's no need to hide,' I tell him. 'Bernie isn't here this morning. He probably has more sense than to drag his owner out in this sort of weather.'

'You'd be surprised,' says Lily. 'Bernie owns an entire wardrobe of clothes. It changes every season. He has a little sunhat to keep the sun out of his eyes in hot weather. Last autumn, he appeared in a tiny Barbour jacket. None of us could keep a straight face. All he needed was a pair of cord trousers and a flat cap. And of course, he has a quilted coat and fur-lined boots for when it snows.'

'Fur-lined?' I ask. 'Aren't his legs already covered in fur?'

'Mrs Ogilvie says you can never be too careful. She told me once that a double layer of fur was safer than a single one. She was a little worried because Bernie can still get snow down his boots if he isn't careful. But he has a heated throw at home, so she wraps him in that after his walk and hopes for the best.'

'I feel as though I'm neglecting Humphrey,' I say.

She hands him his second biscuit. 'He doesn't look as though he's suffering too much. There you go, Humphrey. Try to make it last for more than a couple of seconds.'

He disposes of the biscuit in two bites, flops down, and closes his eyes.

'I promise to make my macaron last a little longer,' I say. 'It would be a shame not to appreciate all Abby's hard work.'

'Is that Lucy?' says Abby, appearing from the kitchen with a stack of cottage loaves.

'I'm afraid so. I'm not banned, am I? You didn't say anything about that last night.'

'Of course, you aren't banned.'

'You might have thought some more about the events of yesterday evening and changed your mind.'

She sits down at my table. 'Not at all. The events of yesterday evening formed a large part of our dinner conversation. Our friends were very interested to hear how the lesson went.'

I groan. 'I hope you told them it was mostly Daniel's fault.'

'I placed the blame where it was due,' she says with a grin.

I don't ask her to elaborate. As long as I don't know exactly what she said, I can imagine she told her friends that Daniel ruined her lesson while I waited patiently for him to get a grip.

'I wanted to see you this morning to apologise,' I say. 'I feel as though we wasted your time, and I'm sorry for that. It's such a busy time of year for you, and you didn't need any extra hassle.'

'I had fun,' she says. 'As I say, it gave us something to talk about over dinner.'

I'm unlikely to meet these friends of hers, so I can live with whatever they think of me. With any luck, the next time Abby has dinner with them, she can tell them how well I've learned to bake now and how the entire world agrees that my cookies throw Daniel's into the shade.

'I'm glad there are no hard feelings,' I say.

'None whatsoever. I should go now. I need to make a fresh batch of Bakewell tarts before lunch. For some reason, our stock is low.'

She gives me a friendly wave and disappears back into the kitchen.

I finish my coffee and wake Humphrey. 'You insisted on coming here, and now you have to walk home again. I refuse to carry you, although you're welcome to give me a ride if the snow gets too deep.'

He yawns and stretches but doesn't move.

'Maybe he could stay here permanently?' I suggest to Lily. 'He wouldn't be any trouble. He'd be perfectly happy lying under this table and eating the occasional dog biscuit. And he could be your guard dog each night.'

'We already have a burglar alarm,' she says.

'He would make a wonderful mascot for your bakery,' I plead.

'We already have one of those too. Bernie was awarded the title a while back.'

'I tried, Humphrey, but it's no good,' I tell him. 'You'll have to walk home in the snow, whether you like it or not. Come on, let's get it over with.'

I pull him to his feet, and he yawns again.

'Is he allowed a biscuit for the journey?' asks Lily. 'On the house.'

'That's kind of you. Your bakery will be seriously out of pocket by the time I leave. What with all those Bakewell tarts, and now a free biscuit for Humphrey. I'll have to ask him what he thinks. He may be full.'

She holds out a biscuit, and Humphrey makes a grab for it.

'Eat it slowly,' I advise him. 'You have a long journey ahead of you.'

As we reach the end of Bramble Close, I catch sight of Bernie in the distance, trotting along with his owner. As Lily said, he's wearing a tartan jacket, and his feet are encased in what I assume are his fur-lined boots. He looks very snug.

I look down at Humphrey, whose legs are soaked with melted snow. He doesn't seem to mind, even though I don't have a heated throw at home in which to tenderly wrap him until he's dried off. A thought stirs in my mind. I watch as Bernie disappears out of sight, obviously going up to the village shops with his owner.

'Stop it!' I tell Humphrey, who's attempting to drag me past the end of our road and continue on to the water meadows. 'We're going home. I don't have time to watch you racing around in the snow looking for birds that probably have more sense than to be out on a day like this. I have more important things to do.'

I call Margery and ask whether she's free to sit with Humphrey for a couple of hours so I can go into Christchurch.

'I could leave him by himself,' I say. 'But I do that whenever I visit Gran, and I know he doesn't like it.'

'No problem,' she says. 'As long as he doesn't expect me to take him out in all this snow.'

'He won't,' I promise. 'He can play in the back garden if he really wants some fresh air. Otherwise, I'll take him for his usual walk this evening.'

She arrives at three o'clock, and Humphrey greets her like a long lost relative he'd been told was stranded on a desert island and whom he had abandoned all hope of seeing again.

'That's enough, young man,' she says, pulling off her coat and scarf. 'You and I are going to spend a cosy afternoon reading my new book on the sofa, not running around the back garden building a snowman.'

'He'd prefer to chase the birds,' I say. 'But they're all safely in their trees for the afternoon.'

I make her a cup of tea, point her in the direction of the cookie jar, and slip out. Humphrey gives me a disapproving look but doesn't attempt to follow. He should be alright with Margery. As Gran said, she takes no nonsense from anyone, even Humphrey. I suspect I take rather too much nonsense from him, but I don't care. I haven't been able to explain to him why Gran isn't here, so I want to work extra hard to make sure he doesn't miss her any more than he has to.

I arrive in Christchurch twenty minutes later and park the car. The town isn't as crowded as I feared. Most people have probably had the sense to stay at home instead of inching along the icy country lanes at five miles per hour. If I'd had more time, I'd have done the same thing. But the cookie club is meeting on Thursday, and I have a lot to do to prepare.

I drive slowly back to Honeywell two hours later and unpack the car.

'You've been busy,' Margery greets me when she sees my bags. 'We haven't. Humphrey has spent the afternoon fast asleep by the window, and I've read seven chapters of my book.'

'Thank you so much,' I say. 'I hope I wasn't away for too long.'

'I have nowhere to be and nothing to do,' she says. 'An enviable position, I'm sure you'll agree.'

'I can't remember the last time I had nothing to do.'

'You'll get there when you're my age,' she says. 'For the time being, I advise you to make the most of your youth and energy.'

'Humphrey will make sure of that,' I say.

I see her off, then return to the living room to find Humphrey hasn't moved. He must be more tired than I thought. Now could be the perfect opportunity to take his measurements.

I pull a tape measure out of my shopping bag and kneel down next to him. He shifts slightly and grunts.

'Shh,' I murmur. 'You have a nice sleep while I get on with this.'

He half raises one paw, then lets it fall again. He opens one eye and looks at the tape measure.

'Don't wake up,' I say in a soothing tone.

He opens his other eye. Time to do something before he realises where he is and what I'm doing.

I take a deep breath and start to sing to the tune of twinkle, twinkle, little star.

Snuggle, snuggle, little pup,
Curl your paws and cuddle up …

To my astonishment, this seems to work. His eyelids droop, and he heaves an enormous sigh as he settles himself more comfortably on the rug.

I quickly measure him from nose to tail and across his enormous shoulders. I jot the numbers down in my phone as I go. He doesn't move, so I tiptoe out of the room with my bags and take them into the kitchen to inspect their contents. Humphrey wanders in half an hour later, still looking drowsy.

'Hi, there,' I greet him. 'Just wait until you see what I've been making for you.'

He walks over to his bowl and takes a long drink. He lifts his head at last, water still dripping from his jowls.

'Better now?' I ask him.

He shakes the water from his fur and runs over to the kitchen door. His meaning is clear.

'Hold your horses,' I say, putting down the headband I've been working on. 'Let me unlock the door rather than you crashing through it and leaving a Humphrey shaped hole.'

I let him out and watch as he romps joyfully through the snow until he finds an almost clear patch of grass. He returns a few minutes later looking delighted with himself.

'I don't suppose I could persuade you to clean up after yourself?' I ask.

He grins at me and shakes the snow off his fur.

'Wait a minute,' I say, picking up the towel I use to dry his paws after one of his muddier walks. 'That's better. Now, I need you to stand still for a few minutes while I try this on you.'

I pick up a green T shirt and slip it over his head. He gives me a startled look but doesn't try to run away.

'Good boy!' I say, slipping the arms over his front paws. Stand still for a moment while I rub some of this green powder into your fur. If you could try to look Grinch-like, that would be great.'

I take a picture of him. 'That's perfect. I see you went for puzzled rather than Grinchy, but that's ok. You're the model. It's your choice.'

He lifts his front leg and inspects it for a moment before trying to chew the fabric.

'Don't be so ungrateful!' I chide him. 'That outfit is the latest in dog fashion.'

He tries to chew the other leg. I sigh and pull the T shirt over his head. 'You aren't cut out to be a supermodel, are you? Never mind. It's early days. Now, why don't you try on this nice reindeer headband?'

I put it behind his ears before he has a chance to object, then take a couple more pictures.

'How about one with you pouting?' I ask. 'No? Well, you're the talent. I suppose you know best.'

I manage to remove the headband before he gets restless and decides to eat it.

'Prima donnas!' I complain. 'With the amount you get paid, I would have thought you'd put up with a bit more than this.'

Humphrey backs himself against the wall and prepares to resist any further attempts to turn him into a well-dressed dog about town.

'You've done very well,' I say, giving him a hug. 'Would you like a walk as a reward for all your hard work?'

Humphrey doesn't have the widest vocabulary in the world, but he knows the words dinner, biscuit, and walk. His ears prick up, and he runs to fetch his lead.

'Why couldn't Gran have broken her hip in the middle of summer?' I ask him as he drags me down the street as fast as his legs will carry him.

He ignores this and heads off in the direction of the water meadows. I don't have the energy to argue. Hopefully, his favourite patch of mud will be hidden under ten feet of snow, and he won't be able to find it.

We stay out for an hour until my toes feel as though they're about to drop off.

'Time to go, Humphrey!' I call.

He ignores me and shoots off in the opposite direction.

'Dinner time!' I shout.

He skids to a halt and pauses with his back to me. I can almost see the thought bubble hovering over his head. He turns and walks over to me.

I clip on his lead. 'I thought that would do it. You're a dog of simple tastes, aren't you? Regular walks, a warm bed to sleep in, and plenty of home-cooked food. And a wardrobe full of designer clothes.'

He snorts and shakes snow all over me.

'I'll take that for full agreement,' I say, setting off back down the path to Gran's house. 'You looked lovely in your photo shoot. That headband really brought out the colour of your eyes.'

Humphrey takes no notice. He quickens his pace as Bramble Close comes into view.

'If you pull me off my feet, we'll never get home,' I warn him. 'And then what will you do? Your personal chef will be lying in the street while you wonder where your next meal is coming from.'

He slows his pace slightly. Perhaps his vocabulary is wider than I thought. Is there a way I could capitalise on that? It would be excellent if I could get Humphrey to do the voiceovers on his own videos. Daniel could never top that.

I abandon the thought. I don't have time to train Humphrey to do anything complicated. I'll just have to rely on his natural charisma and model good looks.

Chapter Twenty-Seven

The second meeting of the cookie club is much less fraught than the last one. For one thing, thanks to a YouTube link Abby sent me, I can now make shortbread cookies that won't be mistaken for something used in the discus-throwing finals of the Honeywell sports association. For another, I don't open the door to anyone until I'm sure Humphrey is safely locked in the living room.

I'm feeling quite pleased with myself by the time the club members assemble with their boxes of cookies. Daniel is one of the first to arrive, carrying an enormous cardboard box also filled with shortbread cookies.

'What a coincidence,' says June when he opens it to show everyone. 'Lucy has made the same cookies as you have.'

'But I've iced mine,' I say, gesturing towards them. 'I went with a Christmas theme – snowmen and Christmas tree baubles.'

'Very nice,' says Daniel. 'They'll look lovely in photographs. I'm sure you've taken a few of those, haven't you, Lucy?'

'Just a couple. The same as you, I expect.'

I've taken rather more than a couple of pictures. I spent most of yesterday evening getting the light as perfect as possible while

I photographed the cookies from every conceivable angle. I even took a few selfies of me pretending to bite into one of them, but the finished results made me look like Hannibal Lecter, so I deleted them.

I posted the best of them on my Instagram account, which I was delighted to see has gained several hundred followers as a result of the pictures I've been posting of Humphrey in his various outfits. I added enough hashtags to sink a small battleship and sat back to await the results.

By four o'clock this afternoon, I had more than three hundred likes for my snowman cookies. If I keep uploading photos of Humphrey, my followers will increase, and next week's cookies should get even more likes. I took a quick look at Daniel's Instagram at lunchtime and was delighted to see he only had forty followers, and he hadn't even got around to posting his cookies. He must realise there's no point, and he'll never be able to compete with me. Score one for the Hollis women.

Phyllis has brought mince pies, and someone else has made a batch of mini pizzas. People talk and laugh while they sort the cookies into boxes, all ready to deliver them around the village over the next few days.

I take advantage of the noise and chatter to speak to Daniel.

'I hope my cookies haven't made you feel inferior?'

'Not at all,' he says. 'I assumed you decided to ice them at the last moment because they weren't evenly coloured?'

'They were perfect – all golden and crisp. They didn't need covering up. I just did that to make them Christmassy.'

'You mean Instagram-worthy?'

'Have you posted yours yet?' I ask, knowing perfectly well he hasn't.

'I'll put the pictures up when I get home,' he says. 'I've been too busy today.'

'Playing with your drones?'

'That's right. And baking fifty perfect cookies. Not a crack or an imperfection in any of them, which meant there was nothing to cover up.'

'I've already told you I wasn't covering up anything. I was being festive.'

'#InstagramBaking and #TisTheSeason?' he says. 'Not very original.'

'So, you've looked at my account?'

'In passing. It gave me something to do while my emails were loading.'

I try not to look smug. 'Three hundred and four likes the last time I checked.'

'Were they for the cookies or for Humphrey?' he asks.

'For the cookies. His pictures got even more likes.'

He laughs. 'That ought to tell you something. Seriously, Lucy, don't you think that was a low trick – dressing up that poor dog for internet attention?'

I help myself to a mince pie and sink my teeth into it. 'Not at all. I would have done that this Christmas, anyway. Lily gave me the idea when she told me about Bernie's various outfits. I didn't want Humphrey to feel left out if he met Bernie on one of our walks.'

'You plan to walk Humphrey through the village dressed as a Christmas elf?' he asks.

'Maybe not. But he looked lovely in his little Santa hat, don't you think?'

'You don't want to know what I think,' he says, taking the last mince pie. 'I wonder if these were made using the little-known turning the pastry into glue technique?'

I pull out my phone and open my Instagram app. 'Three hundred and twenty likes now! You'd better up your game if you want to win this bet.'

June taps me on the shoulder. 'Do you two plan to stand here arguing all evening when there's work to be done?'

'I apologise for Lucy,' says Daniel. 'She doesn't have her head in the game. She's too busy looking at her phone.'

'Three hundred and twenty!' I mouth at him before adding, 'What can we do to help?'

'Take ten boxes of cookies each,' says June. 'Irene has printed out lists of all the houses in the village in groups of ten. Take a list of addresses and make sure all the cookies are delivered as quickly as possible.'

'But take care no one sees you,' adds Phyllis. 'It's better to wait an extra day if you need to rather than risk being caught.'

'How can we be sure we won't be caught?' asks Daniel. 'Don't some people have cameras on their doorbells nowadays? They'll see who's delivering the cookies.'

'That's up to you,' says Margery. 'We don't care how you manage it, as long as it's legal.'

'Last year, Ivy joined a group of carollers,' says June. 'She had the box of cookies under her coat and dropped it on the doorstep as they left.'

'Didn't Phyllis do something with a long stick one year?' asks Margery.

'It was a grabber,' says Phyllis. 'My granddaughter bought it for me when I had that slipped disc a few years ago. She said it was to help me pick up things I dropped. I don't think I ever used it for that, but it struck me it would work just as well for putting things down. I stayed out of range of the camera and popped the box on the doorstep using the grabber.'

'Ingenious,' says Daniel. 'Has anyone tried disabling the cameras?'

'They'd better not,' says Margery. 'We make it clear each year that everything our members do must be legal. No one will put up bail if they're caught doing something they shouldn't. Anyway, it's a test of our ingenuity.'

'Not everyone has a camera doorbell,' says June. 'The trick is to choose a time when people are busy. Or deliver the cookies in the middle of the night and hope no one is awake.'

'Humphrey would bark the place down if anyone tried something like that,' I say.

'You should find out whether there's a dog on the premises first,' says Irene. 'But don't tell them why you're asking.'

'This is far more complicated than I first thought,' says Daniel. 'I'm impressed by your level of organisation.'

'That's Lavender,' says Margery. 'She puts a lot of work into this club. It's a shame she isn't here this year.'

'She'll be home soon if all goes well,' I say.

'Please let me know if she needs anything at all,' she says. 'You too, Lucy. Will you be staying on for a while?'

'I'll be here until just after Christmas,' I say. 'My boss has finally agreed I can use my annual leave until then. I'm not sure what we'll do after that.'

Irene hands out the last of the boxes, and people start to leave. Daniel hangs around until the last person has gone.

'I'm pleased to hear your boss has had a change of heart,' he says.

'I wouldn't put it like that. Having a change of heart implies she had one to start with. She told me HR said she had to allow me to take my leave, but she wanted to make it very clear it was coming out of my holiday allowance, and I would be back in the office the minute it ran out. She's also scheduled a back-to-work meeting for me. I can imagine how that will go.'

'Maybe she'll be overcome by Christmas cheer and offer to let you work from home for the next few months,' he says.

'And maybe I'll win the lottery next week. I shouldn't complain. Caroline can't actually fire me for taking the leave I was due. And she won't find it easy to replace me even if she wanted to. Not everyone is prepared to give up their evenings and weekends at short notice for no extra pay.'

'Try not to worry about it,' he says. 'You have enough on your plate without borrowing any more trouble.'

'Speaking of plates, I must check my likes on my latest batch of cookies.'

'Please wait until I've gone!' he says. 'I'm not in the mood for your gloating.'

'Fair enough. I have to feed Humphrey and take him for a quick walk before bed anyway. You should go home and think about a strategy for delivering your boxes of cookies.'

'I have a few ideas already,' he says. 'I can be creative when I need to be.'

'Not as creative as me. See you next week, Daniel. Don't forget to latch the gate as you leave!'

'I'm never going to live that down, am I? See you around, Lucy.'

I watch him walk down the path, close the gate behind him, then check the latch with elaborate care. I laugh and close the front door.

I take Humphrey for his evening walk and give him his dinner.

'I don't know about you,' I tell him when he's finished. 'But I'm ready for bed.'

He follows me up the stairs and takes his usual flying leap onto my bed. I switch out the light and pick up my phone to set an alarm for tomorrow morning. I may as well take a quick look at Instagram to make sure the site hasn't crashed under the weight of all my likes.

It hasn't, but I'm pleased to see almost five hundred hearts under the picture of my snowmen cookies. Daniel has a lot of catching up to do.

I almost don't check to see whether he's posted his pictures yet. It feels a little mean. He accused me of gloating, and I don't want to be that person. Fine, I do want to be that person, but I don't want anyone to realise that. I intend to be gracious in victory when we finish our competition next week. I can do my gloating in private.

Maybe I'll take a look to save myself from having to log in again tomorrow. I click on his account and give a gasp of horror as I see his latest post. That can't be right! There are over six thousand hearts under the photograph of this week's cookies.

Has he found a way to hack into the system and change the number of likes? That's impossible. If anyone could do that, everyone would be doing it. Has he used some viral hashtag I've somehow overlooked? I check the post again. #MerryChristmas #ChristmasCookies #WhatDoYouThink?

His hashtag game is even worse than mine. But the fact remains that he has six thousand likes. The numbers click up as I watch. I look away when they reach six and a half thousand in case the algorithm is accidentally counting my views as likes.

I stare into the darkness, my heart beating madly. Whatever Daniel is doing is working. I have to find out what it is before his numbers reach the sort of heights I have no hope of reaching. I half close my eyes and peek at the screen again. The numbers have stopped moving, which is a relief.

I open my own account and stare at my pictures, concentrating hard. Nothing happens, which means it isn't my magic gaze that causes the numbers to climb. It's a pity because I'd be more than happy to sit here for the next couple of days doing nothing but stare at the screen. Anything to make sure Daniel doesn't win this contest.

'This makes no sense,' I tell Humphrey, but he just yawns and rolls over. Clearly, he isn't a social media buff.

I flick back to Daniel's account and see to my horror the number of likes is now over seven thousand. What is he doing to cause this? I almost call him to ask, but that would mean admitting I've looked at his account and that I care about the numbers he's getting. I have to figure this out by myself and try to do something about it.

I run my eyes down his list of followers. He only had about forty the last time I checked. He now has four hundred and eighty-five. I scan the list, although I'm not sure why. He and I aren't likely to have any mutual friends.

A name catches my eye, and I stop scanning. Cecily Montford. Why does that name feel so familiar? Maybe he and I do have a mutual friend after all. No, we don't! I stiffen in outrage when I realise why I know the name. Cecily Montford is the woman who's famous for being famous.

She's loosely related to the Royal Family, although I can't remember how. She runs a luxury travel vlog and has some sort of wellness brand. And she's some kind of activist. I saw her on the news only last week, chaining herself to the railings outside a stately home. I can't recall what she was protesting. Probably, neither can she.

She's also a terrible name dropper, although I might be too if I moved in the sort of circles she does. She posts humorous content on the 'struggles' of aristocratic life and the perils of being recognised wherever you go. I can't help thinking that if you don't want to be recognised, it might be a good idea not to turn up in some greasy spoon restaurant at three in the morning, dressed in a couture gown and accompanied by a pack of tabloid newspaper photographers. But, each to their own.

The real question is why she's following Daniel's Instagram account and liking the pictures of his boring cookies. More importantly, why isn't she following my account? If she likes Christmas cookies so much, mine are far more interesting. I've made the effort to ice them and make them look festive. All Daniel has done is put his on a plate.

It's no good. I won't sleep if I don't find out what's going on. I scroll down my contacts list and text Daniel.

Just happened to see your account as I was scrolling through Instagram. I couldn't help noticing Cecily Montford is one of your followers.

I almost switch my phone to silent so I don't have to see his reply. It might be best to let him think I'm not interested in the answer. The phone beeps while I'm trying to decide.

Just 'scrolling through Instagram' and 'just happened' to see my account? I'm not sure what your question is. Cece is an old friend of mine. I didn't realise she'd started following me.

He's the most frustrating man I've ever had the misfortune to meet. I take a deep breath before replying.

I don't suppose this has anything to do with you trying to game the system and cheat at our competition?

He doesn't reply for a minute. I'm not surprised. I've called him out, and he's realised the game is up. Did he really think I wouldn't notice what he'd done? I can't imagine how he thought it was ok to manipulate his numbers like that. Whatever happened to good, honest competition?

My phone pings again. I'd like to ignore it, but curiosity gets the better of me. I look down at the screen. Daniel hasn't written a message. He's simply sent me two emojis – a pot and a kettle, or at least a tea pot that I assume represents a kettle.

I slam my phone down on the bedside table, pull my pillow over my head, and prepare to get some sleep. I need to be well rested if I'm to come up with a plan to get the better of him. He obviously thinks he's won this round, but I'm not going down without a fight.

Chapter Twenty-Eight

My life in London feels increasingly distant the longer I spend in Honeywell. I get the occasional flash of guilt when I remember how I behaved. I'm a professional, and I shouldn't have walked out like that. But I resent being put in the position where I felt I had no other choice. It isn't as though the company has no one else to cover for the most urgent parts of my job. Marie has stepped in several times when I've been in Berlin for meetings.

I also resent the tone of the email Caroline sent to let me know I could take my leave. It was the perfect blend of condescension and annoyance. So much for employee relations. I'm not looking forward to going back to work in the new year, but it would be a shame to allow it to spoil the rest of my time here. I have a sneaking suspicion Caroline will do everything possible to make sure I don't take next year's holiday allowance at a convenient time in case I run away with the idea that the company, and she as my manager, have any of their employees' interests at heart.

I tell myself several times a day it's best not to dwell on my work frustrations. I'm sure everything will look a lot less bleak when I return. I just needed a break and a change of scenery, and that's exactly what I'm getting. People pay good money to come to a place like Honeywell.

A Hollywood producer would be delighted to shoot a Christmas movie here. It's a beautiful little village, especially blanketed with white, as it is right now. I hadn't expected the snow to last for so long, but Humphrey and I are making the most of it while it's here.

We set out together each morning, usually in the direction of the field next to the water meadows. This seems to be Humphrey's favourite walk, and I like it too. I love watching him bounding along ahead of me as though it's the first time he's ever been this way. Each new turning is a fresh adventure to him, and he greets even the most familiar landmark with wild excitement.

I wish I could be more like that with my life in London. It would be great to wake each day and eat my slice of toast as though it was the first time I'd ever come across the concept of hot, crunchy bread. I could follow it by skipping through the streets to the train station, marvelling at every flower and garden wall.

I imagine Caroline's reaction if I flew into the office each morning, exclaiming at the fact two of the chairs have been replaced, or gasping in excitement as I switch on my computer and watch the start-up routine that's exactly the same as every other day. She might be less reluctant to allow me to take my annual leave if I behaved like that.

Humphrey and I enjoy a similar walk together most afternoons and evenings, where he's equally excited and intrigued by every stone and leafless branch. I enjoy the afternoon walks the most. I'm not a morning person at the best of times, and Humphrey's exuberance at seven thirty can be exhausting. But I usually feel more energetic after lunch, and I can appreciate the way the setting sun casts a golden glow over the frozen fields. I love watching the twilight wrap around the tree trunks, causing their shadows to elongate into strips of lace before melting into the darkening snow and disappearing entirely.

I take him out a little earlier than usual on Saturday afternoon. I visited Gran this morning and stayed rather longer than I expected to. Humphrey has been restless since I got back, and I make a note not to leave him alone for more than a couple of hours again.

'I'll take you for an extra-long walk to make up for it,' I tell him. I'm not sure whether he understands the extra-long part of this, but walk is one of his favourite words, and he trots off to fetch his lead.

We crunch through the snow together. I leave a trail of footprints behind me, and Humphrey leaves a mass of scuffed up snow. He loves to run across the field, his legs pistoning wildly, snow flying in all directions and coating his fur until he looks like an overgrown snowball with a wagging tail.

I watch in amusement as he charges back and forth, making zigzags and circles and letting out excited yelps. Every now and then, he stops to shake himself off, sending a spray of white flakes everywhere. There's something so pure and joyful about Humphrey in the snow. He bounds over to me, and I reach down to ruffle his snowy fur.

'I'm glad to see you're running off some of that energy. Maybe you'll sleep well tonight and not wake me at 3 a.m. again because you think you've heard a squirrel breaking into the kitchen to steal your snacks.'

He cocks his head to one side as though considering this, then sprints off. My phone beeps, and I check to see who's messaging me while I'm busy playing with Humphrey. To be fair, whoever it is has no idea where I am or what I'm doing.

The text is from Daniel. *I've just found a recipe for Amaretti cookies. Way beyond my skills, but it should be a piece of cake for you. See what I did there?*

I roll my eyes and prepare to text back. Something about the silence around me catches my attention, and I look up in sudden alarm. There's no sign of Humphrey. He must have run down towards his favourite patch of mud. Why did I take my eye off him, even for an instant? I shout his name, my voice carrying over the snowy field so loudly that half of Honeywell could hear it. I shout again, but there's no reply except the faint echo of my own voice across the snow.

I frantically scan the field, but there's no Humphrey bounding towards me through the snowdrifts. My heart starts to slam in my chest, making me dizzy.

'Humphrey!' I yell. 'Walk! Biscuit! Dinner!'

Still nothing. I start to run, the snow crunching under my boots as I retrace our path to the road. Humphrey knows his way back to the cottage. Has he somehow grown bored and decided to return home? It's unlikely, but that would be the most positive alternative.

I scan the path frantically for paw prints. I can see the marks of my boots walking towards me and various messy areas of snow left by Humphrey's paws, but there's nothing to show he's been back this way by himself. I want to believe he has, but I somehow doubt it. Humphrey loves playing in this field and is always reluctant to leave.

I hesitate, trying to decide whether to run home and check whether he's there or stay and continue searching here. If I go home, and he isn't there, I'll have wasted valuable time that I could have spent searching around the field and water meadows. I think of all the dangers he could have encountered. Why did I ever bring him here? Having done so, why did I take my eye off him? It was just a text. It could have waited. It wasn't even an important text. Just another one of Daniel's stupid jokes.

I circle the field again, peering into the distance, hoping to catch a glimpse of brown fur. My heart sinks as I remember it won't be brown. Humphrey has been rolling around in the snow. By this time, he'll be almost as white as the ground.

Panic grips my chest as I run, calling his name at the top of my voice. The minutes pass, and there's still no sign of him. How could I have allowed this to happen? I stop at the edge of the field, gasping for breath. Should I widen the search? I could start combing the area on the far side of the hedge. But what if I do that, and Humphrey returns here? Will he have the sense to wait for me or will he think I've abandoned him and run off again, maybe for good this time?

I have to stop this. Letting my thoughts spiral won't help either of us. If only there was someone else around I could enlist to search with me. I could do with a second pair of eyes at this moment. Of course! Why didn't I think of that before? I fumble for my phone, my hands shaking, and dial Daniel's number.

His voice is amused as he answers. 'Are you calling to tell me what's wrong with the recipe I sent you?'

For a moment, I can't think what he means. What recipe? It doesn't matter right now. All that matters is finding Humphrey.

'Something's happened!' I begin.

'Lucy? Are you alright?'

A sob escapes me. 'No!'

His voice sharpens. 'What's happened? Where are you?'

'At the field. Humphrey went missing about ten minutes ago. I've searched everywhere, but he's disappeared. I desperately need some help.'

The shock of hearing the words spoken out loud, of making them real, finishes me. I start to sob uncontrollably.

'I'm on my way!' says Daniel's voice in my ear. 'Stay where you are, and keep calling for him. With any luck, he'll be back with you before I arrive.'

'No, he won't! He's gone, and it's all my fault.'

'No, it isn't,' he says. 'Just hang in there, and we'll get Humphrey back. He can't have gone far.'

He's right, but that isn't necessarily a good thing. Humphrey doesn't need to have gone far to get himself into trouble. There are probably a million hidden dangers in this field alone. I wonder why I've never realised that before. If I ever get him back, he and I will stick to sedate walks through the streets. And I'm never allowing him off his lead again.

'I'm on my way,' says Daniel again. 'I'll be with you in five minutes.'

Chapter Twenty-Nine

His car pulls up on the far side of the field a few minutes later, and I breathe a sigh of relief. I couldn't have held it together much longer all by myself. I seem to have lost the ability to think clearly.

He jumps out and runs over to me. 'No luck?'

'Not a trace of him. I can't imagine where he's gone. I've been calling and calling. He's never done anything like this before. I'd never have let him off his lead if I'd known he'd disappear.'

'You weren't to know,' he says.

'Maybe not. But if I hadn't stopped to answer your stupid text, none of this would have happened.'

I'm aware how unfair this is, but I can't help myself. Anger will keep me on my feet for a while. Thinking about my responsibility for this fiasco won't.

Daniel doesn't react. 'Did you see which way he went?'

I point. 'Over there, I think. But I'm not really sure. I wasn't watching him when he left the field. And he's been running around here so much today that I can't trace his paw prints.'

He nods. 'Let's assume for now that he took off in that direction. There's no road for miles, which is a good thing. What's between these fields and the next village?'

'I'm not sure. We've never been down there. I've mostly stuck to this area. There's some farmland nearby.'

A horrible thought strikes me. 'You don't think he's strayed onto the farmer's land, and they've shot him?'

'Absolutely not.'

'But what if he's been chasing their sheep?'

'The nearest sheep are over near Compton,' he says. 'That's in the opposite direction to here. If Humphrey has found his way into a farmer's field, the worse he'll have done is dig up the odd cabbage.'

I feel a surge of relief when I realise he's right. But that feeling is short-lived. We still have no idea what's happened to Humphrey.

'I love him so much,' I say, my voice breaking.

Daniel gives my shoulder a reassuring squeeze. 'In which case, we should get him back for you as quickly as possible. Stay here for a moment.'

He lopes off to his car and opens the boot. He fishes something out and returns a minute later carrying a drone. I stare at it, my mind racing. When I decided I needed a second pair of eyes, I meant Daniel. I didn't consider his drones, which shows what a state I'm in.

'I never thought of that!' I say.

He raises one eyebrow as he sets the drone on the ground. 'Isn't this why you called me?'

'I called because I needed help, and you were the first person I thought of.'

'Fair enough. But this is the best way I can help. Trust me, Humphrey doesn't stand a chance of hiding from this.'

He gives me a quick smile, then crouches down beside the drone. He flips a couple of switches and taps at his tablet. The drone's lights blink into life, and its propellers start to hum, a low buzzing that gradually intensifies. Daniel's eyes are focussed, his fingers moving expertly over the controls. I feel a wave of relief to realise he knows exactly what he's doing.

'Ready?' he asks, glancing up at me.

Before I can respond, the drone lifts off the ground, hovering for a few seconds just above head height. It rises higher, angling its camera to take in the entire field. I step closer, leaning in to watch the view on the screen expand into a bird's-eye perspective of the snowy landscape.

It's surreal to see the field stretch out below the drone – patches of undisturbed white, punctuated by trails and paw prints. Daniel manoeuvres it in smooth arcs, sweeping it back and forth across the field, the camera scanning everywhere.

'See anything?' he asks, his eyes glued to the controls.

I stare at the image, straining to spot any movement. 'Not yet.'

'Don't worry,' he says, steadying the drone and zooming in on a hedge at the far end of the field. 'Humphrey's quick, but this is quicker.'

The minutes tick by with agonising slowness as the drone methodically scans the area. It rises higher, then disappears over the hedge and out of sight.

'Shouldn't we follow it?' I ask.

'There's no need,' he says. 'Let the drone do the work for now. You concentrate on that screen.'

The drone flies over a small spinney and carries on.

'Shouldn't you have checked those trees?' I ask.

Daniel smiles. 'Humphrey is a gifted dog in many ways, but he hasn't yet mastered the art of climbing trees. Much to the relief of Honeywell's bird and squirrel populations.'

'I'm not talking about him climbing trees. But you didn't look on the ground beneath them.'

'I switched on the infrared as we passed over the spinney. If we don't see the runaway himself, it will pick up his body heat.

Humphrey's a big dog, and he's been running around. We should be able to pick him up from a mile off.'

'Then, why haven't you?' I ask, more sharply than I intended.

He glances over at me. 'I will. I promise.'

His tone is so calm and confident that I find myself believing him. I keep my eyes fixed on the screen, willing Humphrey to appear.

Daniel stiffens. 'Is that …?'

He moves one of the controls forward, and the camera tilts steeply as it heads towards the ground.

'Gotcha!' he murmurs.

'Are you sure?'

'Absolutely sure. Look at that shape next to the building.'

I stare at the flickering orange and red blob. 'That could be anything. It could be a sheep.'

'Too large,' he says. 'And sheep don't usually dig holes in the snow.'

He switches off the infrared, and the camera straightens up again. I give a gasp of relief as I see Humphrey industriously scrabbling at a patch of snow. Daniel brings the drone down and lands it on the roof of the building.

'You found him!' I say in disbelief.

'I promised I would.'

The weight of the past half hour comes crashing down on me all at once – the terror of what might have happened to Humphrey, and the fear of never seeing him again. I can't hold it in any longer. I collapse into Daniel's arms, sobbing uncontrollably.

'It's ok, Lucy,' he murmurs against my hair.

'I was sure I'd lost him,' I choke out between sobs. 'And it was all my fault.'

'I thought it was mine for sending stupid texts.'

'I was wrong,' I say in a muffled tone into his sweater. 'I'll never say anything unkind to you again.'

'I doubt that,' he says with a laugh in his voice. 'Are you ready to collect the miscreant?'

I wipe my eyes. 'We'd better go before he decides he's had enough of digging that hole and wants to move on.'

'We'll find him if he does,' says Daniel. 'I almost dropped the controller when you lunged at me like that, but it's still in one piece. If Humphrey makes a move, we'll find him again. Let's get going before he does. He's about five hundred metres in that direction.'

I break into a run, and he follows me. When we reach the hedge at the far end of the field, I see a large gap in the branches.

'This must be where he scrambled through!' I say.

'Or he simply launched himself at the hedge,' says Daniel. 'And that hole is the result. Either way, we should go through it.'

We push through the gap and find ourselves in a second field. The snow is deeper here, and I sink up to my knees in several places. I spot the building I saw on the screen a few minutes ago.

'That's it!' I say.

'And there's the man himself,' says Daniel. 'Heading towards that fence. He must have got fed up with digging a hole in the snow and decided to move on. I'll retrieve my drone while you go and have a few words with him.'

I sprint across the field as fast as I can, shouting for Humphrey. Hearing my voice, he turns and smiles amiably, for all the world as though we've arranged to meet here, and he's wondering what took me so long.

I drop to my knees and wrap my arms around him, burying my face in his fur. He gives my arm an awkward lick.

'Never do anything like that again,' I tell him as soon as I can speak, careful to keep my tone calm and neutral. He doesn't respond well to raised voices.

Daniel appears and smiles down at the pair of us.

'For once, it's you in trouble and not me,' he tells Humphrey, who wags his tail frantically.

I pull Humphrey's lead out of my pocket and clip it to his harness. 'This is never coming off again.'

'Don't listen to her,' Daniel advises Humphrey. 'She's annoyed because she couldn't find you, and my toys could.'

I straighten up, clutching the lead. 'I'll never call them toys again. I'm more grateful to you than I can say. I don't know what I'd have done if you hadn't answered your phone.'

'You would have done exactly what you needed to,' he says. 'You'd have widened the search until you found him or he decided he'd had enough and came to find you.'

'Maybe,' I say. 'But I'm not sure I'd have stayed calm enough for that. It felt like one more thing I couldn't prevent.'

He nods but doesn't comment. I'm not sure what made me say that. The important thing is that Humphrey is safely back with us. That's enough for anyone.

We climb back through the hedge and make our way towards Daniel's car. Humphrey doesn't chase a single bird on the way. Either he's trying to show how sorry he is for his behaviour this afternoon or he's too tired after digging up half a field of snow.

'I'm sorry I can't offer you a lift,' says Daniel. 'But I barely fit into this car as it is. I can't imagine what Marcus thought he was doing hiring me a Mini Metro while I was down here. If we try to fit Humphrey in too, we'll end up looking like one of those clown cars as we pass through the village.'

'That's ok,' I say. 'Humphrey gets car sick, anyway. We're better off walking, so we can have a talk on the way. He and I need to discuss the concept of trespass.'

Daniel ruffles Humphrey's fur. 'Sucks to be you, mate! Lucy can be scary when she wants to be.'

'Not tonight,' I say. 'I'm too relieved to have him back safe and sound. I'll be cooking him an enormous piece of steak and tucking him in with a hot water bottle and a bedtime story.'

'Sounds good,' says Daniel. 'If you put some Christmas pyjamas on him and a cute little nightcap, you can post it on your Instagram account. It might get you a few more followers. And you desperately need those if you want to stand any chance of beating me when we add up our totals next week.'

Chapter Thirty

Humphrey wakes me for his walk a few days later. For once, I don't burrow under the quilt, pleading with him for another five minutes. I ignore the cold and jump out of bed, taking even him by surprise.

'Breakfast and a walk,' I tell him. 'I've decided to let you off your lead again today. But only if you behave yourself. We'll go to the field because you like it so much there, but one hint of trouble and we're leaving. After that, we need to come home and clean up. The doctor told me yesterday that Gran should be coming home today or tomorrow, and I don't want her to be disappointed with the way you and I have kept the house.

For a moment, I feel like someone telling their young child the truth about Santa. Would it have been better to have kept the news about Gran a secret and just allowed Humphrey to enjoy the surprise? I smile to myself as I remember he doesn't understand what I'm saying. I'm turning into Mrs Ogilvie and treating Humphrey like my baby. There are worse ways to approach the business of being a pet owner. Bernie is a happy little thing, and Humphrey is a happy giant thing, so all is well in both their worlds.

We eat our breakfasts, then I bundle up in as many layers as I can find to brave the icy morning.

'I don't suppose I can persuade you to put on your reindeer outfit?' I ask Humphrey. 'It would go down a storm with my followers, and it might get me some much-needed likes.'

I can't be too upset with Daniel after what he did to help me find Humphrey. But seriously, who cheats at a competition like this? I had to work hard to increase my followers, whereas all he had to do was ask his famous friend to share one of his pictures on her stories, and the rest of the sheep followed.

His cookies didn't even look that good. I put a lot of effort into mine, icing their little noses to look like carrots and tracing zigzag patterns onto the Christmas ornaments. Ok, they weren't perfect, but I did my best. And Daniel just asked some influencer woman to do it all for him.

My teachers used to tell us about the satisfaction we would feel if we did our work by ourselves without asking someone else to do it for us, even if it resulted in a lower grade. But I don't feel any particular glow as I stride along the streets of Honeywell behind Humphrey. Perhaps that's because it's so cold, and my hands and feet are already numb. Maybe I'll feel a sense of pride in my achievement once Humphrey and I are safely back in the warm.

I try not to think about the fact I'm about to lose my competition with Daniel. 'Live in the moment!' I instruct myself. I seem to tell myself that quite often these days. Not, I suspect, because I'm morphing into some Zen-like creature who's learned to take joy in the tiny things of life and is ready to write a self-help book, but because I'd prefer not to think too much about my immediate future.

Does Cecily Montford practise this same sort of Zen thinking? If so, she's bound to be twenty times better than me at it. According to her followers, there's nothing she can't do perfectly, and they hang on her every pronouncement. If she'd made outfits for Humphrey, they would have attracted millions of likes within the first few minutes of her posting them.

I catch myself. Why am I thinking negative thoughts about a woman I've never met and who's never done me any harm? All she's done is play the cards life has dealt her and built up a successful business for herself. On the surface, it may seem as though she was dealt a better hand than most people, but appearances can be deceptive. She may have had just a difficult upbringing as someone born in less affluent circumstances.

I can't help wondering how Daniel knows her. Did he perhaps meet her at some drone-flying competition? I don't follow her myself, so I have no idea about her possible hobbies. Or did they meet somewhere else and start dating? Surely not. Cecily only dates famous people – sportsmen and actors. Daniel is neither. Didn't she once date a famous chef too – that Italian guy who talks about pasta being less of a meal than a way of life? If that's the sort of man she's into, Daniel doesn't stand a chance. His last lot of cookies were adequate, but I can't imagine anyone describing them as a way of life.

We've reached the field next to the water meadows – or the ice meadows, as I suppose I should call them this morning. The frost has turned the grass into a field of silver. Humphrey tugs at his lead until I unclip it, then bounds away in his eternal quest to reduce the bird population of Honeywell to a manageable size. His breath forms little clouds in the frosty air, giving even the sleepiest bird notice of his approach.

He catches sight of a rook sitting on a low branch and lumbers towards it. It gives him a sarcastic look and flies away. Nothing daunted, he catches sight of another and changes direction. This takes him several seconds, and the second bird waits even longer before taking to the skies. It watches Humphrey with what I like to think is an amused expression before giving a leisurely flap of its wings and flying off, leaving him to chase its shadow with as much enjoyment as he chased the actual bird.

I have to admire his philosophy. If you can't get the thing you really want, pursue something else with equal enthusiasm. The joy is in the quest, not the outcome. I could learn from that. I can't entirely disregard the outcome in the way that Humphrey can. I have to eat and pay the bills. But I could certainly learn to live in the moment a little more and not sweat the small stuff.

What does it really matter if Daniel ends up with more likes than me on Instagram? The important thing is that I've learned a new skill and had fun doing it. It may take a while for my brain to catch up with this philosophy. It's still telling me it would be even better if I could both enjoy the journey and also get the outcome I want, which means crushing Daniel and showing the world how much better a baker I am than he is. Perhaps I should sign up for one of Cecily's mental wellness courses. Or Cece, as Daniel called her. I refuse to speculate why that may be. His personal life is his own business.

I come back to reality with a start. This was supposed to be a quick walk. I've promised myself to have the cottage in perfect order before Gran returns, which means doing some serious cleaning. I know how house-proud she is, and I don't want her wishing she'd remained in the hospital.

I whistle for Humphrey, who's immediately afflicted with his usual deafness. I turn away and pretend to look at the willows at the far side of the water meadows.

'What splendid specimens!' I exclaim. 'I could stand here all day studying them. I'm so glad Humphrey is busy. It gives me plenty of time to appreciate their glorious something or other.'

Humphrey ambles over to find out what I'm doing, and I grab his collar and clip on his lead.

'I thought that would do it! You're extremely predictable. And extremely contrary. Sorry about that, but we have to go. It's time for me to redeem your promise to clean the entire house for me while I lie on the sofa and watch.'

My phone rings a couple of hours later. As I expected, it's Gran.

'They've told me I'm allowed home this afternoon!' she says. 'I asked whether I could use the phone at the nurses' station. I wanted to call you before they changed their minds.'

'They won't do that,' I reassure her. 'I'm sure they're as anxious to get rid of you as you are to leave. They'll be looking forward to a little peace and quiet.'

She laughs, but her voice is anxious. 'Will you be able to come and get me? I could take a taxi, but they said they'd prefer someone to collect me.'

'Of course! I can drive over as soon as you like.'

'No rush,' she says. 'The doctor won't be doing her ward rounds until after lunch. Could you come around two o'clock?'

'I'll be there,' I promise. 'And don't worry if there's any delay. I have a babysitter all lined up for Humphrey.'

I make us both an early lunch.

'You're having Kibble,' I tell Humphrey. 'And I'm having a toasted sandwich. I'll try not to get them confused.'

I text Daniel while I wait for my sandwich to grill.

Any chance of you dog-sitting today? I'm collecting Gran from the hospital around two o'clock.

His reply comes back almost immediately.

Delighted to come over and sit on your dog. Or I could take him for a walk if you prefer. I can be there by one-thirty.

'That's a relief,' I tell Humphrey. 'I may be gone for some time, and it will be nice for you to have someone to play with. I want you to behave yourself for Daniel and promise not to mess up the house. It took me ages to clean it, and you were no help at all. What's the point of keeping you if you can't run a duster around occasionally?'

I'm glad Daniel's coming over. He can take Humphrey for a nice long walk, which should mean he's not too boisterous when Gran gets home. She'll be tired after her journey, and the last thing she needs is a giant dog landing in her lap. Knowing her, she'll make up some excuse for him, but it's best not to put it to the test.

Humphrey greets Daniel with enthusiasm when he arrives.

'He's had his lunch,' I say. 'And he's ready for his second walk. I've put his lead on for you, but there are several spare pairs of socks in the laundry basket if you need them.'

His eyes crinkle with laughter. 'Thank you for thinking of me, but I don't believe they'll be required. And we won't be walking past that house again. I went round to apologise, bearing a box of chocolates, but the man who answered the door was a little short with me.'

'You returned his socks, all nicely washed. What more did he want?'

'I'm not sure he accepted my explanation of why I'd removed them in the first place,' he says. 'If only you'd allowed me to take Humphrey with me to apologise, I might have avoided a painful scene.'

'How painful was it?'

'Let's just say I doubt I'll be receiving a Christmas card from him this year. But he took the chocolates, which was a good sign.'

'Grumpy old thing,' I say. 'I'm glad you didn't take Humphrey with you. He doesn't like loud voices, do you, sweetheart?'

Humphrey gives an enthusiastic bark, and Daniel laughs.

'I'd better get going,' I say. 'If I know Gran, she'll be sitting on the edge of her bed counting the minutes. And woe betide any junior registrar who suggests she stays for an extra night.'

'Another Hollis woman who knows her own mind?' he asks, taking Humphrey's lead from me and following me down the drive.

'I come from a long line of women who know their own minds.'

'Come on, Humphrey,' he says. 'We'd better get going before we get ourselves into any more trouble.'

Chapter Thirty-One

As I predicted, I find Gran waiting for me when I arrive at the hospital. She isn't sitting on the edge of her bed, but she's in a chair by the window.

She looks delighted when she sees me. 'They're just filling out the paperwork, and then we can go.'

'I told you they couldn't wait to get rid of you. And we can't wait to have you home. Humphrey has been preparing a special dance for you. He doesn't always remember the steps, but I'm sure you can fill in the gaps.'

'I've missed him so much,' she says. 'I can't tell you how much it's meant to me knowing you were with him.'

'I've loved every minute of it. I'll miss him when I go back to London after Christmas.'

'Did you say someone is looking after him while you're away?' she asks.

'That's right. You remember me mentioning Daniel – the man who gate-crashed our meeting?'

'Of course.' She gives me a searching look. 'He's the one looking after Humphrey today?'

'He offered ages ago. I wouldn't have asked him otherwise.'

She smiles but doesn't say anything more.

The nurse appears a few minutes later. 'All set? I've found you a wheelchair. If you'd like to hop in, I'll take you down.'

She helps Gran into the wheelchair. Hop may have been a slight exaggeration, but Gran is far more mobile than I expected. I drop off the flowers and chocolates I've brought with me at the nurses' station and thank them for everything they've done for Gran. I had considered baking them some cookies, but I decided they have enough to contend with at this time of year. I'm confident my baking is edible by now, but it's safest not to take any chances.

The nurse helps Gran into my car and issues her with last-minute care instructions. We say goodbye, and I drive slowly away.

'How does it feel to be going home?' I ask.

'Wonderful,' says Gran. 'Although I'm a little nervous in case anything goes wrong.'

'It won't,' I assure her. 'I've turned the living room into a bedroom for you. It's lucky the bathroom is downstairs. You won't need to use the stairs for a while.'

'Humphrey won't be happy,' she says, looking worried. 'He doesn't like his routine being upset.'

'I've upset his routine in every conceivable way this past fortnight,' I tell her. 'And he's handled it like a champion. Please don't worry about him.'

She doesn't look convinced. I don't say anything else but concentrate on driving as smoothly as possible. Gran isn't one to complain, but it can't be comfortable taking a journey like this on her first day out of hospital.

We chat about my week as I ease the car along the country lanes. I tell her about the last meeting of the cookie club and my attempts to deliver the cookies without being discovered.

'I don't know how Santa does it,' I say. 'I was almost caught delivering one box, whereas he has to climb down millions of chimneys without being discovered. My targets came home unexpectedly early from their evening out. Still, I managed to hide behind a bush until they were safely inside.'

'It doesn't matter too much if the adults see you,' says Gran. 'As long as the children don't. There's so little magic in the world nowadays. I like to think we can provide some at Christmas.'

She wouldn't say there was no magic in the world if she'd seen Humphrey in his elf outfit. But it may be better not to mention that. I've decided not to bother telling her about his recent costume changes.

We pull up outside Rose Cottage, and I help her out. She takes a deep breath. 'What a relief to be home.'

I open the gate and gesture for her to go through. 'Someone else will think so too.'

The minute I put the key into the door, we're greeted by an ear-splitting bark. A second later, Humphrey comes into view. Daniel has had the sense to keep him on his lead, but it's as much as he can do to hold him.

I step in front of Gran before Humphrey can send her flying. He cannons into me in his effort to get to her.

'Steady there!' says Daniel, pulling him back.

Gran bends down and puts her arms around Humphrey's neck, and I'm touched to see how gently he responds to her. It's as though he senses she needs careful handling. She buries her face in his fur for a long minute. When she raises it at last, her eyes are full of tears.

'Thank you for looking after him for me,' she tells me in a choked voice. 'I'll never forget it.'

'Not just me,' I say. 'It takes a village, remember? Everyone helped. The staff at the bakery gave him biscuits, and Margery babysat him while I went shopping. Even Daniel –'

He laughs. 'I can't wait to hear what you have to say. Any sentence that starts with *Even Daniel* is bound to end badly for me.'

I smile back at him. 'Not at all. You've been great. Just wait until you see the rail Daniel's fitted in the bathroom for you,

Gran. And it was kind of him to look after Humphrey today. I didn't want us to arrive home and find he'd got into the living room and eaten your pillow.'

Humphrey gives me a shocked look that makes it clear he would have a low opinion of any dog behaving in that way.

'You haven't introduced me yet,' says Gran.

'I'm sorry,' I say. 'I'd forgotten you and Daniel haven't met. He's been such a part of my life while you've been in hospital that I feel you must already know him.'

I catch Daniel's eye and see he's smiling.

'A reluctant addition to your life,' he says. He holds out his hand to Gran. 'I'm Daniel, the newest member of your cookie club. It's a pleasure to meet you.'

'Temporary member,' I can't help saying.

'Temporary member,' he agrees.

'I'm Lavender Hollis,' says Gran. 'I've heard all about you.'

'I've barely told you anything,' I say. I don't want Daniel thinking he's formed a large part of our conversation during my hospital visits. Nothing could be further from the truth.

'Not from you,' she says. 'But I've had plenty of other visitors. They've told me about him.'

'I'll understand if you'd like me to leave at once,' says Daniel, and she laughs.

'Not at all. You must stay for a cup of tea. I want to hear everything that's happened while I've been away. Starting with Humphrey here.'

We sit at the kitchen table while I fill her in with all the news. Humphrey lays his head on her lap as I talk, and she gently scratches his head. Looking at the two of them makes me want to cry. I hadn't quite realised until now what a huge part of each other's lives they are.

'Which just about brings us up to date,' I say. 'I left Humphrey with Daniel and came to fetch you. I'm sure they had a good time together.'

'We did,' says Daniel. 'We went for the usual walk towards the water meadows. He has strong opinions on where he likes to walk, and I don't like to argue with him, although it's a little muddy there at the moment. Most of the snow has melted, and the ground is fairly squishy if you leave the path.'

'Which I have no doubt you did,' I say.

'Not by choice,' he says with a grin. 'But Humphrey saw a group of magpies, so, you know …'

'He didn't catch one?' I ask anxiously.

'I wouldn't have let him off the lead if I'd thought there was the slightest chance of that. But he got within about thirty metres of them, so he was happy enough. They moved to a higher branch to continue their conversation, so I don't think they were too bothered by him.'

'These cookies are excellent,' says Gran. 'Did one of you bake them?'

'Don't worry,' says Daniel. 'You're quite safe. Irene dropped them off while Lucy was gone. She asked me to tell you she'll pop in tomorrow morning.'

'I wasn't worried,' she says. 'Lucy tells me she's improved her baking skills no end since she arrived in Honeywell.'

'That wasn't difficult,' I say. 'I had absolutely no skills when I arrived. Even learning how to combine butter and sugar in the correct proportions was a huge step forward.'

'And keeping them in the bowl while you did it,' adds Daniel.

'The less said about that, the better,' I admit. 'But you were no more skilled than I was when we started.'

'I wasn't,' he says. 'This competition has been good for both of us.'

'Competition?' asks Gran.

'He means club,' I say quickly. 'He's saying the cookie club has been good for both of us.'

'I don't think that's quite what he meant,' says Gran. 'Was it, Daniel?'

His eyes are full of laughter as he meets my gaze. 'Help me out here, Lucy.'

'I can't. You're on your own.'

'Tell me!' says Gran.

I reluctantly tell her about our competition, with Daniel helpfully chipping in with all the more embarrassing details. I'm not sure why Gran needs to know quite how badly I performed during our cookery lesson with Abby. Especially since I'm now confident enough to tackle basic recipes. But Daniel refuses to omit a single thing.

'And that's when Lucy and I decided to make it into a competition,' he finishes. 'We knew there was no point in asking the club members to vote. They would have told us to stop wasting their time.'

'They're an efficient bunch,' I agree. 'For some reason, they all seem more focussed on the actual purpose of the meetings than telling us how wonderful our cookies are.'

'So, we decided to run a competition ourselves,' says Daniel.

I'm pleased to see Gran doesn't look annoyed. But I didn't expect her to laugh quite so hard.

'I don't quite understand the part about followers and stories,' she says. 'But do I take it you're trying to find out how popular your cookies are with the general public?'

'That's right,' says Daniel. 'So far, the general public appears to be on my side.'

'This is a happy day,' I tell him. 'So, I won't spoil it by arguing with you. Or explaining to my grandmother exactly how you've been cheating. We can leave that until another time.'

'Agreed,' he says. 'As long as we're both clear about my lead. You have as much hope of catching me as Humphrey has of bringing home a pheasant for your Christmas dinner.'

'Speaking of dinner,' I say, 'I'd better make a start on ours.'

He looks alarmed. 'Your grandmother is only just out of hospital. Are you sure it's wise to inflict a home-cooked meal on her on her first day back?'

'No need to worry,' I say. 'Angela Carson dropped a casserole round last night. Even I'm capable of heating that up without burning it, and preparing some vegetables to go with it.'

'How kind of her,' says Gran. 'Is there enough for three, Lucy?'

I want to tell her there's only enough for two. But that wouldn't be fair to Angela Carson, who's provided enough dinner for a small army. Or several people and one Humphrey.

'If you mean me,' says Daniel, 'I'm seeing friends this evening. If you mean Humphrey, the answer is no, there's never enough food for him.'

'I did mean you,' says Gran. 'Humphrey can't eat the casserole, but there's usually some steak in the freezer. Lucy can cook that for him if she doesn't mind.'

'I don't mind,' I say. 'But we don't want him getting ideas. He's supposed to be having dry food this evening.'

'It's a celebration,' says Gran. 'He and I haven't seen each other for such a long time. We must do something to mark the occasion.'

'Quite right,' says Daniel. 'Perhaps Lucy can dress him up in his spinning bow tie.'

He catches my eye and smiles. 'Yes, I saw your post last night. He looked very smart. But it won't do you any good. I have a feeling Cece is about to share my latest post on today's Instagram story.'

Chapter Thirty-Two

Gran goes to bed soon after dinner, saying she's tired. I help her with everything she needs and settle her onto the sofa bed.

'Please call if you need anything in the night,' I say. 'Daniel brought you this bell when he came over to sort out the handrail in the shower.'

'He seems like a very nice man,' she says. 'You didn't mention that when you told me about him.'

I'm annoyed to feel myself blushing. 'I barely told you anything about him.'

'I know,' she says. 'And I've wondered why. But my friends have kept me up to date. They're laying bets on how long it takes for the pair of you to get together.'

'That doesn't sound likely. You must have misunderstood what they meant. Maybe they're laying bets on which of us murders the other first.'

'I may be old, but there's nothing wrong with my memory,' she says. 'There's nothing wrong with my eyes, either. You could do a lot worse.'

'So could he!' I say, and she laughs.

'That goes without saying. I'm only teasing you, Lucy. Your love life is none of my business. For all I know, you may be seeing someone up in London.'

'Not recently. I don't have time.'

'Or he could be,' she goes on.

It's quite likely Daniel is involved with someone, although I'm a little surprised he hasn't mentioned it. He's talked about everything else. Is it really possible he and Cecily Montford are an item? Is that why she's so happy to share his posts with all her followers? I don't know him very well, but I can't imagine him getting together with someone who lives her entire life through social media and sells expensive homeopathic cold and flu cures on her website. On the other hand, she's extremely beautiful. Most men would be delighted if a woman like that showed an interest in them.

'Lucy?' says Gran.

'I'm sorry. I was thinking about Humphrey's basket,' I say, not entirely truthfully. 'Would you like him in here with you tonight? He's been sleeping on my bed while you've been away. But it's up to you.'

Humphrey answers the question by scrambling onto the sofa and flopping down next to Gran.

'You can't do that,' I say. 'Gran needs her space. I'll bring your basket.'

I fetch it from the kitchen and put it next to the sofa. 'In you get!'

I say it without much hope. To my surprise, he hops down and obligingly curls up in it.

'Wonders will never cease,' I say.

'He's very good at times like this,' says Gran. 'He's a sensitive soul, and he seems to know when people really need him to do something.'

'I needed him not to lie on my feet and cut off the circulation each night,' I say. 'But he didn't take any notice of that.'

'There's a difference between a want and a need,' she tells me. 'Haven't you learned that yet?'

'It appears Humphrey has. But if he changes his mind and causes you any bother, please ring the bell. I'll leave my bedroom door open so I'll be able to hear you.'

She settles herself more comfortably and blows me a kiss. 'Goodnight, Lucy. Sweet dreams.'

'No need for those,' I say. 'I'm getting the entire bed to myself for a change. What more could I ask for?'

I half expect to hear the bell during the night, but I don't. I tiptoe downstairs when I wake, not sure what I'll find. I put my head around the living room door to see Humphrey fast asleep in his basket. Gran is asleep too, her hand hanging down and touching his head. I smile at the picture they make. If anyone wanted to paint a portrait of unconditional love, they need look no further than this.

I switch on the kettle and return to find Gran opening her eyes.

'I don't know what was in those tablets the hospital gave me,' she says. 'But I had a wonderful sleep.'

Humphrey stirs and yawns.

'From the looks of it, so did he,' I say. 'Did he move at all after we put him to bed?'

'Not an inch. Haven't I always told you what a good dog he is?'

'You have. But I didn't fully appreciate it until now. I'm glad you slept well. I'll make us some breakfast, then take him for his walk.'

We spend the rest of the day quietly. Various people pop in to see Gran, but they don't stay for long. Apparently, Angela Carson has arranged some sort of visiting rota and encouraged everyone to stick to it.

'You're a popular woman,' I tell Gran as I help her get ready for bed that evening. 'It must be nice to live in a place like this where you know everyone, and everyone knows you. I've barely met anyone while I've been in London.'

'How about your workmates?' she asks. 'Do you get on well with them?'

I think of Caroline constantly telling me I'm failing to meet her arbitrary deadlines, and Mark undermining me at every opportunity. And Dave and his IT minions treating us as though we're the lowest possible life form if we ever dare to suggest they might pop along to fix our computers.

'They're fine,' I say at last. What else can I say? Gran has only been home from the hospital for one day. The last thing I should be doing is telling her things that are bound to worry her.

'It always takes a while to settle into a new job,' I add. 'I'm sure I'll get to know my colleagues better as time goes on.'

Gran looks distressed. 'I've taken you away from your job at the worst possible time of year.'

'Not at all,' I reassure her. 'It was about time I took some days off. I've only taken a week's leave this year. And they don't like us rolling our holiday allowance over into the following year, so I've done them a favour.'

'It's very nice of you to put it like that,' she says. 'But I know it isn't true. Maybe we can find someone to come in to help me each day, and you can go back to London. There's still almost a week until Christmas. I'm sure they'd be happy to see you.'

I'm rather less sure, but I don't want to argue with her.

'I'm enjoying the break,' I say. 'I'll return to work feeling more energetic. The nurse will be coming in for the next few days to check your stitches are healing, and you start physio next week. But you'll still need someone to cook and clean. And Humphrey can't walk himself. Please don't worry about me. I'm having a lovely time with you both. Now that I'm not so worried about leaving Humphrey by himself, I can get out and see more of the area.'

'That's true,' she says. 'Have you been to the Christmas Fair yet?'

'Humphrey gets a little over-excited when he's around too many people.'

'He's better with a few people at a time,' she says. 'And he's so large that he tends to knock things over.'

'Is the fair worth a visit?'

'Oh, yes! I'm disappointed to miss it this year. But you can tell me all about it. Tomorrow is the last meeting of the year for the cookie club, so you won't want to visit it then, but how about Friday evening? I'll ask Margery whether she'd like to pop over while you're gone. She can fill me in with everything that's happening in the village.'

I tuck her into bed and settle Humphrey into his basket.

'I thought he might wander up to visit me last night,' I say. 'But he didn't move. It's obvious who his favourite person is.'

'He's a very loyal dog,' says Gran. 'But I can see how much he likes you. You've done a wonderful job with him.'

I sit beside her. 'I've been wondering about something, but you may be too tired to talk right now.'

'Not at all,' she says. 'Is it about your work?'

'What makes you ask that?'

'Oh, I don't know. It feels as though there's something you aren't telling me.'

'It isn't about my job,' I say. 'It's about the cookie club. The other members told me all about its history. But none of them mentioned Mum. And she's never talked to me about the club. It struck me as odd, that's all. She's a Hollis woman too. Why has she never said anything about it?'

Gran is silent for a long moment, stroking Humphrey's head.

'It's my fault,' she says at last. 'Nothing to do with your mother. When she was growing up, I always thought she would stay here in Honeywell, just as I had, and my mother before me. I planned to pass the leadership of the cookie club on to her when she was old enough. But it soon became clear she planned to move away as soon as possible. She didn't want to stay in such a small place. She wanted to travel and see other places. Your grandfather encouraged her, and he wouldn't let me say a word about it.'

'Mum always told me I should leave home and find my feet in a new place,' I say. 'She said I should snatch every opportunity and try new things to discover what I wanted in life.'

'She was right,' says Gran. 'But I couldn't see that at the time. All I saw was that my daughter wanted to leave us. It took me a long time to realise how selfish I was being. And by that time, she'd already left.'

'Are you saying you and she never got past it?' I ask, and she laughs.

'Goodness, no! We made up that quarrel long ago. I saw how happy she was when she left to work in London. And then she met your father and moved to Coventry with him. She found her place, just as Ed and I had found ours.'

'So, why didn't you tell her about the cookie club then?'

'I didn't set out to keep it a secret,' she says. 'I assumed she knew I was running something of the sort. But she never mentioned it, so neither did I. It always felt to me like a symbol of everything she didn't like about living in a village – doing the same thing each year with all the same people. I was worried she might look down on it, just like she'd always looked down on her life here.'

'I don't think that's true,' I say. 'Mum has always talked fondly of her childhood in Honeywell and told me what great parents you and Grandpa Ed were. Just because she wanted to move on didn't mean she didn't appreciate what you'd given her. You gave her the confidence and self-belief to feel she could set off on her own adventure.'

'That's what Ed told me,' she says. 'You remind me a lot of him, Lucy.'

'You must miss him very much.'

'I do. But life goes on. And now I have Humphrey to look after. He gave me a new lease of life after I lost Ed.'

'It works both ways,' I say. 'You did the same for Humphrey. Look what a difference you've made to his life.'

She glances down at him with a fond smile. 'We're both very lucky. I've been meaning to ask you, Lucy. There seems to be a greenish patch of fur behind his right shoulder. Has he been rolling in the grass or something?'

Humphrey opens an enquiring eye as though interested to know what I have to say about his green fur. I wink at him.

'It's nothing to worry about,' I tell Gran. 'He's just been doing a bit of method acting while you've been away.'

Chapter Thirty-Three

I'm looking forward to spending an evening at the Christmas fair. I've done most of my shopping online this year, but it would be nice to do some in person too. This has always been one of my favourite things about Christmas – selecting the perfect gifts for people. Especially my family. My parents made it such a special time of year for me growing up, and I have so many happy Christmas memories.

I won't be seeing Mum and Dad on Christmas Day. Dad can't travel down here, and Gran isn't going anywhere for a while. Much to Humphrey's relief, I suspect. She wasn't joking about his travel sickness. I tried to take him for a walk in the forest the first week I was here, but we only got a mile down the road before he started showing unmistakable signs of nausea.

I had no wish to spend an entire day cleaning Gran's car, so I turned around and came home again. I haven't repeated the experiment, and I don't intend to. So, Gran, Humphrey and I will spend Christmas in Honeywell, while Mum and Dad celebrate in Coventry. It can't be helped. At least none of us will have such a terrible day as we did last year, when Dad was still in the hospital and no one knew what sort of recovery he would make.

I rang Mum a few days ago to update her on Gran's progress, and we promised each other that we would have a second Christmas together as soon as I can get to Coventry. I'm determined to make that happen before going back to work. Caroline has done without me so far. She can do without me for a couple of days longer.

I say goodbye to Gran and Margery as I leave for the fair. They're already deep in conversation, and I doubt they'll notice my absence. They must have a lot to catch up on. Humphrey thumps his tail as I pat him goodbye but makes no move to follow me. He's adapted very well to Gran's return home and has calmed down considerably. He seems to have adopted the role of protector and guardian and rarely leaves her side. That suits me fine. I don't want him running down the road after me, demanding to be taken out for a glass of mulled wine and a piece of Stollen.

I close the gate carefully, just in case, and look up and down Bramble Close. No dark figure emerges from behind a nearby hedge wielding a drone, which is a good start. I walk up to the village, enjoying the crisp night air and the crunch of snow beneath my feet. This feels like the perfect evening for me to visit the Christmas fair. Except for running the cookie club, I haven't yet managed to get into the spirit of the season.

My stay in Honeywell feels like a dream – a blur of dog walking, baking, and trips to the hospital. I don't feel as though I've achieved very much, but I'm oddly exhausted. Maybe that's always the way it is with holidays. It's been so long since I've taken one that I can't remember how you're supposed to feel when you get back home at the end of them.

I resolve to be far stricter about this when I return to work. I've been too quick to accept Caroline's rulings about how I'm allowed to use my free time. She's always told me the company will collapse if everything isn't done by yesterday, and I see now that isn't true. They've managed fine without me since I came down here, and they can manage fine without me the next time I need a break. If they can't, they'll have to hire more staff. It isn't up to me to run myself ragged to make up for their inadequate planning.

The Christmas fair is being held on the green at the far end of the high street. I can hear the music and laughter from quite a distance away. I was right to think Humphrey wouldn't enjoy it, but it's exactly what I need after all this time on my own. My spirits lift as I walk more quickly towards the entrance.

The smell of mulled wine and roasting chestnuts drifts through the air, mingling with the scent of pine from the decorated trees lining the path. Twinkling fairy lights are strung over most of the stalls, casting a festive glow over everything.

I make my way through the crowd, taking in the stalls selling handmade gifts, warm hats and scarves, and the boxes of glittering ornaments. It's all so wonderfully ... *Christmassy.* Exactly the kind of spirit I've been missing until now. Speaking of spirits, I notice a stall called The Snowball Saloon. It appears to be selling mulled wine and eggnog. Just what I need to start the evening. I'm wearing my thickest boots, but my feet are still cold. Not for long though.

'One glass of eggnog, please,' I tell the man.

'Make that two,' says a voice.

I turn, with a feeling of inevitability, to find Daniel standing behind me.

'What are you doing here?' I ask.

He pulls out his wallet. 'I'm in charge of the drone display.'

'Really?'

'Not really. I wouldn't trust my precious drones anywhere near this place. You've seen the sort of riff-raff the fair attracts.'

'You're here, so I see what you mean.'

'I've got these,' he tells the man.

'There's no need!' I protest, but Daniel has already handed over his card.

'I've been looking for a way to apologise,' he says, 'And this seems the perfect opportunity.'

'Apologise for what? Knocking the cookies out of my hands?'

He hands me my glass. 'I was thinking of the time I let Humphrey escape, but you're right – there are so many things I need to apologise for. One glass of this won't be enough.'

'How about you cheating in our competition and getting fifty times more likes than I did?' I ask, and he laughs.

'I have nothing to apologise for there. It isn't my fault that a friend thought my cookies were so amazing she wanted to share them with all her followers.'

'Just a coincidence, then?'

'Coincidences happen more often than people realise. On an unrelated subject, I've been admiring your pictures of Humphrey dressed in an increasingly bizarre set of outfits.'

'They're Christmas-themed,' I say. 'There's nothing bizarre about Christmas.'

'Dressing him up as the Grinch may have been Christmas-themed. And the reindeer ears were quite festive. But what about the tuxedo and bow tie?'

'People like to dress up smartly for the holidays. There's nothing wrong with that.'

'I'm not sure Humphrey agrees,' he says. 'His expression in the picture of him standing next to the tray of wine glasses was less than festive. He looked as though he'd like to throw them at someone.'

'He was hungry. He hadn't had his dinner.'

'That would account for it.'

'I'd like to see you do any better,' I say.

He raises an eyebrow. 'Isn't that what started all this – you telling me you'd like to see me do better?'

'You're right. I take it back.'

'I'm glad you did say that. If you hadn't, I wouldn't have joined your cookie club and got to know you and Humphrey better.'

There's a warmth in his eyes that makes my heart skip a beat. I'm not sure how to answer this. Do I regret accidentally inviting him to the cookie club? I thought I did at the time, but now I'm not so sure.

'Shall we look around the fair now we're here?' he asks. 'How long do you have? Is Margery staying for the entire evening?'

'How did you know Margery was visiting Gran?' I ask.

'Didn't you mention it?'

'No, I didn't. So, how did you know?'

He appears to be fishing around for some explanation, then laughs. 'Your grandmother told me.'

'Gran did? How?'

'Or rather, she sent a message to me via Margery that you would be visiting the fair this evening. She wondered whether I might enjoy it too if I hadn't already visited it.'

'Did she indeed? And had you already visited it?'

'Twice,' he says. 'But I didn't dare tell her that. And Margery didn't so much ask whether I'd like to come along as command me. You know how I am around strong women. I can't stand up to them at all. I just do as I'm told.'

'I hadn't noticed. But neither of them is here now, so there's no need for you to stay. I'll tell Gran I met you here. I won't mention that you only stayed for five minutes.'

'What if I want to stay for longer?' he asks.

I gesture towards the stalls. 'That's your call. You're a grown man, and you can do as you like.'

He smiles down at me. 'What if I'd like to stay here and spend the evening with you?'

My heart seems to have sped up. It must be the eggnog. I should ask them what they put in it.

'That's up to you,' I manage.

'And you,' he says. 'I don't intend to stalk you around the fair against your will. If you really don't want me here, I'll finish my eggnog and go home.'

My instinct is to tell him I don't want him here. It's become so much of a habit to put him in his place that I've never stopped to wonder why I'm doing it. Maybe because it's fun, and I haven't had much fun over the past year. But it occurs to me now I may be cutting off my nose to spite my face.

'Well?' he asks gently.

'You should stay,' I tell him. 'I'd enjoy spending the evening together.'

We spend the next half hour inspecting the stalls.

'It's important to take your time Christmas shopping,' says Daniel.

'I used to agree. But the last two years, it's been a struggle to buy anything at all.'

'Your father's accident?' he asks sympathetically.

'Yes. That was last December. And this year, I've been too busy at work to spare a thought for Christmas. Even down here, I've had my hands pretty full. So, I've been ordering most of my presents online. Humphrey hasn't enjoyed that. I've had to put a note on the front door asking the delivery people not to ring or knock.'

'He's showing you what an excellent guard dog he is,' says Daniel.

'According to Gran, he's the opposite of useful in an emergency. But she took him on after some difficult circumstances, and she knew in advance there would be times when he was a bag of nerves.'

'Poor Humphrey,' he says. 'I'm sorry he had a bad start in life.'

'Me too. But his luck changed the day he met my grandmother. She loves him exactly as he is, and she puts up with all his foibles. And in return, she has a gorgeous pet to keep her company and love her back. She always tells me she has the best end of the deal.'

'They're both lucky,' he says. 'And he seems very comfortable with you.'

'He wasn't to begin with, but he's grown to trust me. Which is fortunate, seeing that he's been lumbered with me over the past two weeks.'

'Are you enjoying taking a break this evening?' he asks.

'It's nice to get out by myself for a while without having to wander around the field in the cold and dark while Humphrey eyes up the local wildlife.'

'Ornithology can be a very rewarding hobby,' he says.

'Not the way he does it. Speaking of hobbies, how's yours going?'

'I assume you're talking about my job. Fine, thanks. We've almost finished this roof survey. The council seems pleased with us. As long as they're pleased enough to pay our invoice, that's all Marcus and I care about.'

'What's next for you?'

'I haven't decided yet. We've been offered a contract in Scotland helping to survey deer populations. And another one not far from here assessing coastal erosion. Marcus and I need to decide soon. We'll have to split up and do one job each, but we haven't figured out which of us will do which.'

'I'd like to go to Scotland,' I say. 'Possibly not at this time of year. But I've always wanted to visit during the summer.'

'What's stopping you?'

'Work, I suppose. I've taken all my leave for the year, and it will be a while before I accrue more. Even when I do, there's no guarantee my boss will let me take it at a time that works for me.'

'Don't ask her,' he advises. 'Just tell her that's what you're doing.'

I feel a flash of irritation. 'Things aren't that simple.'

'Why not?' he asks.

'Because they're not. Maybe you've forgotten what it's like to work for someone else, but that's what I do. If I want to further my career and get something worthwhile on my CV, I'll have to put up with for a while longer.'

He glances over at me. 'I've annoyed you. I'm sorry.'

'You haven't annoyed me. Not really. But life is never as simple as we want it to be, and none of has as much choice as we'd like.'

'Have you finished your eggnog?' he asks. 'Would you like another?'

'Not before I finish my shopping. I don't know what they put in it, but it has quite a kick.'

'Rum,' he says. 'But we could have brandy in our next one.'

'Maybe later. I need to keep my wits about me if I don't want to end up buying a bottle of rose-scented shower gel for Dad and a skateboard repair kit for Gran. Even worse, a *World's Best Boss* mug for Caroline.'

Chapter Thirty-Four

Daniel buys us a bag of caramel almonds, and we eat them as we browse the stalls. I buy a warm scarf for Mum and a jar of chutney for Dad. We stop at a stall with the intriguing title of *A Boxful of Christmas*, where I buy a box containing a selection of scented candles and toiletries for Gran. We get everything wrapped at the charity gift wrap station.

'I'm not sure what to buy for Humphrey,' I say.

'A French maid's outfit?' suggests Daniel.

'Do they make them large enough?'

'I'm not sure. But it might gain you a lot of new followers if you post it on Instagram.'

'I'm definitely not putting that to the test,' I say. 'I've decided to quit the Instagram game. I saw what happened when you put up the pictures of this week's cookies and Celia shared them. I can't compete with that.'

'It had nothing to do with her,' says Daniel. 'People were intrigued by my baking. I wasn't surprised. It isn't often you see Christmas cookies in the shape of drones.'

'There's a reason for that. And it had everything to do with her. Even with your hashtags, no one would have had the faintest idea what those cookies were. I thought they were Lego bricks until I read the captions.'

'That's because you have no technical knowledge,' he says. 'It was clear to the most casual observer that my propellors had been accurately iced.'

'I thought they were flowers.'

'I even included the camera lenses,' he says.

'They looked like buttons. I thought you must have got them mixed up with my snowman cookies from last week.'

He shakes his head. 'Science education in the UK is seriously lacking these days. Shall I critique your last batch for you?'

'They were seasonally appropriate. Gingerbread people epitomise Christmas.'

'Drunk ones?' he asks.

'They weren't drunk! A few of their limbs may have been uneven, but they were all as sober as a judge.'

'Drunk,' he repeats. 'Several of them had eyes going in different directions, and one unfortunate gentleman had lost his nose altogether. I assume in a bar fight. They were a motley crew.'

'They were wonderful! I'm sure the children lucky enough to receive them will be delighted.'

'They'll be suffering nightmares for weeks,' he insists. 'You'd better hope word never gets out who made them or you'll have irate parents chasing you all over the village.'

'We're getting away from the point,' I say. 'I'm trying to tell you I've withdrawn from the contest. You've won. Congratulations.'

He gives a slight bow. 'That's very kind of you. I'd like to thank my parents, who gave me the courage to believe in myself, my preschool teachers, who –'

'I'll leave you to it,' I say. 'It looks as though this could take a while, and I want to see the rest of the fair before it closes.'

'You're right. I haven't had time to prepare my remarks as fully as I would wish. I'll save the rest for a more appropriate time. Perhaps I'll post the entire speech on my Instagram account under the caption *Local Man in Stunning Victory.'*

'You aren't local,' I say. 'And it would be more appropriate for the caption to read *Newcomer Cheats His Way to Undeserved Win.*'

'You're a sore loser,' he says. 'I hate to see it. Shall we put the painful subject behind us and enjoy the fair?'

'That's the plan.'

He links his arm in mine, and I don't object. It would be a pity to lose each other in the crowd and have to waste time searching.

We stop at a stall selling mince pies and sample several flavours.

'I think I like the apple and brandy best,' I say. 'But the orange and cranberry is a close contender.'

'I'm leaning towards the ginger and apricot,' he says. 'But I can't help thinking the pastry isn't as light as it could be. Maybe they forgot to toss the butter onto the floor before mixing it with the flour.'

I point to the Christmas trees. 'I wish I could buy one of those huge trees for Gran. But her living room is quite small, and I wouldn't want to scare Humphrey.'

'I like the little tree you've put up,' he says. 'I was admiring it during our last meeting. Is it real?'

'It's the one Gran uses each year. She told me where to find it in the attic. Humphrey was a little too interested in helping me with the decorations, but I got there in the end.'

'I noticed you posted it on your Instagram account,' he says. 'It didn't receive as many likes as it deserved.'

'Perhaps you could point it out to Cecily in case she missed it?'

'I'm afraid not. She told me once when we were at university together that she never mixes the personal with the professional.'

'Did you really know her at university?' I ask.

'I did. She and I didn't mix in the same circles, but we got on well whenever our paths crossed. She and Marcus dated for a few months, which is how …'

'You persuaded her to like your account?' I say.

'Cecily is a woman who recognises quality when she sees it. I wouldn't be surprised if one of her staff approaches me in the coming months to suggest a cookie collaboration for her next year's wellness promotion.'

'I'd be extremely surprised. But you won fair and square-ish, so I'll say no more about it.'

'What makes me think that may not be true?' he asks.

I laugh. 'I thought we'd declared a truce for the rest of the evening.'

'You're right,' he says. 'It's entirely in the spirit of the season. I approve.'

We stop at a small enclosure labelled *Nativity Petting Zoo.*

'Would you like me to buy you a ticket?' asks Daniel.

'Why not? I love petting zoos. It isn't often you get the chance to stroke,' – I glance at the sign – 'goats, sheep, and more.'

'It's the "more" that's worrying me,' he says, following me into the enclosure.

'No donkeys?' he asks the man running the attraction. 'I would have thought they were the obvious choice for a nativity scene.'

'We offered,' says the man. 'But the organisers thought it might be too risky in this sort of environment. Those things can kick!'

I bend down to stroke a tiny goat who's looking up at me appealingly. 'You would never kick, would you?'

'Probably not,' says the man. 'But she'll eat everything in sight, so don't let her see any food you may have bought this evening.'

He hands us both a bag of pellets. 'These are included in the entry price. They're safe for all the animals we have here.'

'Even the rabbits?' asks Daniel. 'I don't remember those being mentioned in the original nativity story.'

'Aren't they gorgeous?' I exclaim. 'Look at this one eating the pellets out of my hand!'

We spend a while inside the small hut playing with the chickens and the tortoise. To be fair, most of the playing is done by me. Daniel watches with an amused smile.

'You must be kicking yourself that you didn't bring your camera with you,' I say when the man tells us our time is up. 'You could have got your wildlife photography badge with no trouble at all. Your Akela would have been delighted with you.'

'I don't need my camera,' he says. 'I have my phone.'

Before I have time to realise what he's doing, he takes a quick picture of me lowering a guinea pig back onto the straw.

I straighten up. 'That photo had better not end up on your Instagram account. It would be humiliating if it received fewer likes than your awful cookies.'

'I'm sure it would have been equally popular,' he says. '#CutestThingEver – who knew there were #GuineaPigs at the #Nativity?'

'I'm not sure you understand how hashtags work. It ought to be something like #BunnyLove or #FamilyFun. But we'll never know how many likes the photo would have got because our competition is over. Doesn't it seem strange to you that so many people live their lives as a series of hashtags?'

'Are you talking about Cece?' he asks.

'Not particularly. She's seen an opportunity and made the most of it. Good for her. I'm speaking more generally. People reduce even the most intense experiences to a set of tags instead of enjoying them. I was looking through my Instagram feed, and there were loads of pictures of rainbows and firework displays, all hashtagged to death. It made me wonder whether they'd stopped to enjoy the moment or simply pulled out their phones and uploaded the pictures to see how many likes they would get and how quickly they would go viral.'

'Each to their own,' he says. 'I can't say I spend too much time on social media. Real life is far more fun.'

'It can be,' I agree.

He looks down at me with a smile in his eyes. 'I'm all for living in the moment.'

I stare back at him, my heart speeding up again. It can't be the eggnog this time. It's been a while since I drank that. He leans in, his hands sliding to my waist, anchoring me. The world seems to shrink until it's just the two of us, a quiet bubble suspended in time.

'Lucy?' says a voice, and I jump and pull away from him.

'I thought that was you!' says the voice, and I recognise Phyllis standing there.

She claps a hand to her mouth. 'I'm so sorry. I didn't realise –'

'It's fine,' I say. 'Are you having a good time at the fair?'

'Lovely, thank you. I apologise for disturbing you.'

She gives Daniel an embarrassed smile. 'You must be wishing me anywhere but here.'

'Not at all,' he says politely. 'It's always a pleasure to see a fellow member of the cookie club.'

'Not so loud,' I tell him. 'The stalls have ears.'

'I should be going,' says Phyllis. 'Give my love to your grandmother.'

She waves and disappears into the crowd.

'That's just great,' I say. 'She'll be on the phone to Gran the minute she gets home. I wonder whether there's time for me to cut the phone lines before she gets the chance.'

'I could call Marcus to send one of our drones over to do the job,' Daniel suggests. 'But it seems a slight overreaction to a chance meeting.'

'I suppose so.'

I stare at my feet, embarrassed. The moment I let my guard down with Daniel, something like this has to happen. What will he do next? In a romantic movie, he would pull me towards him, murmuring, 'Now, where were we?' and I would melt into his arms. I find myself hoping he doesn't do anything so cringeworthy. I needn't have worried.

'Is this a hashtaggable moment?' he enquires.

'It could be. #Excruciating #WhyMe?'

'That's a negative way of looking at things,' he says. 'How about #SeizingTheMoment #TakingAChance?'

'I'm more concerned about my grandmother's friends than taking a chance,' I say.

'I'd noticed that.'

'What does that mean?'

He shrugs. 'Just that you aren't what anyone would call a risk-taker.'

'I take plenty of risks.'

'Such as?'

I struggle to come up with a concrete example. But that doesn't mean there are none. No one should be expected to think clearly under this sort of pressure.

'I'm sorry,' he says. 'Let's not spoil a great evening by arguing.'

I want to agree, to get back to where we were when Phyllis interrupted us. But I can't. I don't know why his words should have stung me so much, but they have.

'Not until you tell me what you mean,' I insist.

'I would have thought it was obvious. You're working in a city you don't like, doing a job you hate for people who treat you like dirt. Yet you won't do anything to change it. That doesn't scream madcap adventurer to me.'

My voice shakes as I answer. 'You have no idea what you're talking about. You've only just met me. How is it any of your business what I choose to do with my life?'

'Lucy, I don't –'

I feel a wave of anger rising inside me that takes me by surprise. 'My life is my business, Daniel, not yours. And I resent being lectured by someone who only knows the smallest fraction of it. I was right about you when we met. You're thoughtless, arrogant, and you think you can fix anything by being charming. It's about time you realised you can't. Other people aren't just there for your entertainment. They're real people, with real feelings, and real problems. And no amount of joking around is going to change that.'

I can't read his expression, but for once it isn't amusement. If I didn't know better, I'd say he looked stricken. But that may be how he looks when he's angry. I don't care. He can be as angry as he likes. I've said what I wanted to say, and he can deal with it.

'Lucy, you have entirely the wrong idea,' he says. 'You think that –'

My anger, which had been dying down, flares up again. 'Don't tell me what I do and don't think! I don't need any stupid mansplaining from you.'

Is that a flicker of laughter in his eyes?

'#Mansplaining?' he asks.

How dare he make fun of me? He may not understand why I'm so upset. Even I don't understand why I am. But it's typical of him to reduce everything to a joke. It's a sign he doesn't really care about other people.

'I'm going home,' I say abruptly.

'Lucy, there's no need for –'

'There's every need,' I say. 'I've been here for far too long. I have responsibilities at home. I can't hang around all night arguing with someone who will never begin to understand that.'

I turn on my heel and march away. I stop after a few steps and turn to face him. 'In case I haven't made myself clear, let me put it in terms you'll understand. #GoodbyeDaniel #DontCallMe.'

I don't wait for him to answer but run across the carpark and set off down the high street by myself.

Chapter Thirty-Five

Margery is just leaving when I arrive home.

'Did you have a good time?' she asks when I walk in.

'Fine, thanks,' I say curtly, and she and Gran exchange surprised glances.

'Just fine?' Gran asks. 'We hoped you'd be more enthusiastic than that.'

'Did you meet anyone nice there?' Margery asks with a knowing smile.

I mustn't be rude to one of Gran's guests, so I can't say any of the things that rise to my lips.

'I'm afraid not,' I say.

She looks at Gran, then back at me. 'Are you holding out on us?'

'I'm not sure what you mean. I didn't meet anyone nice this evening. But I had a good time, and I finished my Christmas shopping. I came home to take Humphrey for a walk if he's ready.'

I give them both a fake smile, grab his lead, and bundle him out into the chilly night air before either he or they can protest.

Humphrey is usually the one dictating the pace, but tonight he has to run to keep up with me.

'We'll stay in the grassy area,' I tell him. 'It's too dark down by the water. I don't fancy a midnight swim in these temperatures.'

I pull out the ball I stuffed into my pocket as I left the house and throw it for him. He gives a delighted bark and runs after it. Or rather, he runs straight past it. His coordination needs work, but his enthusiasm more than makes up for it. I throw the ball for him for an hour. I prefer not to go home until my temper has cooled. None of this is Gran's fault, and I don't want to end up arguing with her as well.

When even Humphrey has tired of the game, I clip on his lead, and we walk more slowly back to Bramble Close. I find Gran preparing for bed and feel a pang of guilt that I've stayed out for so long. She doesn't seem to mind.

'You've had a lovely walk, haven't you?' she asks Humphrey as he leaps up to lick her face.

'Careful!' I warn him, but she just laughs.

'I'm a lot steadier on my feet than I was when I first came home. I think Humphrey senses that.'

I'm not convinced, but there's no point in arguing. All I want is to get the pair of them settled, then retreat to my bedroom. I'm exhausted, and not just because of my recent ball game with Humphrey.

I help Gran into bed, count out her tablets, and fetch her a glass of water.

'How did tonight really go?' she asks as I plump up her pillow.

'I've told you. It was great. I finished my shopping and had some eggnog.'

'All by yourself?' she asks.

I turn to face her. 'I know you sent a message to Daniel telling him I'd be at the fair tonight. I'm not sure why, but –'

'I thought you might enjoy some company.'

'I can find my own company if I need it.'

I see her expression and relent. 'I don't mean to be snappy. I know what you were doing, and maybe it's a grandmother's prerogative to match-make for her grandchild. But you've missed the mark with this one. Still, there's no harm done. Can I get you anything else before I go upstairs?'

She settles back on her pillow. 'Humphrey and I are fine, thank you. I'm sorry if –'

'Don't give it another thought.' I bend to kiss her cheek. 'You can't win them all. Night, Gran.'

I feel somewhat better the following morning. I'm still annoyed with Daniel, but that isn't Gran's problem. I go about my day as usual, taking Humphrey out for some exercise and stopping in at the village shop for the list of groceries Gran has given me. It isn't until mid-afternoon that she mentions the fair again.

'Phyllis called this morning.'

'Is that right?' I say, determined not to give her any help. With any luck, she'll let the subject drop.

She doesn't. 'She told me she saw you at the fair last night.'

'I may have bumped into Phyllis at some point,' I say. 'There were lots of people there.'

'You told us last night you didn't meet anyone.'

'I told you I hadn't met anyone nice,' I say. 'And I hadn't.'

'So, you and Daniel …?'

'There is no me and Daniel. I'm not sure who told you there was, but they were wrong. Perhaps you could spread that around to all your friends before they get carried away.'

'No one had to tell me,' she says. 'I have eyes in my head. It's obvious that young man likes you very much. And I thought –'

'That's wishful thinking on your part,' I say. 'Even if you were right about him, it takes two to make a successful relationship, and I'm not interested.'

'Why not?' she asks.

'I'm just not. Can we please drop the subject?'

'If you like. But I'm worried about you, Lucy.'

'Because I don't have a man in my life? Times have changed, Gran. No one needs a man to live a happy and fulfilled life.'

She smiles. 'They never did. I'm not as old-fashioned as you think. My mother told me never to settle for someone unless I was sure I couldn't live without them.'

'Like Grandpa Ed?'

'Exactly.'

'That's great,' I say. 'And I know how happy you two were. And how happy my parents have been together. But I agree with your mother. I've never met anyone I'm sure I can't live without.'

I'm hoping this will put an end to the conversation. But of course, it doesn't. This is Grandma Lavender. She's a Hollis woman, and she comes from a long line of Hollis women, all of whom are known for speaking their minds.

'You're not listening to me,' she says.

'Yes, I am. You've told me not to settle, and I don't intend to. I realise you and your friends have decided it would be fun to set me up with Daniel. But that's not your decision to make.'

'I'm aware of that,' she says. 'But you're deliberately misunderstanding what I'm saying. No one meets someone and immediately realises this is the person they want to spend the rest of their lives with. Or if that happens, it's very rare. But we meet someone we get along with, and we take a chance and see where it goes.'

'I don't get along with Daniel,' I insist.

'I'm your grandmother. I know you extremely well.' Her tone softens. 'What happened last night?'

To my horror, I feel the tears prick my eyes. 'Nothing.'

She pats the chair next to her. 'Why don't you sit down and tell me all about it?'

I sniff. 'Humphrey needs his afternoon walk.'

'Humphrey is fast asleep in his basket. You've walked him off his legs. You don't have to talk to me, Lucy, but you might feel better afterwards.'

I try to tell her yet again that she's wrong, but my voice cracks, and the tears start to my eyes. Gran doesn't look perturbed. She pours me a cup of tea and waits.

'We had an argument,' I say at last.

'About what?'

I try to remember. 'Daniel was being his usual obnoxious self.'

She smiles. 'He's never struck me as particularly obnoxious.'

'That's because you don't know him.'

She takes a sip of her tea. 'What did you argue about?'

'My job.'

She considers this. 'That doesn't sound like a contentious subject.'

'He implied that I hate it, but that I'm too cowardly to change it.'

'Why does he think you should change it?'

'Because he's an interfering know-it-all.'

I catch her amused smile and add, 'It's true! He's known me for a couple of weeks, and he thinks he knows everything there is to know about my life.'

'Is he wrong about your job?' she asks.

'No, but that isn't the point.'

She hands me the plate of cookies. 'Are you sure? You haven't seemed happy for a while. I've been worried about you.'

I select the largest cookie. 'You're allowed to be worried about me. He isn't.'

Her eyes dance. 'I suppose you told him that?'

'I told him I never wanted to see him again and not to call me.'

'I realise I'm old,' she says, 'and your generation sees things differently to mine. But that strikes me as rather an overreaction. From what I can tell, he was just expressing concern for you.'

'I didn't ask for his opinion,' I say. 'Maybe it was an overreaction. But he hit a nerve.'

'I thought so. Out of interest, why have you stayed at that job for so long when you hate it so much? Is it because of your father?'

There's never any point in trying to hide things from Gran. She always puts her finger straight on the point, whether or not I want her to.

'I can't bear to let my parents down,' I say. 'They were so upset at the thought of Dad's accident affecting my life too. I tried to tell them several times that I'd made a mistake in taking that job, but they thought I was trying to make them feel better about the idea of me leaving it and coming home to help. In the end, I gave up. It won't hurt me to stay there for a while to gain experience. And it will stop them worrying. They have enough on their plates without that.'

Gran is silent for a while. She looks up at last and meets my gaze. 'Why didn't you tell Daniel all that? I'm sure he would have understood.'

'Because he made me so angry,' I admit. 'I don't know why. I'm not usually an angry person, but these past few months have felt different. Everything makes me snappy. It's as much as I can do to be polite to people sometimes. Maybe I need a proper holiday.'

'I think you do,' she says. 'But it isn't just that, is it? Have you ever talked to anyone about your father's accident – not just the facts of it?'

'Not really. There's not a lot to say. He was almost killed. We thought he might never walk again. He's had a year of painful physiotherapy and still doesn't know how well he'll recover. The man who did it will be out of prison soon and free to go about his business with no consequences, while Mum and Dad serve a possible life sentence for what he did.'

'I doubt that young man's life will be entirely consequence-free,' she says.

I feel the familiar flare of anger. 'That's what Mum said the last time I talked to her about it. It made me angry, but there was nothing I could say. She and Dad have been so positive about this whole thing. It would be wrong for me to bring them down. They have the right to handle it in any way they like.'

Gran's eyes are full of understanding. 'You have the right to your own feelings too, Lucy. Don't let them get lost in all this.'

Tears prick my eyes again. 'What's the point? All the anger in the world won't turn the clock back to last December and the decision that man made.'

'It won't,' she says. 'But pretending you don't feel anything won't make it magically disappear either. I was angry when your grandfather died. No amount of reminding myself we'd had more than fifty happy years together stopped me feeling that way.'

'What did?' I ask.

'Talking to my friends about it. Telling them how I felt and how confused and guilty I was. And hearing the ones who had gone through the same thing say they'd experienced similar emotions, and I wasn't a bad person for feeling what I felt.'

'I don't know anyone whose father's life has been upended by a drunk driver,' I say.

'But you know people who have felt grief and anger and pain and come through it. It doesn't have to be exactly the same situation for someone to understand what you're going through.'

'You're right,' I admit. 'But I don't have many close friends. We all went our separate ways after university, and I haven't made any new ones in London. I thought Daniel was becoming a friend, but he turned out not to be. He's just like everyone else. He'll never understand how I feel. He showed me that last night.'

'He won't understand if you don't let him,' she says. 'Why not give him a chance?'

'It's too late for that now. And frankly, I don't have the energy.'

'So, talk to someone else,' she says.

'You mean a therapist?'

'Or me, if you prefer. I promise not to tell you how you feel, and I make an excellent cup of tea. We could add a little something to it if that helps. Just to keep the cold out, you understand. The bottle is in the larder.'

This makes me laugh. I wipe my eyes. 'Thanks, Gran. I have to walk Humphrey soon, and I don't want to get lost, so I'll stick to regular tea. But I think it might help to talk to someone.'

She pushes the plate of cookies towards me again. 'There's no time like the present. Humphrey won't be awake for a while.'

I pick up another cookie and take a bite without tasting it. Then, leaning back in my chair, I start to talk.

Chapter Thirty-Six

I wake the following morning feeling lighter than I have for months. I'm not sure why talking to Gran made such a difference, but it did. I told her all the things I've been pushing down inside me for an entire year, and she wasn't shocked or horrified. She just listened.

It took quite a while. When I finally finished, she gave me a hug and told me I'd done wonderfully well, and that Mum and Dad were lucky to have a daughter like me, which made me cry again. Then she asked me to peel the potatoes for supper and check whether Humphrey had enough dried food left to last for the Christmas week.

I did as she asked. After that, I took him for his walk and helped Gran make a shepherd's pie for dinner. We watched a murder mystery together while we ate it. It was lovely to have a normal, uncomplicated evening. I was worried that if I opened the lid of that box, it would be impossible to nail it shut again. But, to my relief, it doesn't seem to work like that. I was able to tell Gran how I've been feeling, then go about my regular life without collapsing in a broken heap. Not for the first time, I'm glad to have someone like her in my life.

We spend the next few days quietly. I'm too tired to make more than the most basic preparations for Christmas, and Gran assures me she prefers not to make a fuss this year. She seems to mean it, which is a relief. I'm distinctly lacking in enthusiasm for the festive season. I wonder whether I'll ever recover it. Maybe I'll end up like Scrooge after all – before the ghosts visited him. I wouldn't blame them for taking one look at me and deciding to give the whole thing a miss and move on to a more receptive target.

Gran and I haven't talked about Daniel since the night of the Christmas Fair. I'm grateful to her for respecting my privacy. I don't intend to think about him again if I can help it. I'm not sure what happened between us, or didn't happen. But I don't have the capacity to do anything about it. He may be on his way to Scotland by now, if he isn't there already, and that's a good thing for both of us.

I have a sudden vision of him driving up the motorway in his hired car, closely pursued by a flock of drones in close formation. I remember my resolve not to think about him and force myself to resume my regular routine with Gran and Humphrey.

It's a shock when I wake on Tuesday to realise it's Christmas Eve. I feel completely unprepared for tomorrow's festivities, but Gran doesn't seem worried.

'There's plenty of time for any last-minute touches,' she tells me over breakfast. 'When I was a child, we didn't even decorate the tree until Christmas Eve.'

'I know you don't want a fuss, but I had visions of you coming home from the hospital to a beautifully decorated house with carols playing in the background and the smell of mince pies baking. I'm not good at this Christmas thing.'

'Lucy, you looked after Humphrey for me. That was all I cared about – not some Hallmark version of Christmas. Besides, we have the whole of today. We can get a lot done in a day if we want to.'

'I won't have you climbing up ladders to hang mistletoe,' I warn her. 'Humphrey wouldn't cope with you disappearing off to the hospital again. But I'd be grateful for a few hints.'

'Isn't it time for Humphrey's walk?' she asks. 'We can talk about everything else when you get home. He's been especially frisky this morning, so I'd appreciate it if you could give him an extra-long run.'

I grab his harness and open the front door. Gran is right. It may be almost Christmas, but that's no excuse for neglecting Humphrey's exercise regime. He has no idea today is Christmas Eve. I try to suppress the thought that I'd prefer not to know either. The idea of spending a week on a remote island in the Caribbean and ignoring the entire holiday season is appealing.

'Don't be such a Scrooge,' I chide myself. 'You'll be posting *Bah, Humbug!* memes on Instagram soon. Or you would if you hadn't deleted your account after your crushing defeat.'

I know that wasn't very sporting of me, but I don't care. There's a good reason I stay away from social media. I should never have allowed myself to be sucked into using it for our ridiculous competition. I have no idea what got into me to make me agree to such a thing. A treacherous little voice tells me it was fun, but I tell it to pipe down. It was a stupid thing to get involved with, and deleting my account ensures I won't be tempted to do anything like that ever again.

I stay out for as long as possible, watching Humphrey charge around the field. There aren't many birds about today. Possibly, word has spread. But he manages to flush a pheasant from the undergrowth. It rises into the air with a whirr of its wings and a look of utter contempt on its face.

'Poor you,' I console him, fixing his lead back on. 'You can't catch a break, can you? Never mind – you shall have some turkey tomorrow.'

He pricks up his ears and gives me a considering look.

'Don't worry,' I say. 'No one will expect you to dress up as Santa or one of his reindeer. I'm done with all that. We'll have a lovely, quiet day with Gran. You can open your stocking in the morning when you wake up. And if there's enough snow, I'll take you outside for a snowball fight. You'll enjoy that.'

He sets off happily towards home. I envy his life. It's so simple and predictable. I don't want to live exactly as he does – too many walks, for one thing – but I find myself wishing things could be as uncomplicated for me.

He prances up the garden path, then stops at the front door, looking up at me with a worried expression.

'What's wrong?' I ask him. 'Can you hear something? Or do you think another delivery driver has been here while we were away? There's nothing for you to worry about. I know you don't like them, but they've been useful this year.'

He stiffens his legs and refuses to move. I bend to stroke his head.

'It's alright, Humphrey. Shall I go in first and check the coast is clear? If it's a delivery driver, they won't have stayed around. They're far too busy at this time of year – almost as busy as Santa.'

I put my key in the door and push it open, to be greeted by a wave of noise and laughter. Is Gran having a party? Does she do that each time I leave the house? She was quite insistent on me taking Humphrey out for a long walk. Maybe she keeps a selection of friends in the garden shed, bringing them out whenever she manages to get rid of me.

'Lucy!' calls a voice, and I see it's Irene. 'Come on in. Everyone's here!'

Everyone who? I keep a tight hold on Humphrey's lead as I step inside.

'Did you have a pleasant walk?' asks another voice. It takes me a moment to place where it's coming from. I catch sight of Phyllis, precariously balanced on a step ladder, fixing a piece of tinsel around the hall window.

'What's happening here?' I ask.

'A special meeting of the cookie club,' says Margery, bustling out of the kitchen with a tray of glasses.

'But we've delivered all the cookies,' I say, confused. 'I saw the final list. We didn't miss a single house.'

'We're not here to deliver cookies,' she says. 'We're here to decorate your Gran's cottage for Christmas.'

I look around, stunned, trying to take in the transformation. The once-plain hallway has been draped with garlands of evergreen. Glittering silver tinsel catches the light and sends it shimmering across the stairwell. Someone has twined a string of fairy lights up the banisters, casting a warm glow across the hall below. And a sweet, spicy scent fills the air.

June opens the front door to hang a wreath above the door handle. I instinctively tighten my hold on Humphrey, but he doesn't make a dash for freedom. He sits on the mat and looks around him with interest. Someone has fixed sprigs of mistletoe and holly to the ceiling. The red and white berries reflect the shine of the fairy lights.

Several more garlands have been strung above the kitchen door, and there are paper snowflakes along the walls and windows.

'You did all this while we were gone?' I say.

'Of course,' says Margery. 'It doesn't take long when you're all working together.'

'Where's Gran?' I ask, and she points.

Humphrey and I walk into the living room, and the sight takes my breath away. The Christmas tree has been transformed. Gran's old decorations have disappeared, and it's now adorned with shimmering glass baubles and tiny silver ornaments. Gold tinsel twists through the branches. Someone has removed the tired-looking angel from the top of the tree. In its place is a delicate silver star that flashes and glows in time with the lights twinkling beneath it. It looks as though someone has stretched out a hand and picked it straight from the night sky.

There's a red velvet tree skirt draped around the base of the tree, embroidered with little snowflakes and reindeer. I feel as though I've landed in the middle of one of Hans Christian

Andersen's fairy tales. Several brightly wrapped packages are lying on the velvet cloth.

'We'll have to move those before Humphrey sees them,' says June. 'But we wanted you to see the effect.'

'It's amazing,' I say.

Gran smiles up at me from the sofa. She's wrapped in a red checked shawl I haven't seen before. 'I told you not to worry about Christmas.'

I sit next to her, still holding Humphrey's lead. 'You did, but I had no idea what you meant. Did you know they were coming over to do this?'

'Of course, she did,' says Phyllis. 'She called the moment you left the house and told us the coast was clear. We'd hoped to finish it all before you came home, but Vera spilled a box of glitter, and it took a while to clear it up.'

'I wouldn't have spilled it if you hadn't left those cups and plates for me to trip over,' Vera defends herself.

'Please don't quarrel on my account,' I say. 'You've done an incredible job. And it's my fault for coming home early. Gran asked me to give Humphrey an extra-long walk, but my feet were so cold I was worried I might be developing frostbite, and I was hungry.'

'We have just the thing for that,' says June.

She points to the coffee table next to the window, where I see a tray of mince pies dusted with powdered sugar, looking as though a light snow has fallen on them. There's also a plate of gingerbread people, all perfectly iced. Their limbs are going in the correct direction, and every button and bow tie is in place. They clearly haven't been at the eggnog, as mine had.

'Spiced cider?' asks Margery.

'Is that what I could smell when I walked past the kitchen?' I say.

'That's right. But don't think I'll telling you what's in it. It's an old family recipe, and I'm sworn to secrecy.'

'I'd love some,' I say. 'And I promise not to ask any inconvenient questions.'

She disappears, returning a minute later with two large glasses, each with a stick of cinnamon sticking out of the top. She hands one to Gran and the other to me.

'I still can't believe you've done this,' I say, taking a sip and feeling the warmth make its way straight to my toes. Maybe they won't develop frostbite and drop off after all.

I take another gulp. It's delicious – full of warmth and spice, with a hint of something fruity. I'm sure I can taste honey too. There's something else I can't quite identify, although I recognise the comforting blend of cinnamon and cloves that always says Christmas to me.

'It's like drinking a warm hug,' I say.

'It's supposed to be,' says Margery. 'I remember my grandmother making this cider for us each Christmas. She left out the secret alcoholic ingredient when I was small and would never tell me what it was. But it still tasted wonderful. Of course, it tasted even more wonderful when I was old enough to drink the real thing.'

I glance around the room. 'I can't believe the entire cookie club is here.'

'Except for the other temporary member,' says June, and Gran shoots her a warning look.

I pretend not to notice. I'm not sure how I'd have felt if Daniel had been here today. My brain feels like my best friend from university's almost permanent Facebook status – It's complicated.

'I bumped into him at the shops recently,' says Irene. 'He was telling me about the new contract he's been offered. Somewhere in Scotland, he said. I can't remember where.'

No one looks at me. I clear my throat and hand my glass back to Margery. 'I'd better see about Humphrey's lunch.'

'No need,' she says. 'We brought him a beautiful piece of steamed salmon. It doesn't seem fair for him to miss out on all the Christmas fun.'

'He'll love that,' says Gran. 'Aren't you a lucky boy, Humphrey?'

He licks her hand and allows Margery to lead him to the kitchen.

'Are you alright, Lucy?' Gran asks me in a low voice.

'Of course. Why wouldn't I be? I'm just stunned by everything your friends have done for you today.'

'We're a team,' she says. 'We look out for each other. We always have. This is much more than a cookie club. It's a family.'

'That's right,' says Phyllis, reeling past holding a large glass of cider. By the looks of it, this isn't her first, or even her second. But who cares? These women have just performed a miracle, and they deserve to party.

'We're like the three musketeers,' says June. 'All for one, and one for all.'

'Except there are ten of us,' says Gran. 'But the principle is the same.'

I look around at the laughing, chattering women. This Christmas may not be exactly what I was expecting. But that's no reason for me to wish it was cancelled. It's like most things in life – it promises one thing and delivers another. Sometimes better, sometimes worse. All you can do is go with the flow and meet it cheerfully.

This must be what my parents decided to do after the accident. No one could have predicted what would happen to Dad, but it happened all the same. They had the choice to allow it to crush them and take away all their hopes and dreams or to adapt and make the most of what they still had. I wish I'd talked to them about it more. It might have helped me let go of some of my bitterness and anger.

Gran has done a lot to help me. And so has this party. I doubt any of the women here has led a completely trouble-free life. But they've made the most of it and kept going and supported each other through everything. They're an inspiration.

The party continues for most of the afternoon. Humphrey grows bored around three o'clock and takes himself upstairs to nap on my bed. As well as the mince pies and cookies, the club members have brought sausage rolls and quiches and tiny sandwiches cut into festive shapes. There's an enormous platter of cheese and crackers with tiny sprigs of rosemary tucked alongside them. June produces a bowl of spiced pecans and walnuts, which disappear in minutes.

Margery wanders around the room, topping up our glasses, while the members share stories of past meetings, each more hilarious than the last. At one point, a conga line forms in the hallway, led by Phyllis.

No one mentions Daniel again, which is good. I don't want to think about him for a while. I'm glad he's going to Scotland. It means I won't bump into him around the village this week. He's probably left already. He's completed his contract for the town council, so there's nothing to keep him here. And no reason for me to think of him ever again.

The afternoon slips by far too quickly. The sound of carols plays softly in the background, blending with the crackling of the fire and the occasional bursts of laughter. I wish it would never end.

But, like everything else, it does. June looks out of the window at five o'clock and sighs. 'It's dark already. We should be going. Don't worry, Lucy. We won't leave you a huge mess to clear up. We'll take it all with us when we go. You'll never know we were here.'

'But I want to know you were here,' I say. 'This has been one of the best afternoons of my life. I never want to forget it.'

'You have plenty more afternoons like this to look forward to,' she says.

'I hope so. But it will take a lot to top this. Thank you all so much. I wasn't in the Christmas mood when I started, but I am now.'

They're as good as their word. They gather up the paper plates and cups and put them into a large garbage bag. Margery wipes down the kitchen counters, while Irene stacks the empty boxes next to the front door.

'Get to bed early,' she advises me and Gran. 'Remember, Santa only visits when you're asleep.'

'I doubt he visits here,' I say. 'Humphrey would wake the entire village.'

'You never know,' she says. 'Christmas Eve is full of surprises. I've always enjoyed it more than Christmas Day. There's still so much to look forward to.'

Humphrey comes downstairs to see them off. Or, as June suggests, to make sure all the unwanted visitors have departed.

'That was quite the afternoon,' I say when they've gone.

Gran smiles. 'Whatever you do in life, Lucy, make sure you find a group of friends who will do what these women did today, and you won't go far wrong.'

'I'll do my best. But you must be exhausted after all that partying. Can I make you a cup of tea?'

'I'm not tired at all,' she says, glancing at her watch. 'Goodness! It's nearly six o'clock.'

'Are you counting how many hours until Santa arrives?' I ask.

'Something like that. I'm almost sure I heard his sleigh outside. Could you just check for me?'

I laugh. 'How many glasses of cider did you drink?'

I'm surprised to see she isn't smiling.

'I'm sure I heard a noise out the front,' she says. 'Take a look for me, would you, Lucy?'

'Of course.' I walk down the hallway and look through the peephole. 'I can't see anyone.'

'I know I heard something,' she insists.

'I'll go and check. Keep a hold of Humphrey, would you? It's snowing, and I don't want him to disappear.'

I open the door a crack and peer down the driveway. An unfamiliar blue van has drawn up outside. Is this another Christmas parcel? I'm surprised they're still delivering at this time on Christmas Eve.

'I'll see who it is,' I tell Gran. 'I don't want anyone leaving the gate unlatched.'

Just as I reach the gate, the driver's door opens, and Mum climbs out. She catches sight of me and beams. 'Lucy! I'm so glad to see you.'

I stop dead, staring at the van. 'What are you doing here? Whose van is this? And where's Dad?'

The passenger window rolls down, and Dad leans out. 'Hi, sweetheart. Happy Christmas!'

Chapter Thirty-Seven

I wake early on Christmas morning and lie in bed, thinking back over the extraordinary events of yesterday evening. I used to stay awake for hours waiting for Santa's sleigh, but the arrival of that blue van was even more magical.

There's no sound from downstairs, but I'm not worried. Humphrey will let me know when he and Gran are awake. I lie back on my pillows, feeling more relaxed than I've done for a long time. I hadn't been looking forward to Christmas very much. Last year was enough to make me wonder whether I ever would again.

And then the cookie club arrived and turned the cottage into a Christmas wonderland. Not only that, they helped me to understand what's really important in life. Mum and Dad's arrival was the icing on the cake – the best Christmas delivery in the history of Christmas deliveries. Whatever Santa may have loaded onto his sleigh this year can't top that.

I should get up. Mum and Dad are staying in a bungalow a few miles away so they don't have to worry about the stairs. I have no idea what time they'll arrive this morning. And Humphrey will soon want his walk. I tiptoe downstairs and take a shower. There's still no sound from the living room. That's good. It was an exciting evening for Humphrey and Gran too, and they need their sleep.

It was sweet to see how pleased Humphrey was to see Mum and Dad last night. He saw Mum a couple of weeks ago, but he hadn't seen Dad in over a year. He sat by Dad's chair all evening, looking up at him with huge, soulful eyes. None of us could understand it until Dad admitted he'd filled his pockets with dog treats before leaving home.

I dry myself off and return to my bedroom as quietly as possible to put on some warm clothes. A glance outside tells me it's been snowing in the night. By the look of the sky, it won't be long until it starts again. Humphrey and I may be making that snowman after all.

I pull back the curtains more fully, and something catches my eye. It's a large bird flying slowly across the patch of grass beyond Gran's back fence. I'm not great at identifying birds, but it's nothing like the crows and jackdaws whose acquaintance Humphrey is always attempting to make. Is it a heron or a stork? Do we even have those in this country? Perhaps they make a special appearance on Christmas Day.

It rises higher, hovering like a bird of prey. I rub my eyes and look more closely. It's not a bird at all. It's a drone. It slowly rises into the air and flies over the fence and into our garden, where it hovers about ten feet away from my bedroom window and starts to play music. Is that Jingle Bells?

This has to be one of Daniel's drones. Doesn't he know I'd be within my rights to shoot it down as an enemy aircraft? I'm not up to date on the finer points of British aviation law, but I'm sure I'm at least allowed to throw my hairbrush at it.

A banner has been fixed to its struts. The letters are large and slightly crooked, clearly painted by hand. I squint to make out the words.

'*Permission to enter hostile airspace?*' the banner reads.

A laugh bubbles up inside me. I step closer to the window, watching the drone as it drifts back and forth. How am I supposed to communicate with it? I remember the drone Daniel used to locate Humphrey. It had a small camera at the front and underneath.

I raise a hand and wave. The drone waggles its wings in acknowledgement, then turns and disappears over the back fence. I watch it go, baffled. Why has Daniel sent a drone to my window, only to recall it a minute later? Just to show he can violate enemy airspace at will? I've been watching too many World War Two movies with Dad.

As I stare into the garden, trying to make sense of this, the drone reappears. This time it's carrying something, although I can't be sure what. It's wrapped in green and red Christmas paper, with a silver ribbon that sparkles in the morning sun. It hovers next to my window for a few seconds, then flies over the roof of the cottage.

I pull on a thick sweater and run downstairs. I open the front door and peer outside, unsure what to expect. I spot the drone hovering next to the hedge. As I watch, Daniel appears at the gate. He isn't holding a remote control. How is he doing this? Has he programmed it in advance and set it on autopilot?

Apparently not. Just as he's closing the gate, the drone gives a violent wobble, the claws open, and the package crashes to the ground, narrowly missing the privet hedge.

'That wasn't supposed to happen,' he says.

I walk down the path to meet him. 'What are you doing here? And why is half your drone stock flying over my house with cryptic messages?'

'Not cryptic,' he says. 'It's basic drone etiquette when flying over potentially hostile territory. Always obtain the landowner's permission first.'

'I'm not the landowner,' I object, and he grins.

'Shall we call your grandmother to sign a waiver?'

'She's still asleep. But Humphrey may wake up at any moment and decide it's a rogue magpie that needs taking down.'

'Too late,' he says, waving to the drone, which turns and drifts away over the hedge.

'How are you doing that?' I ask.

'I'm not. Marcus is. And I'll be having strong words with him later about his delivery technique.'

'I don't understand,' I say. 'I thought you'd gone to Scotland.'

'Who told you that?'

'Irene mentioned she'd met you in the village. She said you'd finished your work here and were off to Scotland for your next contract.'

'I said I might be. I told you we'd been offered two contracts – one in Scotland, and one locally. Marcus and I haven't yet decided which one of us should take on the Scottish contract.'

I stare at my feet. 'How will you decide?'

He takes a step towards me. 'I thought I'd leave that up to you.'

My breath catches as he puts his hands on my shoulders and looks down at me. There's a slight smile playing around the corners of his mouth, but there's an unfamiliar look of anxiety in his eyes.

'Up to me?' I ask, my voice barely above a whisper.

He nods, his gaze steady. 'If you'd rather I stayed around for a while, I will. If not, I'll take a train to Scotland tomorrow and spend the next few months wishing things had turned out differently between us.'

I can't speak for a moment. I thought I would never see him again. After my behaviour towards him at the fair, I didn't think he would ever want to see me. Yet here he is, telling me he wants to make this work. The question is, do I?

I look into his familiar brown eyes and realise this isn't even a question. I nod.

'Just to confirm,' he says, leaning a little closer. 'That's a yes to me staying?'

I can't speak, so I nod again. He pulls me into his arms, and his lips meet mine, soft and warm in the cold morning air, snowflakes drifting down around us. It feels as though we're the only two people in the world as I kiss him back. When he finally draws away, I look up at him and smile.

'I didn't think I'd ever see you again.'

'I was worried I'd never see you again,' he says. 'You and I had unfinished business. I wanted to find out what it would be like to kiss you without being interrupted by Phyllis.'

I flush as I remember the Christmas fair. 'I'm sorry I was so awful to you that night. It's a complicated situation, but I shouldn't have taken it out on you.'

'I was the one to blame. I had no right to tell you what you should do with your life. I'm sorry, Lucy. I won't do that again.'

'I may have overreacted slightly,' I say. 'I've done that quite a bit over the last year.'

His eyes soften. 'I can imagine. You told me what had happened to you and your family. I should have been more understanding.'

'I didn't give you the chance. I've been holding people at arm's length all year and refusing to allow anyone to help me deal with it. Gran helped me to see that. I didn't understand it at first. But then all her friends turned up yesterday to make sure she and I had a wonderful Christmas. And I realised what a difference it makes if you let people help instead of shutting them out.'

'I heard about the emergency meeting of the Honeywell Christmas Cookie Club,' he says.

'I'm sorry you weren't invited,' I say, conscience-stricken.

'I was. Irene told me all about it and suggested I come along.'

'No one mentioned that to me.'

'That's because I told her I'd prefer to sit this one out and wait until I'd talked to you alone. It didn't seem fair to land on your doorstep without giving you the chance to decide whether you even wanted to see me.'

'I could have thrown you out if I didn't,' I say. 'Or got Humphrey to do it for me.'

He laughs. 'I was worried about that too.'

'It would have been publicly humiliating. I understand why you might have wanted to avoid that.'

'I have my dignity,' he says.

'I've watched you trying to bake. No, you don't.'

'No, I don't,' he agrees. 'But I still wanted to see you alone.'

I move closer to him. 'We're alone right now, and there don't seem to be any more drones around.'

'So we are,' he says, his arms tightening around me. 'I think we should make the most of it.'

He leans down, his lips brushing against mine. His kiss is gentle at first, but when I respond, nestling closer to him, it deepens. His hands find their way to my waist, and I wrap my arms around his neck, pulling him in as though the world outside has disappeared, and he and I are the only two people left.

I barely notice the noise of an engine coming up the street or the sound of it pulling it up to the kerb.

'Oh, my goodness!' says a voice, making us both jump.

I turn my head to see Mum standing by the garden gate, looking at us with a stunned expression on her face.

Chapter Thirty-Eight

I try to take a step away from Daniel, but it's too late. She's already seen us standing there wrapped in each other's arms. And what excuse can I make – Daniel was testing the fabric of my hoodie to check it's properly waterproof?

'Hi, Mum,' I say in a carefully casual tone. 'This is Daniel.'

Her face lights up. 'I've heard so much about you!'

'No, you haven't,' I say. 'I've never mentioned him in any of my calls.'

'But your grandmother has. She's mentioned him several times.'

'Lovely to meet you,' she tells Daniel. 'I'd give you a hug, but you seem a little … tied up at the moment.'

'Just a temporary state of affairs,' he says. 'It's lovely to meet you too, Mrs Hollis.'

'You can call me Liz,' she says. 'I have a feeling we're going to be seeing more of each other.'

'I hope so,' he says. 'Does your husband need help getting out of the van?'

Mum claps her hand to her mouth. 'I'd forgotten about Robert!'

'Poor Dad,' I say. 'First you drag him all the way down here, and then you abandon him in the freezing cold.'

'It's lovely and warm in there,' she says. 'I told you the insurance came through last month. There was enough left for us to buy a properly adapted van. And I made sure it had an excellent heater. I hate having cold toes when I drive.'

'You can tell us more about your temperature preferences later,' I say, freeing myself from Daniel's arms and walking over to hug her. 'Meanwhile, Daniel can make himself useful and do whatever needs doing.'

'I'm happy to,' he says. 'While I'm doing that, maybe you could pick up the parcel over there?'

'Why is it lying in the snow?' asks Mum. 'Did the postman throw it over the hedge? He ought to be more careful.'

'Don't blame the postman,' I say. 'There are no deliveries on Christmas Day. This arrived by … other means.'

I try to catch Daniel's eye, but he's already walking towards the van.

'I'll tell you later,' I say to Mum. 'Or Daniel can.'

'Is he coming in for a while? I do hope so. Your father and I have been looking forward to meeting him.'

'I haven't asked him,' I say. 'But I'm sure the answer is yes. Daniel has a habit of turning up when he's least expected and finding any excuse to stay.'

She only smiles and returns to the van. I retrieve the parcel from the snow. I give it a gentle shake and hear a slight rattling noise. I hope it isn't something fragile like wine glasses. Even Daniel should know better than that. I carry it into the house and put it on the hall table.

'Is that you, Lucy?' calls Gran's voice from the kitchen.

'Happy Christmas!' I say, giving her a hug. 'And to you, Humphrey. Has Santa visited?'

'He has,' she says. 'I noticed Humphrey's stocking had been filled when we woke up this morning. Santa must have been extremely quiet. Humphrey didn't bark at all.'

'Perhaps Santa waited until you were both asleep,' I suggest. 'Is that your parents I heard outside?'

'They arrived a few minutes ago.'

'I thought I heard a noise in the back garden earlier,' she says. 'I must have been mistaken.'

'That was Daniel. More precisely, it was one of his drones.'

She looks pleased. 'Did he accompany it?'

I smile back at her. 'He did. He and I have decided to … we thought that …'

'I'm delighted to hear it,' she says. 'Several members of the cookie club stand to make a fair bit of money from the news – including me.'

'I'll pretend I didn't hear that.'

The front door opens again, and Dad comes in. He's leaning heavily on his sticks, but he's walking by himself. Mum has obviously been keeping secrets from me, just as I have from her.

'I've met Daniel,' he says as I help him off with his coat. 'He seems like a pleasant lad. He's been telling me about his drone company.'

Daniel appears in the doorway behind him. 'Don't get your daughter started on the subject of drones. She has a low opinion of them.'

'Not always,' I say, remembering the night Humphrey got lost. 'But I wouldn't recommend you sinking all your money into starting a delivery business. Look what happened to that parcel.'

'It's fine,' he says, handing it to me. 'I wrapped it in several layers of paper.'

I tear open the package to find a smaller box inside containing a whisk, a spatula, a Christmas apron, and a tiny rolling pin.

'It's beautiful,' I say. 'But I didn't get you anything. I wasn't expecting to see you today.'

'You didn't throw me out on my ear the moment you saw me,' says Daniel. 'That's more than enough for me.'

'Don't stand in the hallway getting cold,' says Gran. 'Come through to the living room. I've lit the fire.'

I hold out my hand to Daniel. 'No need to ask whether you're joining us.'

'I don't want to intrude,' he says. 'I can come back another time.'

'Don't even think about it,' says Mum. 'There's plenty of room for us all.'

This isn't quite true, particularly when Humphrey joins us. But we all squash in. Dad sits in the armchair by the window, while Mum and Gran sit together on the sofa with Humphrey between them. I hand Gran Humphrey's stocking, and Daniel and I sit on the rug by the fire to watch him open it.

Gran dips her hand in, pulls out the first parcel, and holds it out to Humphrey, who stares at it thoughtfully.

'He may need a little help,' I say.

She unwraps it and hands him a large rubber bone. He snatches it from her and sinks his teeth into it. It makes a loud squeaking noise, and he drops it at once.

'It takes a bit of getting used to,' I reassure him. 'Why don't you see what else you have?'

Five minutes later, there's a small pile of gifts in front of him. As well as the bone, Santa has brought him a teddy bear with triple reinforced seams, a bag of treats, a warm blanket, a large rubber ball, and some fur-lined boots.

'You're a lucky dog,' Gran tells him, but he's too busy with his treats to respond.

'I should put the turkey on,' says Mum. 'I saw it defrosting last night. It looked big enough for the entire village.'

'I should go,' says Daniel. 'I had no intention of gate-crashing your Christmas meal. Marcus's parents don't live too far away, and they've invited me to join them if I don't have any other plans.'

'Don't bother arguing,' I advise him. 'You'll be staying for Christmas dinner if Mum has to lock the doors to prevent you from leaving. You've already told me you can't say no to the Hollis women. My advice is to give in gracefully and do as you're told.'

'I wouldn't dream of locking the door,' says Mum. 'But we'd love it if you would stay. Isn't that right, Lucy?'

'It wouldn't be the worst thing,' I say, and Daniel laughs.

'I'm keen to hear more about this cookie club,' says Dad.

Daniel turns to me. 'Would you like to tell them or shall I?'

I smile at Gran. 'I think this is your story, don't you?'

Mum and Dad listen while Gran tells them the history of the cookie club and brings them up to date with the goings on this year.

'I'm sorry I didn't tell you all this before,' she says to Mum. 'I've been regretting that for a while now.'

Mum slips an arm around her and gives her a hug. 'I can see why you didn't. I was a horrible teenager. I didn't value what I had here until I'd lost it. And why shouldn't you have something of your own? From what you've told me, it sounds like a pretty special club.'

'Not that special,' says Daniel. 'They made me a temporary member.'

'If you're still around next year, we'll consider making it permanent,' says Gran. 'Lucy too.'

'Are you coming down from London next December?' Mum asks me. 'How lovely.'

I hadn't meant to talk to her about my future until later, but the opportunity is too good to pass up.

'I won't be in London next year,' I say. 'I've given in my notice. I emailed Caroline yesterday and told her. I may have to go back and work out my notice, but I suspect she'll be only too happy to get rid of me.'

Mum opens her mouth to speak, and I hurry on. 'I've hated every minute I've spent there. I tried to make it work, but it isn't for me. I've decided to do what I've always wanted to do and set up for myself, translating novels into German. I've registered with a couple of sites, and I'm going to give it a chance. I know you and Dad were keen me to spread my wings, but I don't want to do it like this.'

I take a deep breath and turn to Gran. 'I was wondering whether I might stay with you for a while? I'd pay rent, of course. But it struck me this could be the perfect solution to both our problems. I'll need somewhere to live while I try to make things work with my career, and you'll need someone to help look after you and Humphrey while you recover.'

Gran's face lights up. 'Oh, Lucy. That would be lovely.'

'I think it's a fantastic idea,' says Dad.

'You do?' I ask.

'Of course, we do,' says Mum. 'I had no idea you hated your job so much. This would be perfect for you.'

'Even though it means living in Honeywell?'

'What's wrong with Honeywell?' she asks.

'I thought you'd see it as a backward step. I'll be returning to the place you were so desperate to leave.'

'But that was me,' she says. 'I never wanted you to follow my dreams. I wanted you to find your own and follow those. And if that turns out to be here in Honeywell, that's wonderful.'

'I'm glad that's sorted,' says Dad. 'And now I want to hear more about this drone company. Did Lucy say something about you using them to deliver parcels, Daniel?'

'Not so much deliver them as hurl them from a great height,' I say. 'We're lucky I'm not lying in hospital at this very moment suffering from a severe concussion.'

'We haven't perfected our delivery system yet,' admits Daniel. 'That's why I didn't attempt to deliver you a cup of a coffee or a bottle of wine.'

'I thought at first it might be some kind of bomb,' I tell him. 'Cunningly disguised as a Christmas gift.'

'It was more like a peace treaty,' he says. 'Although it wasn't one I was sure you'd accept.'

'At least you dropped the parcel in the front garden. For one terrible moment, it seemed as though you planned to drop it onto the roof, and I'd have to risk life and limb climbing up to retrieve it.'

'It's an intriguing idea,' says Dad. 'Not the part about you scrambling over the roof in the snow. But the idea of replacing Santa with drones. It would give the reindeer a well-deserved rest.'

'That's very true,' says Daniel. 'In a way, you could say Santa was the first prototype drone delivery system. It shouldn't be a surprise. He originated from Germany, and they've always been at the cutting edge of technology.'

'When I first saw it hovering over the back garden, I thought it was a Christmas Eagle,' I tell him.

'Is there such a thing?' asks Mum.

'Humphrey would like to think so.'

'I've brought him something too,' says Daniel, reaching into his pocket and producing a small parcel. 'I'm afraid I don't have anything for the rest of you. I didn't expect to get any further than the garden gate this morning. But I'm excellent at washing up, so that can be my gift to you all.'

'Don't be ridiculous,' says Mum. 'We're delighted you're able to be here with us today.'

'Are you about to tell him his presence is present enough?' I say. 'Please don't. It's bad for his ego. What did you get for Humphrey, Daniel?'

He hands the parcel to me, and I pull out an envelope containing a large sticker saying *Beware of the fierce guard dog!*

'It's for your front door,' he explains. 'To stop unwanted people knocking and upsetting him.'

'That's very thoughtful of you,' says Gran. 'Humphrey will appreciate that.'

'If that doesn't do the trick,' he says, 'I've found an online store selling doorbells that make a loud growling sound whenever someone presses them. Humphrey will never be bothered by visitors again.'

'I must make a start on the meal,' says Mum. 'Lucy, would you and Daniel like to give me a hand?'

'We should drink a toast first,' says Gran. 'It's been a while since we've had three generations of the Hollis women together in the same room. That's surely something to celebrate. There's a bottle of sherry and some glasses on that shelf.'

Daniel fills five glasses, and I hand them around.

'What are we drinking to?' asks Dad.

'You being here today,' I say, smiling affectionately at him.

'And to Lucy moving to Honeywell,' says Gran.

'And to Daniel's almost successful package delivery business,' I add. 'And to Mum and Gran for teaching me how to follow my dreams.'

'Such a lot of things to drink to,' says Daniel. 'I hope I'm up to the task.'

He slips his arm around me, and I rest my head on his shoulder.

'#TakeTwo #WorthTheWait,' he murmurs into my ear.

'There's one more thing we should drink to,' says Dad.

'Are you sure?' I ask. 'We don't want to run out of sherry.'

'We can't miss out on this toast,' he says, raising his glass and smiling around at us. 'To the Honeywell Christmas Cookie Club. May it never run short of ingredients!'

I hope you enjoyed this book. If you did, please consider leaving a review on Amazon. It helps new readers find my books, and I really appreciate it.

Join my mailing list to be the first to be notified about my upcoming books.

rosemarywhittaker.com/signup

A Tale of Two Christmases

Annie never comes home for Christmas. There's too much chance of running into Alex. He broke her heart, and she never wants to speak to him again.

Alex always comes home for Christmas. He's desperate to talk to Annie about what went wrong between them.

Faced with a family crisis, Annie reluctantly agrees to spend the holidays with her parents. It shouldn't be too difficult to avoid Alex for just one week.

But she didn't expect to arrive in the middle of the wedding of the year. The entire village will be there, and no one will be able to avoid anyone else.

It's a battle of two Christmases, and only one can win.

Snuggle up in front of a roaring fire with a mug of hot chocolate and enjoy this sparkling Christmas romance.

Available now in paperback and Kindle ebook

A Boxful of Christmas

For Emma, Christmas is more than just a season. It's a way of life.

When she arrives in the enchanting village of Honeywell to sell Christmas boxes at the local fair, she's on a mission to spread as much festive cheer as she can.

Tom, who has grown up on the local Christmas tree farm, can't quite understand the fuss.

When fate puts the pair of them side by side at the bustling Christmas market, sparks fly as Emma's festive fervour clashes with Tom's determined indifference.

Can Emma's unwavering love for the season melt Tom's icy resolve, or will their blossoming romance turn into a festive fiasco?

With its perfect blend of laugh-out-loud scenes and sparkling dialogue, A Boxful of Christmas is guaranteed to get your holiday season off to a magical start.

Available now in paperback and Kindle ebook

A Sugarloaf Valentine

When the ingredients for love turn into a recipe for disaster…

Lily's world is turned upside down when her ex-boyfriend Stephen walks into her bakery, hoping to buy Valentine's cookies for his new girlfriend. To make matters worse, he wants Lily to decorate them with a message of love.

Determined not to let him see her heartbroken, Lily tells him she has met someone else too and has never been happier. It's a risky deception, but luckily, she knows just the man to help her out.

She doesn't count on ending up on a double date with Stephen and his new girlfriend. Nor does she expect her fake boyfriend to have a secret of his own.

As Valentine's Day approaches, and Lily struggles to create the perfect cookies, she wonders whether the recipe for happiness has been in front of her all along.

With a cast of charming characters, and a dash of sweet romance, A Sugarloaf Valentine is a delightful read that will have you falling in love with love all over again.

Available now in paperback and Kindle ebook

About the author

Rosemary Whittaker wanted to be an author as soon as she was old enough to hold a book the right way up. From that moment on, she was the despair of her teachers, who attempted to impart the basics of an education while she stared out of the window, making up characters and situations.

Having accidentally absorbed enough to graduate and become a teacher, she spent the next few decades moving around the world with her husband, children, and menagerie of unexpected pets.

She accidentally found herself in Australia some years back and intends to stay there for a very long time. She currently spends her time writing, sourcing English marmite and salad cream and wrangling her two determinedly destructive house bunnies – Pumpkin and Midway.

Rosemary has written several light-hearted romance novels set in the different countries in which she has lived. She also writes children's books as R J Whittaker – in particular a series of books about a recalcitrant monkey named Pom Pom, who is not in any way, shape or form based on her experience of raising her own four boys.

Printed in Great Britain
by Amazon

52195560R00155